PRAISE FOR BARBARA WOOD

"A master storyteller. She never fails to leave the reader enthralled."
—Elizabeth Forsythe Hailey, author of *A Woman of Independent Means*

"Barbara Wood is an entertainer."
—*Washington Post Book World*

"An accomplished storyteller."
—John Jakes, *New York Times* bestselling author

"Wood makes her fiction come alive with authentic detailing and highly memorable characters."
—*Booklist*

YESTERDAY'S CHILD

YESTERDAY'S CHILD

BARBARA WOOD

TURNER

Turner Publishing Company

200 4th Avenue North • Suite 950
Nashville, Tennessee 37219

445 Park Avenue • 9th Floor
New York, New York 10022

www.turnerpublishing.com

Yesterday's Child is a work of fiction. Although some events and people
in this book are based on historical fact, others are the products of
the author's imagination.

Cover design by Gina Binkley
Interior design by Mike Penticost

Library of Congress Cataloging-in-Publication Data

Wood, Barbara, 1947-
Yesterday's child / Barbara Wood.
p. cm.
ISBN 978-1-59652-868-0
1. Americans--England--Fiction. 2. Family secrets--Fiction. I. Title.
PS3573.O5877Y47 2012
813'.54--dc23
2012006393

Printed in the United States of America
12 13 14 15 16 17 18—0 9 8 7 6 5 4 3 2 1

With great love and admiration
I dedicate this book to
Naomi Pemberton,
my Nana

Why was it that now, approaching the parlour door, I should feel the crawl of terror over my skin, a gripping, sinking feeling deep in my bowels that I should not pursue this further? Why should I be afraid now when I wasn't moments before? It was as though the air about me were evil, as though the hellish tragedies that had taken place in this house all those years ago were now contained in this one spot, and that I foolishly entered it.

The sensation was a familiar one. I had felt it two nights before when I had found Victor standing over my bed. It had been the air then, a terrifying aura that had emanated from the darkness as though some evil horrors lurked there. This was the same feeling now, as I left the safety of the sitting room and delivered myself into the dark catacomb of the hallway.

It was almost as though something were waiting for me.

YESTERDAY'S CHILD

CHAPTER 1

THERE WAS SOMETHING WRONG WITH THE HOUSE ON GEORGE Street. I sensed it the moment I walked in.

I had just stepped through the front door and was staring down the long, dim hall at the woman who was gliding towards me. In the oblique shadows I saw that she was tall, erect, and graceful, that she wore a floor-length old-fashioned gown, and that her thick black hair was swept neatly to the top of her head in a knot. I stared for an instant at her as she approached me with arms outstretched, then I turned briefly to my aunt, who had come up the garden path and now stood at my side.

"Andrea," my aunt said, "meet your grandmother."

I turned to the woman who came towards us and blinked in surprise. The long dress and rich hair were gone.

Instead, I found myself gazing at a small, stooped woman who wore a simple house dress and wool sweater, and whose grey hair was covered by a linen cap.

"Hello," I heard myself say.

The old woman seized my hands and drew near to kiss me. Suddenly, I realized how very tired I must be. The jet from Los Angeles had taken eleven hours, and then one more from London to Manchester. The time lapse was obviously getting to me.

We embraced and regarded one another in the frail light of the hall. It is difficult now for me to recall exactly how my grandmother had appeared to me in that brief first moment, for my eyes, fatigued from the journey, had trouble focusing. Her face seemed in motion; now ugly, now radiant. It was hard to seize upon her features, they seemed to ebb and flow as if unstable; her age would have been impossible to guess. I knew she was eighty-three, yet there was such youth and vitality to her eyes that I was held by her gaze. Her lingering traces of past beauty, not giving way to the ravages of time, made me liken her face fleetingly to a rose pressed between the pages of a book.

As I was drawn down the hall to the open door of the sitting room, I couldn't shake the curious confused feeling I had. Later, lying in bed that night, it occurred to me that it was the house that affected me. There was a strangely compelling atmosphere about the place; it seemed to have some palpable energy of its own, which I felt closing in around me immediately. It seemed to be embracing me and drawing me in.

As I walked down the hall, which was illuminated by one naked bulb, the amber light of which did not reach the floor, the shadows seemed to gather in the corners, crouching, endowing the hall with an ambience of waiting.

With that moment when I first stepped through the door of the house, it seemed that a change had taken place, as though my entrance had caused a shift in the atmosphere. And lying in bed that night I realized I had sensed it in that first moment, as I shook the English damp from my shoulders and as I shuddered briefly with the strange sharpness of the air. Now I understand that the uncanny chill of it came not from temperature but from something else, something older than time.

While I knew this was absurd, so consuming was the feeling later as I lay in that cold bed that the house seemed to be closing in on me, that I screwed my eyes shut tight against the darkness. Why was I here? To try and control my rising panic, I thought back over the unusual turn of events that had brought me to England. I thought that perhaps in this way I might calm myself and find an explanation for my strange mood.

I tried to tell myself that it was the suddenness of being in a strange town in a foreign country; it was the result of the plane flight, the peculiar circumstances of my arrival, the sudden unexpected summons, the recent turmoil of my personal life, and my unsettled state of mind.

And yet, try though I did, I could not shake the feeling that the house had been waiting for me.

I told myself at the time that it was my imagination, that my emotional state of mind had actually begun back in Los Angeles, when I had decided to come in the first place.

Three days before, two letters had arrived addressed to my mother in L.A. The first was from my grandmother, the second from my aunt. The letters were written to my mother explaining that her father, my grandfather, lay gravely ill in Warrington General Hospital and was not expected to live.

The news was extremely distressing to my mother. There was no way she could possibly make the journey because of health reasons. And it drove her nearly to hysteria.

The reason for her anxiety was this: Twenty-five years before, my parents and my brother and I had emigrated from England to a better life in America. I had been only two at the time, my brother, seven. When my parents had become

U.S. citizens, so had we, automatically. Our home was Los Angeles, our speech American, and our tastes Californian. Until the arrival of the two letters I had given little thought to England or to my being English by blood and birth. None of us had ever looked back.

In recent years my mother and father had occasionally spoken of a trip "back home" to see the family again, but many excuses and reasons for not going had kept them away until now, it seemed, it was too late.

The letters were most untimely as my mother was just recovering from a foot operation and could barely hobble around on the crutches that she would have to use for the next six weeks. In the meantime, she feared, her father would die.

At first I was surprised when she asked me to go, to be with the family in this time of need and to "represent" the American kin. And then it seemed that while the letters from my aunt and grandmother asking my mother to come to see her father one last time had come most inopportunely for her, they had arrived as a disguised godsend for me. I had been, at that time, searching for a way to escape my own life for a while.

I had broken up with Doug, had made him pack his things and move out, and had been toying with the idea of an impromptu vacation when my mother had called about the letters.

"One of us should go," she had said over and over again. "our brother can't. He's in Australia. Your father can't leave his work. And besides, he isn't a Townsend. And of course I should go, but I can barely move. You should go see your grandfather while you can, Andrea. After all, it's been twenty-five years. You were born there. All your family is there."

From that moment on things happened so rapidly that they remain now as a blur in my memory; talking to the stockbroker I worked for, explaining the emergency, fishing my passport out of a box of mementoes from a trip to Mexico, reserving a seat on the British Airways polar express, and finding within myself an urgent need to be running away from the unhappiness and bitterness of the end of a love affair.

It was strange flying over the North Pole, thinking about what I was leaving behind and wondering about what lay ahead. I thought of the guilt that had made my mother almost hysterical with remorse; guilt that she hadn't gone back to England before this and that it was her own fault that her father would die without seeing his daughter. I thought also of Doug and the painful way we had said our good-byes.

This then, I told myself, was the reason for my confused state of mind as I stood apprehensively in the terminal of Manchester's Ringway Airport, wondering if I was doing the right thing.

I had been told that my Aunt Elsie and her husband would meet me here. In fact, we had no trouble finding one another. Aunt Elsie resembled my mother enough for me to identify her at once, and I suppose my own likeness to my mother aided Elsie in picking me out of the disembarking passengers. And for the same reasons, this pleasant, jovial woman, smelling faintly of Yardley Lavender, bore some similarity to myself.

There is a trait peculiar to our branch of the Townsends, one which I have been told has come down to us from ancestors long dead. It is a small vertical furrow between the eyebrows just above the nose, the Townsend groove, which gives us a defiant, angry look. I have had it all my life, ever since childhood, and it appeared now on the face of this woman who came through the crowd.

"Andrea!" she cried, enveloping me in an unexpected embrace and stepping back with tears in her eyes. "How like Ruth you are! So like your mother! Look, Ed, isn't it our Ruth come back to us?"

A smallish man, somewhat diffident, stood slightly apart. He smiled, muttered something, then awkwardly took hold of my hand. "Welcome home," he said.

I allowed myself to be led away from the clamour of Ringway Airport and out into the cold night, a cold that shocked my body. Although November, it had been eighty-five degrees in Los Angeles. In Manchester, England, it was thirty-four.

My Uncle Edouard, who was a Frenchman, hurried off in the direction of the parking lot while his wife and I stood at the kerb outside the terminal with my one suitcase. We occasioned a glance at one another and made gestures that Uncle Ed had better hurry.

That I was ill at ease was to say the least. In the whole of my life I had never known what it was like to have a family; that is, in the sense of relatives and blood ties beyond my own parents and brother. I had never experienced fondness or affection for someone who was bound to me by family lineage. I had never learned to accept the love of a stranger or to give it in return simply because he or she sprang from the same font. In my life, friends were what counted. You chose them for private, noble reasons, and you cleaved to them not because you had to but because you wanted to.

But now, all of a sudden, people with unfamiliar faces and who spoke in a strange dialect were to be the automatic recipients of my affection simply because of the accident of birth. Knowing nothing about this man and woman, nor of the people I was soon to meet, I was nonetheless expected to accept them with fondness and sentiment, no questions asked.

It was a new concept to me and one which did not settle well.

"How was your flight, love?" asked the woman with my mother's face. She spoke in a thick Lancashire accent which was difficult at first for me to understand.

"The flight was great," I replied, my knees cramped up almost to my chest in the backseat of Uncle Edouard's Renault.

"I expect you must be very tired."

I nodded and looked away from my aunt. Her resemblance to my mother—to me—was most unsettling. This stranger with our face. Instead I concentrated on watching the traffic, which fascinated me, being on the wrong side of the street as it was.

"It was good of you to come, Andrea, seeing how poorly your mum is. How glad your granddad will be to see you. It'll be like our Ruth being here, won't it, Ed?"

I bit my lower lip. And what would it take to make it seem like *me* being here?

I tried to rest back in the seat and recuperate. That it was going to be an arduous visit I had prepared myself for. But to what extent I could not know. My mother and I had not even spoken of time limits. The length of stay had been nebulous and not really talked about. I supposed a week, maybe two. Long enough to renew old ties.

And to get over Doug. If that was possible.

"Welcome home," my Uncle Edouard had said at the airport. I closed my eyes. Home was Los Angeles.

"Andrea."

I opened my eyes.

"Andrea, look."

I brought my head up to regard my aunt. She had pronounced "look" like "moot." She was pointing out of the window. "Do you know what that is?"

With the heel of my hand I wiped away a circle of fog on the window and peered out. A monstrous black edifice loomed nearby, spattered here and there with dim lights, but basically unrecognizable.

"That's General Hospital," she said softly. "That's where you were born."

I twisted my head and looked again. Too soon it was gone, and terraced houses were now flitting past. How strange, to be told by this woman with the incomprehensible accent, in this freezing little box of a car, driving on the wrong side of the street eight thousand miles away from home, that that black and forbidding spot had been the place of my birth.

I smiled weakly. She returned it. My aunt was trying too hard. I wasn't trying hard enough.

There was something undefinably unsettling about this small English town; the streets looked cold and deserted, and reflecting on shiny cobblestones were the occasional glows of Victorian streetlamps. Driving through Warrington was like driving back in time.

"You'll have to forgive me . . . Aunt Elsie, but the flight from Los Angeles was eleven hours and then I had a two-hour wait at Heathrow . . . "

"Oh aye!" she blurted. "Jet lag they call it. Proper tired, you will be, and here's me playing tour guide. Well, you don't have to worry about the rest of the evening. No one expects to see you tonight, not even Granddad. Time enough tomorrow for that. Right now you'll want some hot tea and a good sleep. Ah, here we are."

Uncle Edouard jerked the car to a stop so that we all fell forward. I had to rub another circle on the window to look out. It was a street like all the other streets we had gone down; just another endless line of red-brick terraced houses and their tiny front gardens.

"Where are we?"

"Your nana's," Aunt Elsie grunted, getting out of the car. As I, too, struggled out and felt again the shocking slap of cold night air, I heard her say, "We all thought it would be best if you stayed with your nana, seeing as how she's all alone now and could do with the company. William or I would have been glad to have you, and it would have been better for you, too, what with our central heating like, but your nana insisted. As soon as Ruth called to say you was coming, Mum got the front bedroom all nice and ready. So here's where you'll be staying, love."

I straightened up and gaped at the house. A tall, two-storey dirty brick affair with a rotten old garden in front and a dark bay window protruding over it, my grandmother's house, attached on either side by identical houses, was dark and without signs of life.

My initial impulse, beneath the onus of jet lag and fatigue and confusion and a growing sense of loneliness, was to turn to my aunt and ask her to take me to her central heating.

But then there was Uncle Edouard already plodding up the broken path with my suitcase and pushing a key into the door lock.

I felt a gentle pressure on my back, Aunt Elsie's hand. "Come on, love. A nice hot cup of tea and a good sleep. That's what you want. And then you'll feel better in the morning."

I walked ahead of her, stiff from my long journey, tired from tension and apprehension, and hungry too, and headachey. So I went up to the house of my grandmother on George Street and stepped over that threshold.

I have already said that it was obvious my grandmother must have been quite beautiful in her youth, but I have not mentioned her striking resemblance to my mother. Staring into the eighty-three-year-old face of my grandmother was a little like looking into the future and seeing my mother as she would appear in twenty-six years.

There was the high-bridged nose of the Dobsons—"aristocratic" "some have called it—and the unusual eyes with grey irises outlined in black. Her eyebrows were thin and delicately arched. Her cheekbones were high, her cheeks hollow, her chin gently pointed. Although the skin sagged and was webbed with a thousand wrinkles, the underlying bone structure could still be seen—elements which even now, in certain plays of light, made her appear quite lovely.

She fascinated me immediately, this woman who was my mother's mother and who, in some remote, undefinable way resembled me, so that I continued to stare at her. Water rose in her grey eyes and she said in a frail voice, "Andrea . . . "

She balanced herself on her cane, threw a surprisingly strong arm about my neck, and murmured against my cheek, "Thank God you've come. Thank God . . . "

And I thought, This is how I will look in fifty-six years. It made me shudder, all of a sudden, thinking for a moment that I had taken a step into the future.

How ironic it is to look back now and realize that, at the very instant of my thinking such a thought, what I had really done by entering the house on George Street was to take a step backward in time.

Nana's was an incredibly small house. When these terraced houses had been built, insulation was poor against the English winters, and the only heating came from the one fireplace in each room. As a consequence, rooms were small, and any uninhabited space, such as the hall and stairwell, were phenomenally narrow and low-ceilinged.

This surprised me. I had always pictured old English Victorian houses as being large, elegant affairs. Perhaps, for the upper class. But for the great middle class, which the English Industrial Revolution had given birth to, it was the smaller practical houses that were so popular. Therefore was the Townsend house on George Street the example rather than the exception and was merely one of hundreds of thousands of others just like it all over England.

"What do you think of my little house?" she asked when Aunt Elsie and Uncle Ed had left and we had settled down in the sitting room. She was buttering some bread that lay on a plate in her lap.

I looked around the room. Uncommonly old and bulky furniture, dingy walls with peeling paint, faded photographs standing on a wormy sideboard. Black leather books with gold printed titles. Heavy velvet drapes. A small, cluttered, Victorian sitting room. Time seemed to have stopped long ago for my grandmother.

"It must have quite a history," I said.

"Aye, it does. Your Uncle William is always trying to get me to move out of here and into a council flat. But I don't want to live off the government. Not like everyone else in England these days. I've got my little house and I want to keep it.

"He's always talking about having central heating installed. But I've always said that we've done with fireplaces for sixty-two years so I guess it's good enough now."

"Is that how old this house is?" Despite the heat from the gas heater that had been built into the fireplace, I still felt the outer cold penetrate the back of my body.

"Oh my heavens no! That's how long I've lived in it! Sixty-two years. When I married your grandfather he brought me to live here."

"How old is the house?"

"It was built in 1880. That makes it nearly a hundred years old."

"Has it ever been modernized?"

"Aye, it had to be. We've got electricity, you can see that for yourself." She dipped into a jar that was cradled in her lap and drew out on her knife a dollop of bright yellow. It spread thickly and stickily on her bread, which she then stuffed in her mouth, wiping her hands on her sweater. "And we've got a toilet upstairs. It got so we were the only ones left on the road who were still going outside. So we had plumbing put in. But it's old now and you have to be gentle with it. There's a bathtub, too."

Shivering with the damp cold of the room around me and yet feeling my face and shins grow hot from the gas flames, I imagined my grandmother's archaic bathroom and decided that of all the things I should miss most during my stay here it would be my comfortable apartment back in Los Angeles.

And it was while I was pondering the personality of my temporary home and trying politely to get some of Nana's sweet tea down my throat that several strange things began to happen.

A draught blew into the room, causing me to tremble. Nana, seeming not to notice it, turned to an old portable radio that stood on the table by her side and turned it on. I thought I heard her say, "It's time for my favourite music programme."

But I wasn't sure of what she said because her back was turned to me and her voice came out garbled.

As the whine of Scottish bagpipes came out of the small radio, I was suddenly gripped with a terrible fit of shivering, so bad that I nearly spilled my tea and dropped the plate on the floor.

Nana turned about, startled. I shook uncontrollably.

"You must be freezing!" She started to struggle to her feet. "It's this English cold we've got. And you in them skimpy California things."

I tried to speak but my teeth started to chatter. I couldn't hold my mouth still.

I watched in bewilderment as my nana took the things out of my lap,

placed them on the table, and then shuffled to the sofa, from which she retrieved a folded blanket. Draping this over me and tucking it in all around,
she said soothingly, "I like a nap of an afternoon and often have this 'round
me. It's good Shetland wool and will keep the cold off."

"G-God," I chattered. "I can't b-believe th-this . . . "

Then I began to tremble more violently.

It was not the cold from the air. I could feel where it was coming from
and could have told Nana her blanket would do no good. It was coming
from *inside me,* an icy breath that sprang from somewhere in the pit of my
body and blew out through my flesh. My face grew hot, my skin warm and
dry. But still I shook with the terrible cold that had gripped me.

Faintly, then, as if coming from a great distance, I heard a piano.

It played a hauntingly familiar melody against the foreground of blaring
Scottish bagpipes. I stared at the radio and then at my grandmother, who
had resumed the ritual of spreading lemon jam on her bread.

The piano continued to play, barely audible above the bagpipes. I turned
my head this way and that, trying to pinpoint its source. Yet I could not, for
it seemed to be coming from all directions at once.

After a moment, the melody came to my mind: "Für Elise" by Beethoven.
And from what I heard, it was being played by an awkward, unpractised
hand. Certain parts were played over and over again, as if it were a lesson,
and then there were halts and pauses as the person stumbled over the difficult parts. It sounded almost like a child playing.

"Nana . . . " I began.

She spread the jam on her bread, lifting it to her mouth. She was humming along with the bagpipes.

Then I noticed something else. The clock on the mantel had stopped
ticking. I looked at it. It was silent.

The air was filled with the clamour of the pipes and in the background,
almost dreamlike, "Für Elise" by some young hand.

"Nana . . . " I said more loudly. "Your clock has stopped."

She looked up. "What?"

"The clock. It's stopped ticking. Listen."

We both stared at the clock over the fireplace. It was ticking again.

Now my teeth chattered more loudly, and try though I did to say something more, I could not.

And then, in the next instant, as unexpectedly as it had started, the shivering stopped.

My body was suddenly, strangely still.

"It's all right," said Nana. "The clock hasn't stopped. You just didn't hear it over the pipes."

"Or the piano." I wrapped the blanket tighter about me.

"Piano?"

I looked at my grandmother. It was amazing how a face could be so old and yet retain traces of such uncommon beauty. "The piano," I said loudly. "Listen."

We both listened. Then Nana reached over and turned off the radio. All that could be heard was the whispering tick of the clock.

"There's no piano."

"But I heard one."

"Where was it coming from?"

"Well . . . " I shrugged my shoulders, looking around the tight room.

"Maybe it's Mrs.. Clark's telly. That can happen in these old terraced houses. She's just on the other side of that wall. Sometimes, of an evening, I can hear through."

"No, it wasn't a TV. It sounded as though it were just being played in the next room. Does Mrs.. Clark have a piano?"

"Dear me, I don't know. But she's as old and arthritic as I am."

"Who lives on the other side of you, Nana?"

"That house is empty. Has been for months. No one wants to buy these days, not when you can get a central-heated council flat for nothing. I tell you the Social Service system in England is just deplorable! Letting all those Pakistanis in—"

"I really thought I heard something . . . " My voice trailed off.

"You're tired, love." Nana reached over to pat my knee reassuringly. "A good night's sleep and you'll feel better in the morning. I'm glad you could come, Andrea. It'll please your granddad."

"What's wrong with Granddad?"

"He's old, Andrea. He's had eighty-three years of a full and sometimes hard life. But they've been good years, too. We've been through a lot together, your granddad and me."

Now she turned to face me, her eyes filled with tears, her lips quivering. "I've had a good life with that man, I have. And I shall be forever thankful for it. Not many women is as lucky as I am. By no means no! And him having gone through what he did in the war . . . " She shook her head sadly.

"Was he in the war?" This was a part of family history I was familiar with, for I had often heard tales of my father's experiences in the RAF during the Battle of Britain.

Her eyes gazed at me steadily for a minute, then they creased in a bit of amusement, causing the tears to fall. "Aye, love, but not *that* war! I meant World War One. The Great War! He was in the Royal Engineers, was your granddad. Served in Mesopotamia, he did."

I blinked at her. This was something I had never heard before.

"You didn't know, did you? I can tell by your face. Did your mum never tell you stories about us? No? Well . . . " She looked down at her hands and twisted her fingers. "In a way I can understand. Because before your grandfather and I got married, the Townsends had a dreadful history."

"Dreadful?"

She went on as if I hadn't spoken. "I 'spect your mum just told you stories about her own childhood like. About her and Elsie and William. Aye, and well I can understand. But you must know something of your grandparents, now mustn't you, love? After all, you're part of us, too. Your granddad and I had some times together, we did. Do you know"—she thrust a finger at me—"do you know that the very day we got married back in 1915 he was sent overseas? And did you know that I didn't see your grandfather for two years after that, and when he did come home he was such a changed man that he was a stranger to me? He had gone away a boy and come home a man."

I watched her old lips move as she spoke the strange dialect. She pronounced love like book.

"Aye, he was a different man. And when we finally went to our marriage bed, two years after the wedding, and me a virgin mind you, it was like going to bed with a stranger."

I found myself swallowing hard and staring at the dancing blue flames of the gas heater. I tried to picture this man I had never seen, this man who was my mother's father, who now lay dying in the hospital nearby, who had lived in this house for sixty-two years. And then I tried to imagine Nana as a young girl again, twenty-one years old and shyly going to the bed of her new husband.

Then I thought of Doug, of our last night together and of the hurtful words we had said to one another. But when his winsome, smiling face swam before my eyes, I immediately shut the memory out. It was over. Doug and I were finished. These pains would pass, his memory would fade, and I would be a free woman again.

"I guess when you're young you don't think much of the past, do you?" Nana asked. She rubbed her hands together and held them out before the gas fire. "I know I never did. I thought I would live forever. When you're young you never think about death either. You don't have a past to look back on yet, and you're so far away from death that you think it won't happen to you. But when you get old, Andrea, and death is just around the comer, the past is all you've got."

She worked her teeth over her lower lip for a moment and then, as if remembering something, started to rise out of the chair. "I've something to show you."

I watched her shuffle to the sideboard, holding on to the back of the easy chair and leaning on her cane. Her legs bowed outwardly and her shoulders sloped beneath her curved back.

A bit of rummaging in a drawer, and then: "Here's something you've never seen."

She extended a photograph to me. I took it gently in my fingers, recognizing it to be very old, and stared down at the face of an incredibly beautiful woman. The portrait was veiled in faded sepia, "Who *is* she?" I asked.

"That's your granddad's mother," I heard her say, close to my ear.

I continued to stare down at the photograph, unable to take my eyes away from this lovely face. "His mother? Does Granddad look like her? How old *is* this picture?"

"Oh well, I don't rightly know. Let me see. This was taken before Robert—that's your granddad—was born, and she was, I think, twenty when she had him . . . "

I felt myself become drawn into those dark sad eyes that stared out from behind a pale brown mist. This uncommonly beautiful creature, with her hair piled modestly atop her head in a knot and with a cameo about her throat, seemed to be smiling sweetly and sadly at me, as though she were a reluctant sitter for the portrait. And her young eyes, heavy and forlorn, seemed filled with a special melancholy that bespoke the quiet nature the girl must have had, and I began to imagine her as she must have been when she lived. A shy, sad, bewildered beauty.

"Maybe 1893," Nana said. "Isn't she beautiful?"

I nodded. My grandfather's mother. My great-grandmother.

"Her maiden name was Adams. She used to live on Marina Avenue, but before that her family came from Wales. Prestatyn, I think it was."

"What about Granddad's father? What did *he* look like—her husband? Do you have a picture of him?"

There was no reply.

"Nana?" I looked up. Her face seemed hard. I repeated, "Don't you have a picture of my great-grandfather as well?"

Nana reached down and took the picture from me. As she turned to replace it in the sideboard, I watched out of the corner of my eye as she sadly shook her head over the photograph.

When she returned to her seat in the chair next to me, propping her legs nearer the fire, the conversation was changed. "It's been such a lovely Jubilee Year for the Queen . . . "

CHAPTER 2

B Y TEN-THIRTY THAT NIGHT I WAS NODDING IN MY CHAIR AND could not keep my eyes open. I felt a gentle nudge on my shoulder and saw that Nana was already standing. I saw also with a pang of guilt that the cups and plates had all been cleared away.

"Did I doze off? I'm sorry, Nana, I didn't mean to leave you with—"

"Nonsense! I wouldn't have you working around here while you're my guest! And it was rude of me to keep you up this late after such a long journey. You must feel at death's door. Up to bed with you."

She was right. I was uncommonly tired, and, in fact, I felt as if every atom of energy had been sapped from my body. Being in strange surroundings was fatiguing, and then there had been that odd fit of shivering and the piano I thought I had heard.

As soon as I stepped from the sitting room into the hall that bizarre feeling came over me again; this time it seemed even stronger. It was almost an air of hostility. I hesitated at the foot of the narrow stairwell and stared up at the darkness at the top. I held back.

"Is something wrong?" Nana was at my side.

"I was . . . wondering which is my room . . . "

"I've fixed up the front bedroom for you nice like, Ed's put your case up there, and Elsie put a hot-water bottle under the clothes for you. I'm sorry it doesn't have a heater. You see, the front bedroom hasn't been used in many years. Not since our William got married and moved out. I 'spect that would be over twenty years ago now. Up you go then, love."

I mounted the stairs warily, amazed at their steepness, and placed my hands flat on the wall at each side. I tried not to look up at the blackness at the top and tried also to pretend the cold of the stairwell didn't bother me.

But it did, and it got worse as I neared the top. I started to shiver. Steam was coming from my mouth. Behind me, a few steps below, Nana scaled her way up the stairs laboriously, and I wondered if she could see me just ahead of her.

At the top step my teeth began to chatter again. I hugged myself and tried to search the wall for a switch. Trying to keep one arm around my other bare arm, I slid my hand over the damp wall in this blackness that was deeper than night.

I struck something.

"Have you found the light?" puffed my nana as she reached the top.

"I . . . don't—"

Her arm shot out and instantaneously the light overhead came on. I looked at the wall. It had been the light switch that my hand had struck.

"That's it. Turn to the right," she said out of breath and leaning against the wall.

Directly at the top of the stairs was the bathroom door, and next to it, the door to my grandmother's bedroom. But around the corner and down a short hall was another door.

"Now if you want anything in the night, you know where it is, don't you? If you use the toilet, don't flush it, will you? And be sure not to leave the light on. There's a love."

Rubbing my arms and dreading the cold, I made my way down the hall to the front bedroom and pushed open the door. It creaked as it swung away from me, yawning into a great black pit. Hurriedly I ran my hand over the inside wall and was able to switch on the light.

I smiled with relief. A delightful room. A nice double bed with big fluffy pillows and a gaily coloured eider-down comforter. A thready but quaint Persian carpet on the floor. Against one wall an antique wardrobe with one door standing open to reveal a rack and empty coat hangers. On the opposite wall a marble fireplace, now boarded up, with an ornate old mirror hanging above it. By my bed there was a small table with a lace doily and a leather-bound copy of the Bible.

It all looked very comfortable, and I felt a bit silly about my groundless fear on the stairs. Turning around to bid good night to my grandmother, I saw the empty hallway before me, heard no sounds, and assumed she had already gone to bed.

So I stepped into my own room, closed the door, and kicked the sausage into place. From then on I had to move quickly. The small bit of warmth I had retained from the fire downstairs was gone now and the icy cold of the room was beginning to numb my body. Already my fingers had grown stiff so they fumbled with the clasps of my suitcase. My nose and chin were bitten with the cold.

I had never experienced anything like this before. Surely if the temperature outside had been thirty-four degrees a few hours ago, then what must it be now? And what was going to keep this ancient, uninsulated house from turning into a deep freeze?

Hanging up my jeans and T-shirt in the clothes wardrobe, I threw my bathrobe on over my pyjamas and went to the window, where I parted the curtain a little.

Beyond the frost-covered pane was a night blacker than any I had ever seen, with no moon or stars, and only one old lamp down the street giving off a bit of illumination. The houses across from us, all connected and identical and lined up like pieces in a Monopoly game, were dark and quiet. The cobblestone street, with an occasional car, so anachronistic, parked at the kerb, was shiny beneath a coat of dew.

I let the curtain fall. By now I was so frozen through that I decided to sleep in my robe. First turning out the light and then making a blind running leap for the bed, I dived under the mountains of covers and pulled them over my head. The water bottle, still hot, I hugged to my abdomen and curled up on my side.

Except for the occasional chatter of my teeth there was nothing but silence about me; a heavy cloak of absolute soundlessness that made me aware of the beating of my own heart. I wondered if I should ever fall asleep under such conditions, with my fingers and feet frozen, my body shaking, and lying on this lumpy mattress. I must have lain staring into the darkness for at least an hour, thinking of Doug and trying to ignore the uneasy feeling I had about the house before I finally fell asleep.

I have no idea what time it was when I awoke. Nor did I know what woke me.

Suddenly, my eyes flew open and there I was, lying in the darkness and clutching the mattress with my painful fingers. I was already frightened; there had been a fear that had begun in my sleep and that had awakened me, but fear of what I could not see. My eyes strained against the night, realizing that it was not the darkness itself that now sent my heart racing in terror of the unknown, but something else in the room. Something present that I could not see . . .

I struggled with my thoughts. I tried to remember who I was, tried to recall where I was and what I was doing here. But my mind was imprisoned in a cage of amnesia. I could remember nothing. I had no memory. My mind was as black as the night around me.

And as I lay wrestling with my thoughts, trying desperately to remember, I discovered the thing that had awakened me.

A tremendous pressure lay upon my body. An intangible force, without substance, pressed me down into the bed, almost suffocating me. I wanted to cry out but could not. The breath in me was stifled.

Something was pinning me down.

My terror quickly turned to panic. A mounting hysteria drove me to struggle against the unearthly pressure. I fought for air, feeling each icy gulp stab my lungs.

I had to get to the light.

My mind raced wildly. Was I paralysed? How could such a force lie atop me without my *feeling* anything?

I concentrated on freeing my arm. My breath came in short gasps. I had to see.

I had to see.

Suddenly my arm was out of the covers. Reaching up for the bedstead, I pulled with all my might and was able, with great effort, to draw myself up to a sitting position. And still the suffocation lay upon me, like an immense gravitational pull, as though the atmosphere were collapsing inwardly and crushing everything in its path. I fought against it, sucking air, trying to keep my mouth open, pushing my arms outward against the force until I was able to stretch far enough from the bed that, as I frantically dashed my hand over the wall, I accidentally hit the switch.

The instant the light came on the pressure snapped off me. I was left panting and gasping for breath.

I had also perspired so heavily that my pyjamas were damp, causing me to tremble so badly in the cold air that I shook the bed. I sat huddled against the bedstead for some time, rubbing my arms, bouncing my legs up and down for warmth. And I reflected on what had happened.

I could not remember what it was that had awakened me. If it had been a dream, or the cold, or simply the strangeness of a new bed.

Or something else . . .

And that queer pressure. Had I imagined it? Had it all been a dream until the moment when, in my sleep, I had been able to reach the light switch?

The idea made me shudder. It hadn't seemed like a dream. It had seemed starkly real, too real for comfort.

As I drew the covers up to my neck and shoulders, I discovered how heavy they were. With several blankets, a comforter, and a cumbersome bedspread, it occurred to me that I had been sleeping beneath a tremendous weight.

Of course. That was it! I now laughed softly for courage. Back home I was used to sleeping with just one light blanket, and so it must have been that in my sleep, feeling the great weight of all these covers on me, I had dreamed that some mysterious thing was holding me down.

How strange is that twilight edge between sleep and consciousness. How bizarre to wake up not knowing who I am or where. But of course understandable now, in the light of the overhead bulb. I had had a nightmare. And it had merely seemed more real than most. Even now, sitting up and finding small comfort in the warm water bottle, I still shuddered from the remaining bits of fear that had first gripped me upon awakening.

But all of it imagination. None of it real.

As I reached up to flick off the light I paused and, for reasons not known to me, turned my head to look over my shoulder.

The mirror over the fireplace.

What was wrong with it?

I held myself in that attitude for a long minute, frowning at the mirror, wondering what had made me turn to look at it, wondering why I continued now to stare at it. Yet stare I did, unable to take my eyes away, as though some small voice whispered at the back of my head, telling me I must not look away.

But why? It was an ordinary enough mirror. Old, antique perhaps, with a dull gilt frame. There was nothing strange or unusual about it. All it did was reflect the interior of the room, focusing mainly, I saw, on the wardrobe opposite.

And yet I continued to be held by it, staring in fascination, almost as if I knew what it was I was looking for. As though it sat just at the very edge of my mind what magic the mirror held. I could almost grasp it . . . .

But then, shaking my head and casting off the notion, I drew away from the light switch and sank back under the covers. I was more jet-lagged than I had realized. More fatigued than I had suspected.

I forced a smile to bolster myself and, resting secure with the light on overhead, reassured myself that tomorrow everything would be all right.

I awakened the next morning to the smell of bacon and eggs cooking, and after as fast as possible a visit to the freezing bathroom, I came downstairs in a pullover sweater and jeans to find a nice warm sitting room and a laid-out table. While my flighty imaginings of the night before were dispelled by the sight of sunlight streaming through the window, I continued to experience an indescribable discomfort. I had dreamed little, and those dreams I could recall were patchy, disjointed, and meaningless. And when I had opened my eyes in the sunlit bedroom and had felt refreshed and more like my usual self, it had been dismaying to discover the disconcerting spell the house continued to cast.

I wondered when it would pass.

"Is this the only room of the house you use, Nana?" I asked, buttering my toast.

"Aye, love. This and my bedroom. The parlour hasn't been used in ever so many years. No need for it. Can't heat it so I use it for storage like. I live in this room most of the time."

I nodded, looking around. There was the sagging sofa, the two easy chairs, the cluttered sideboard, a cabinet with glass doors behind which stood old books and china, and lastly this small kitchen table with its two straight-backed chairs. Portraits of the Queen hung all about. There was an old calendar with Australian scenes on it. A battered sewing box. A vase with brown carnations in it. A filigree frame containing a group shot of Elsie's and William's children, my cousins.

It was a cosy room and warm enough. As we ate we sat by the one window, which looked out at the yard, although it wasn't exactly what you'd call a back yard. From this window to the high wall at the rear couldn't have been more than ten paces. One could literally jump from one end to the other. The ground was inlaid with uneven brick. There was no grass, no garden, just a stretch of earth along the foot of each wall out of which grew (or had once grown, for now they were skeletons) rose bushes. And in the back wall, a gate leading out to the alley beyond and the large field after that.

"Do those roses ever bloom, Nana?"

"No, love. Won't nothing grow in that garden. Never has. Not in all the years I've been here. Them rose bushes are from long ago. Even before I first came to live here."

"Did you ever try to cultivate them?" I held my tea cup against my lips, staring absently at the stark, barren shrubs.

"I did at first, but nothing seemed to help. The soil's bad, I s'pose." She idly stirred her tea. "And do you know, it's a funny thing, come to think of it, but we've never had nothing grow in that garden. And we've never been able to keep a cat or a dog neither. Always run away they did. Something about the soil, your granddad always said."

I pondered this for a moment and then, shaking the odd feeling her words aroused, I said, "How long have you and Granddad lived here alone?"

"Your Uncle William was the last to move out. That must have been twenty or more years ago now. After that, your granddad and I had no use for any other part of the house. But do you know, it's still got most of its furniture that was here the day I moved in sixty-two years ago."

"You're kidding! All this?"

"Every bit of it. And the bed you're sleeping in as well. Original mattress and everything. All brought in around 1880."

"You've got some valuable old stuff here, Nana."

"Aye, and Elsie and William are always after me to sell it all and move into a flat. But how could I? This house has memories for me! I couldn't leave it! I'm part of it, Andrea."

I returned to gazing out of the window at the brilliant blue sky and tried to imagine what it must be like to live in the same house for sixty-two years. The longest my parents and brother and I had lived anywhere was ten years, in a beach house in Santa Monica, and that we had considered an eternity.

"A lot's gone on in this house, Andrea, make no mistake. It's had its share of tragedy."

I turned back to my grandmother.

She avoided my eyes. "Well, and happiness, too. There's some of both in every family, now isn't there?"

The rest of the morning was taken up with clearing the table and listening to Nana talk about the trouble with the British economy. At one o'clock Elsie and Ed let themselves in, shivering and bringing with them a rush of cold from the outside. Their faces were like apples, their fingers white and stiff to move.

"Temp's dropping," announced Aunt Elsie as she rushed to the gas fire. "I hope you'll be warm enough, Andrea."

"I'll be fine. How long are visiting hours?"

"In the afternoon, just one hour. Which is enough for your granddad. We don't want to tire him out. And at night it's an hour and a half."

"Do you go both times?"

"No, love. At night our William and his wife go. It's because Ed is retired that we two can go in the afternoons. At night William and May go after supper. Granddad must never be without visitors, so we share it. Some days Christine goes after work."

I knew a little about Christine. She was seven years younger than I and worked in the typing pool for some nearby manufacturer. My other two cousins, Albert and Ann, were Elsie's children. Ann had moved away to Amsterdam, while Albert was married and lived at Morecambe Bay on the Irish Sea.

My mother and I had been kept apprised of the family's activities over the years, just as she had written them about my college graduation and Richard's move to Australia. I had seen Christine and Albert and Ann only in photographs. And except for basic statistics—Ann worked in an artist's studio overlooking the Dam, Albert and his young wife had a baby girl, Christine had her own flat here in Warrington—except for this I knew nothing about my cousins.

Nor did I care to. Having done without relatives so far, I felt no great urge to generate relationships. After all, in a few days I would be going back to L.A. and these people would be, as far as I was concerned, distant relations.

"Your mum and I had some times when we was girls," said Elsie before the fire. "I don't know how our William could stand us. We were older, see, and bossed him around." She gave out a great laugh. "Oh, I do wish our Ruth could have come with you. But those foot operations are painful, aren't they? You know, Andrea, I helped your mum with you when you was a baby. Did you know that? After you were born, she came down with a problem and had to go back to hospital. So I took care of you. It was like you was my own baby 'cause I hadn't any children of my own just then. Albert was born the next year."

She talked thus for a while longer and then it was time to go.

I bundled up as well as I could, thankful for the woollen hat and mittens Elsie had brought for me, and braced myself against the outside.

"I'll have a nice fish dinner waiting for you when you get back, love," said Nana, shuffling to the front door with us. "I'm not going with you, Andrea, because it's too cold for me to go outside. Maybe Sunday, if I'm up to it. Make it a nice visit, will you?" As Elsie and Ed ran down to the car,

Nana stayed me a minute with her hand and said in a low voice, "He'll be a stranger to you, Andrea, but never you mind that. He's a Townsend, just as you're a Townsend. Always remember that he gave life to your mum. He's your granddad and he needs you right now. He needs us all." I nodded dumbly and hurried down to the car.

Warrington General Hospital was the same foreboding complex Elsie had pointed out to me the night before. Here was where I had drawn my first breath, between those looming red-brick walls. And here I was again, twenty-seven years later, returning to make a pilgrimage to the Townsend part of me.

We found a small space for Uncle Ed's Renault and all piled out. Stomping our feet for circulation, we then hurried across the damp grass and between the bare trees and finally through the swinging doors of the hospital.

At once the smell hit me. It burned my nose with its horrible pungency— an odour that, at first, made me gag. I watched Aunt Elsie and Uncle Ed. They seemed not to notice the smell. They were busy peeling off their outer layers and draping them over their arms. I did likewise, trying to ignore the sickly air. It was a foul stench, redolent of disease, stale urine, and putrefaction. I couldn't stand it at first and tried to breathe through my mouth.

Uncle Ed and I followed Elsie down the hall and into the ward. Here I was met with another shock.

A large grey room with bare wooden floors and whitewashed walls, the men's geriatric unit of Warrington Hospital was comprised of a row of twenty beds along either wall, a sink at one end and an old-fashioned television set at the other, windows framed by unmatched drapes, and a stack of folding wooden chairs in one corner.

From this last Uncle Edouard helped himself to three chairs, unfolded them, and placed them around the first bed near the entrance.

"Come on, love," he said in his French/Lancashire speech. "Closest to your granddad."

I approached the bed slowly, watching the face of the old man who slept there. I stood over him for a second, looking down at the hollow face, the flaking skin, the tufts of white hair that stood straight up. He looked to have been laid out for a wake, so neat he was, so smooth his covers. My grandfather slumbered in deep repose, as if he had come to his final rest.

I felt myself fumble for a chair. It grated over the wooden floor and echoed throughout the ward, just as did our footsteps and voices. Elsie and Ed sat opposite me on the other side of the bed, with my aunt digging into her large leather bag and bringing out treats for Granddad. A packet of biscuits. A bottle of orange drink. A roll of mints. As she did so she chatted with the recumbent man as if he responded, as if his eyes were open and he was alert. Elsie prattled on and on about the rugby match with Manchester, about the horses my grandfather had so often played, about the Queen's Jubilee on telly, about our Albert's baby girl, how she's growing.

Uncle Edouard, smiling and arranging the treats atop Granddad's small locker, echoed Elsie's words.

I watched them both in amazement. Except for the barest rise and fall of the covers, and except for the plastic bag which hung from the foot of his bed, filled with yellow fluid, and joined to a rubber tube that ran up under the covers and was somewhere connected to my grandfather, except for these small evidences, the man in this bed could easily have been dead. His body was as still as if it were without life. His dry old skin had a peculiar pallor to it. All about hung a sour smell, emanating from this body that was no longer renewing itself.

I searched the face for something familiar. I had photographs of him in my album back home, a hearty and robust man with thick black hair and a ruggedly handsome face. But they were pictures of a stranger, a face without an identity. And now, being in the presence of that man, he remained just as elusive to me.

And yet there it was, barely seen now as his face slept in some pre-death slumber, smooth and unlined, there between his eyebrows and just above the bridge of his nose was the furrow.

I felt my throat tighten. My hands came together on my lap and joined in a steadying clasp.

"I 'spect you wonder why we talk to him," Aunt Elsie said all of a sudden.

I snapped my head up. I had forgotten she was there.

"Well, the doctor told us that even though a person is asleep, he can still hear. Isn't that right, Ed? He said it's the hearing that's the last to go when a person passes away, so that even though someone's asleep they can still hear. And even though Dad seems unresponsive, it's possible that somewhere, deep inside his brain, a part of him will hear us and be comforted by our presence. So I talk to him all the time. After all, it's the least you'd do for a dog, now isn't it?"

She ended her sentence with an expectant look on her face. I knew what she wanted.

I looked back down at that ancient face, at the sunken cheeks, at the lips that fell between toothless gums. I smelled the rancid air, the aroma of bodies decomposing, and looked long at the furrow between this man's brows.

Here was our link.

Inclining myself a little, I gingerly placed a hand on the covers and felt his thin and bony arm beneath. "Hi, Granddad. It's me, Andrea."

My words hung in the air. The three of us bent towards the bed.

Presently Elsie said softly, "He's heard you, love. He knows you're here."

I kept my eyes on that old face. I tried to picture the dashing Royal Engineer that had marched off to Mesopotamia in 1915. I tried to see through this decrepit exterior to find some trace of the man who had once dandled my mother on his knee.

Yet I could not. I was trying to force it. Trying to feel some affection for this wasted human being who was, after all, still a stranger to me. I could feel nothing for him, even though we were closely blood related, and although his gift to me had been the small groove between my eyebrows, I could not manufacture even the barest sentiments towards him. He was, in the end, simply a dying old man.

I looked up at Elsie and forced a smile.

And so it must be with all my relatives. How could I deliver the affection they sought when I had none to give?

Eventually the hour passed. I had thought it would go on interminably. In the interim, other visitors had come to see the other old denizens of this depressing ward, their voices all echoing off the damp walls, their footsteps disturbing the peace. Nurses and Sisters scurried about. Someone turned on the TV. The old man in the next bed fell into a coughing fit and let forth such an explosion that his dentures flew across the room.

Yet my grandfather never stirred. Wherever he was, it must have been an infinitely nicer place than this.

When we departed I tried not to show my relief. I was also thankful that it was not expected of me to make the nightly visit too, with Uncle William and his wife.

"It's too cold for you, love," said Elsie as we hurried back to the car. "I can see that now. All you've known is Southern California. It can't be pleasant for you. But it was good of you to come. Your granddad won't go on much longer and then it'll be over."

Seeing tears gather in her eyes, I reached out and touched her arm.

"You're doing good," she said in a tight voice. Uncle Ed was patiently holding the car door open. "Dad would have loved to have our Ruth at his side in his last moments. But you're just like your mum. You've got her smile. It's like looking at our Ruth again just before she left England."

I turned away and quickly piled into the cramped back seat.

Aunt Elsie fell in next to Uncle Ed and continued, "I do wish your mum could have come back for a visit before this. I 'spect she feels guilty now."

"Yes, as a matter of fact, she does."

"Aye, it's understandable. I'd feel the same way, I would. But time goes on and the years roll by and suddenly you realize that no one lives forever."

I played with the cuffs of my mittens. Uncle Ed backed the car out and then jostled us down the gravel drive towards the hospital entrance gate. Here, nailed to the red-brick wall, was a sign that read: Dead Slow.

I had never had any proximity with death before, had never known anyone who died, had never seen a corpse. As a consequence, death had always been a remote concept to me, something almost philosophical, a thing that *never really happened.*

When you live among palm trees and eternal sunshine, when you're twenty-seven and going from boyfriend to boyfriend, when you live for swimming-pool parties and Saturday-night discotheques, somehow you never think of your mortality. You never think of the end of things or of the past or of all the lives that have gone on before you.

We bounced off down the wrong side of the street, Aunt Elsie pointing out places I supposedly had known as an infant, and I could not find the spot in my heart that was supposed to endear me to this land. As far as I was concerned, I was a stranger among strangers, and home was eight thousand miles away.

It was there again, as soon as we fell through the front door, the peculiar gloom the house seemed to cast over me. But this time I attributed it to the mood my grandfather's visit had put me in.

The smell of fish dipped in batter and frying potatoes greeted us as we opened the door of the sitting room. Nana was back in her little kitchen, what she called "the scullery," getting dinner ready for us. It was nearly two-thirty.

Elsie and Ed stayed to eat with us, heaping their plates with crisp fish and scallops and spoonfuls of mashed peas. We doused our plates with salt and pepper and vinegar, and washed it all down with sweet English tea.

"How was he today?" asked Nana, tucking a cosy over the teapot.

"All right, Mum. He was resting."

Uncle Ed stood rubbing his hands over the fire. "He was quiet."

Nana nodded, comforted. Then she eased herself into a straight-backed chair. "He's getting good care at hospital. Always warm, he is, and lots of good food. Was he glad to see Andrea?"

"I think so," murmured Elsie.

"You know, love," said my grandmother, turning to me, "when your granddad fell ill a few weeks ago and he could no longer walk and the ambulance took him away, I wanted to lie down and die right there. It was as if they had cut off one of me arms. And I suffered badly in those first days. But when I saw how comfortable he was in hospital, how kind the Sisters were, I knew it was best for him. So I prayed to God for strength and managed to reconcile myself to what's happened."

Her steady grey eyes beheld me for a moment. Then she said softly, "He'll never come out of there, Andrea."

"Oh, Mum!" said Elsie, jumping to her feet. "No need to go on like that! He'll come home, you'll see."

"No one lives forever, Elsie."

My aunt seized her coat, exclaiming, "Look at the time! It's time we were getting on, Ed."

As my aunt and uncle readied themselves for the harsh outdoors, I sat at the table by the window looking out at the stunning blue November sky and wondered just what I had to do with all this.

I heard Nana see them to the door, push the sausage against the foot of it and draw the heavy drapes in place, then return to the sitting room.

"There, there, love. I know it's been hard, seeing your granddad like that. But he's at peace, Andrea, remember that."

I avoided looking at her, fearing what she would find in my eyes, that she might see the truth there. For the truth was that I had no feeling whatever for my grandfather, just as I would have none for any of the other old men who lay decomposing in that ward. What had cast a gloom upon me was the stark reality of an end that awaits us all, an inevitability to which I had not, before now, given much thought.

It had also started me thinking about Doug.

"I know what you need!" she said brightly—she who seemed to have surrendered to this awful, unfair thing. "You'll do with some hot drop scones, you will. I haven't made any in such a long time, but I have all the ingredients and can whip up a panful right now. Would you like that then, some nice drop scones?"

As she bustled off into the scullery, her cane hitting the floor like a third foot, I drew myself out of the chair and tried to toss off the mood.

"Can I help?" I called out.

"Go on with you! And don't come in here either! Now sit by the fire, there's a love."

I wandered around the small room a bit, coming to rest before the armoire in the corner and stopping to look through the glass doors.

Several books stood on one shelf. I read the titles. Seeing one of interest, I opened the door and drew out the black leather-bound copy of *She* by Rider Haggard. There was a bookplate glued to the inside cover. It read "Cheshire County Council. Awarded to Naomi Dobson for school attendance and progress. Thirty-one July, 1909."

I let the book fall open. Pages flipped by. Long ago, in high school, I had read this adventure of Victorian explorers in uncharted Africa and of the discovery of an immortal queen. When I came to a familiar passage I stopped and read it. "Mortality is weak and oppressed in the company of the dust which awaits upon its end."

And I thought, How true! How oppressed I had become in the presence of the dust that my grandfather was becoming, knowing that the same end awaited me.

It was as I was replacing the book on the shelf that I felt the skin of my neck suddenly crawl.

It was an uncanny sensation, one which moved slowly up the back of my neck and over my scalp. I froze. I had the definite feeling that the air around me had changed. It seemed to have shifted, to have actually *moved*. And it also seemed, as I stood unmoving and staring at the book, that the light in the room had grown somehow dim.

I lifted my head and looked around. The sitting room looked no different. And yet . . . oddly, at the same time, it *was* different.

Unable to discern just how it had changed, and aware also of a sudden, eerie silence, I slowly turned my head and looked at the window.

I let out a gasp.

A young boy, no older than fourteen or fifteen, had his face and hands pressed against the pane and was looking in at me.

I gaped back for a second, briefly thinking that he looked familiar, then managed to find a voice to call out. "Nana!"

The boy remained at the window, his expression fixed on me: an expression of frank curiosity. He had black hair and dark eyes. His forehead seemed wrinkled in a frown, for there was a furrow between his brows.

"Nana!"

I forced myself away from the armoire and went towards the scullery.

"Yes, love?" she rang out.

"Nana, there's a—" I looked back at the window. He was gone.

"There's a what, love?"

She came to the doorway, wiping flour-covered hands on her apron. Behind her was the sound of lard sizzling in the pan.

"There was a boy looking in the window just now."

"What? The ruffians!" She picked up her cane, turned unsteadily, and hobbled back into the kitchen. I followed her through the kitchen and out to the back door, Nana muttering angrily all the way.

Fiddling with the lock, she drew open the door and the arctic cold of the day fell on us. Nana stepped carefully down on to the uneven bricks.

"Young ruffians! Like to torment old people, they do! That's why we never had a doorbell put in. Ring it they do, and then run off. Now then, where is he?"

I looked around the tiny yard and knew that our search would be futile. "He must have gone through the gate," I said lamely.

"What? Oh my no, that gate's not been used in ever so long. See for yourself, it can't be moved."

Shivering, I did examine the hinges and the catch. All rusted permanently shut. Then I examined the small stretches of wall, peering at the brittle rose bushes and damp earth for evidence of his having come over the wall. Then I stood on my toes and looked into Mrs. Clark's small yard and saw the endless chain of yards and wall and dreary backs of old houses.

"What's back there, Nana?"

"An alley that's never used. And then that big field, that's Newfeld Heath, it goes down to the canal. The rascal's long gone now."

"Yes . . . " I absently rubbed my arms. The rose bushes had not been disturbed and it would have been impossible for anyone to come over this wall without landing on them.

I shivered, now more from the strange feeling the episode left me with than from the cold.

"Come back in, love, and forget about it. Just a local lad having a jest."

I followed her back into the house and secured the back door. Inside the sitting room I continued to shiver. No amount of tea or fire or hot buttered scones could shake the bizarre feeling that had preceded his appearance at the window. Or the fact that I felt I had seen the boy somewhere before.

❈

We had tea at six o'clock, an affair of sandwiches and hot milk, after which we took our places again before the fire. I rested back and tried to let myself drift in the heat of the room. Still jet-lagged, as I imagined I would be for a few days, I was already incredibly tired and desirous of going to bed. But since my grandmother obviously thrived on my company and needed someone to fuss over, I forced myself to stay awake.

She talked about this and that for a while, switching now to the problem of Pakistanis in England, then to the happiness of days long gone by. In her broad Lancashire speech she told me tales of my mother's childhood, of William and Elsie and Ruth growing up in this house, of my mother first bringing my father home to meet the family. It was all very interesting, a great deal of which I had already heard from my mother, but after a while I began to notice an almost deliberate avoidance of the deeper past. Nana would only go as far back as her first baby, Elsie, then she seemed to hit a wall which she feared to penetrate.

After a while she said, "I've a box of photographs here somewhere. You shall have a look at them."

I kept my eyes closed against the peace and quiet of the sitting room, sinking into the overstuffed chair and building a mental wall against the memories I had come here to forget. I hoped it would not be too long before I could think of Doug and not feel pain.

"Here we are." Nana, having found the box in the bottom drawer of the sideboard, placed it in her lap as she resumed her seat. "These are all of your mother and William and Elsie when they were young." She rummaged in the box. "Here's one of us at the seaside. Looks like it's around 1935. Your mum is fifteen in this. Elsie's a year older so she's sixteen. And William's just a lad."

I glanced at the blurry photograph and leaned forward to peer into the box. Many photos lay heaped upon one another, some of which I recognized from my mother's collection. They were all glossy and black and white and all from around the same period.

But, sticking up along the edge of the box lay a photograph on its side, bigger than the rest and, from the bit that showed, considerably older.

As Nana chatted on I reached in and fished out the photograph.

I was right. It was indeed older than the others. Much older. Faded and brown with a crack down the centre, it was a portrait of three children standing on the stoop of a house.

I stared at the picture.

My heart stopped beating.

"Nana . . . " I heard myself say.

She looked at what I had in my hand. "What's that one?"

"Nana . . . who *are* they?" The room began to swim about me.

"Let me put my glasses on." As soon as the bifocals were perched atop her nose and my grandmother could see the faces of the three children, she pursed her lips in displeasure. "Oh," she said darkly. "That one. Those are the Townsends, Andrea, Your grandfather's family. That's Harriet and Victor and John. Here, you don't want to be . . . " And she reached out to take it.

But I clung to the picture. I saw that my hand trembled. "Which one . . . " I had to lick my lips. "*Which is which*, Nana?"

"Ay?"

"Which child is which? Name them for me."

"Well let me see then." She leaned forward and tapped a finger to each face. "That's Harriet. That's Victor. And that's John."

The boy in the centre. The one between the girl with the ringlets and the smaller lad in a sailor's outfit, the one Nana called Victor.

He was the same boy who had peered through the window that afternoon.

CHAPTER 3

O H, IT CAN'T BE!" SHE SAID. "YOU'VE IMAGINED IT!"

"I haven't, Nana. This is the boy I saw looking through the window."

"A lad who resembled—"

"Even the clothes were the same, Nana. I didn't think of it at the time, but his clothes weren't modern. He was wearing an old-fashioned shirt and trousers. In fact the same clothes that are in this photograph. I *couldn't* have imagined it, Nana. Not *before* seeing the picture. He was as real as you are to me now."

Nana swung her head from side to side. "Andrea, it's your mind playing tricks. Seeing as you'd just come from visiting your granddad, it's no wonder—"

"What does that have to do with it?" I wrung my hands, trying to keep them from shaking. Down in the deepest pit of my soul I had a horrible sick feeling, a premonition of things to come.

"Your granddad looked a lot like Victor when he was a lad. Now you came home from the hospital in a gloom, I saw that, and you worried over it. You had your granddad's face in your mind, and by some trick, maybe because you was sad, you made him younger. You took his face and erased the years and made him younger. Then you thought you saw him at the window."

I tried to keep myself calm, tried to keep myself from arguing, for my grandmother had become greatly distraught. But I had to find an answer. "Nana," I said slowly, "why should Granddad have looked like this boy when he was young?"

"Because . . . " She chewed her lower lip and her face became distorted with worry. "Because Victor Townsend was your granddad's father."

My eyes went back to the picture.

"Victor Townsend was your great-grandfather."

I was at once mesmerized. Gazing at that youthful but already handsome face, at the thick black hair and the groove between the brows that gave him a defiant look, I felt a strange sensation come over me. For the moment, I was held captive by the old photograph, just as the night before, for an instant, something had made me stare at the mirror over my fireplace.

The three children were standing on a step before a house that was unfamiliar to me. The little girl, maybe five or six years old, had a plain face although someone had gone to great pains to dress her up. The frilly little pinafore and ribbons in her hair only enhanced rather than hid the fact that she was homely. The other boy, younger than Victor and gentler of features, stood awkwardly next to his brother.

Victor Townsend, the eldest, dominated the scene.

"That was taken in front of their old house in London," said Nana in a tone that suggested she would rather not speak of it. "So that would have been in 1880, just before they bought this house. Victor's father, your great-great-grandfather, was with a London manufacturing firm, some sort of supervisor he was, and was sent to Warrington to open a new plant. When they came here, this house was only just newly built. They were the first to live in it."

I continued to gaze down into the faces of 1880. "I've never heard anything about him. Victor," I murmured. "My mother has never mentioned him—her grandfather."

"And never she will either." Nana's voice seemed heavy and ominous.

"Why? Didn't she know him? If he was her grandfather then she must have—"

"Victor Townsend disappeared a long time ago." Nana's stare fell into the blue flames of the gas fire. She did not blink as she spoke. "Even I never knew him, and he was my husband's father. He disappeared one day before your granddad was born and was never heard from again."

I continued to be held by the face in the photo. The hazy features of youth were already showing evidence of the strength and character that would later mark the man. "And no one knows what happened to him?"

"Oh, there's stories. Some say he ran off to sea. Some say he set up house in Norfolk with another woman. Some say . . . "

Finally I brought my head up. "Go on. What do some say?"

But she shook her head angrily. "I've said too much already. Let me just tell you that Victor Townsend was a bad and evil man. He was the Devil himself, was Victor Townsend, and when he disappeared, well, there were no tears shed."

I stared awhile longer at the picture until a cold draught, suddenly blowing through the room, brought me back to the present. Reluctantly I returned the picture to the box. "Are there more pictures of them, Nana? Of the Townsends?"

"Well, there's an album . . . "

"Can I see it?"

Her fingers worked quickly to bury the photograph at the bottom of the box, then she slammed the lid on as if to keep it from getting out. "I don't know where the album is now. The last I saw it was many years ago. But I 'spect it's still in the house somewhere."

"Is it the Townsend album?"

She nodded.

I thought a moment. "Nana, the portrait you showed me last night, the one of the young woman. You said she was my great-grandmother."

"Aye, Jennifer Townsend, poor lass."

"Why poor? What was wrong with her?"

"Because of what Victor Townsend did to her, that's why. Now, that's enough."

I paced in my room. Although I told myself I did it to keep warm, I marched a path on the carpet out of nervousness.

It was easy to convince myself that I was just overtired, that this visit was an emotional strain as well as a physical one. It was simple to explain away the odd happenings as products of fatigue—such as the boy at the window or the feeling of suffocation the night before. And these I could, rationally, accept and explain away.

However, what was troubling me now was not those things, but something else. Something which no amount of logic or reason or forced nonchalance could dispel.

For the idea was growing in me that I had a *feeling* about the house.

Although the previous night when I had arrived, and then all that day, I had tried to tell myself it was only my imagination, this time I *knew*. Something was definitely not right.

And it was for this reason that I now stormed back and forth across the room, my nerves on edge.

A short while earlier I had learned to my great dismay and disappointment that Nana did not have a telephone, for I had decided on an impulse to call my mother. I suddenly needed her, needed contact with her and to be in touch with my true reality eight thousand miles away. And besides, this was her family, these were her people, and above all . . . this was *her house*.

What had I to do with any of it?

Without the telephone I felt suddenly and brutally cut off from the world. A peculiar loneliness which I had never experienced before took hold of me. I felt stranded, abandoned, left alone with a strange old woman in this most disturbing house.

Thoughts of Doug also plagued me. I had used my grandfather's illness and my mother's request that I come here in her place as an excuse to get away from Doug and to work out a way to forget him. As it was turning out, however, I was dwelling on him more than ever. And the strange part was, rather than going over and over that last angry night as a means to rid my heart of him, instead I found myself recalling only the good times we had spent together. And no matter how hard I tried, I could not seem to command my own thoughts.

Why, when in all my twenty-seven years I had had absolute control over myself, why all of a sudden did my mind seem to have a will of its own?

It was nearly midnight when there was a knock at my door. I spun around, startled.

"Andrea, love, can't you sleep?" came Nana's weary voice through the wood.

"Uh . . . I'm fine . . . Nana." I took a hesitant step towards the door and then faltered. Of course, my pacing had creaked the floorboards and she was certain to have heard them. "I'm okay, Nana. Just doing some exercises. Please go back to bed."

"Shall I get you some hot milk?" came her frail voice.

I was stabbed with guilt. I pictured her standing out in the freezing hall in her flannel nightgown, supported by two bowed legs and a cane.

"No thanks, Nana. I'm just going to bed right now."

"Are you warm enough, love? Do you want another water bottle?"

"No, I'm fine."

"Well, be sure the sausage is right against the door so no draughts get in. Good night then, love."

I listened to her hobble down the hall and into her own room where I presently heard the bedsprings creak, and then the house was still once again.

With great reluctance I shoved the bolster hard against the foot of the door, turned out the light, and climbed into my own bed.

Within seconds I was asleep.

It started the same way it had the night before. First my eyes snapped open suddenly, making me sharply awake without being aware of why. Then the brief spell of amnesia. Then the sickening pressure upon my body.

"Oh no . . . " I groaned with a sinking feeling in my stomach. "Not . . . again . . . "

Lying still and trying not to panic, I tried to analyse the feeling, to see if I were indeed awake or just dreaming, to see if it could possibly be only the blankets creating a nightmare in my fatigued mind.

Yet the longer I lay, the more awake and alert I became, and with awareness came alarm. For this was no mere dream. There was indeed an unseen force pressing my body against the mattress, constricting my chest and making it painful to breathe.

Not wanting to give way to my mounting fear, I tried to constrain myself and force myself to be as calm as possible. Taking breaths as slowly as I could, I forced my lungs full of the cold night air, moaning with the pain of it, and found that, if I lay absolutely motionless, I could suffer the ungodly pressure.

My mind raced ahead of my heart. What could be causing this? Not even the fine sweat of terror now sprouting all over my body could cause me to shiver, so great was the unseen weight on me.

Suddenly I sensed another change in the room. Although there was not the faintest trace of light and although the darkness was as dense and absolute as if I were truly blind, I *knew* that I was no longer alone.

My throat rose and fell in a painful swallow. Just where the presence was I could not be sure, for it seemed to come at me from all sides; it pervaded the air and seeped through the walls and came up through the floorboards. It surrounded me, hovered over me, filled the entire room with an unearthly coldness that came not from the air itself but from somewhere *beyond*, as if from the grave . . .

There was a sound at my right.

Afraid to look, and yet afraid not to look, I slowly rolled my head to the side and saw, to my horror, the bedroom door standing wide open.

I wanted to cry out but could not. There was no breath in my lungs. My throat simply closed over a useless whimper.

The door stood wide open.

And from some unseen source on the other side, possibly the hallway, there streamed a ghostly light into my room. Suddenly I saw Victor Townsend standing over me. I screamed. And screamed again.

"Andrea! Andrea!" A feeble pounding on the door.

Blindly I reached out and by some miracle hit the light switch. I sat bolt upright in bed.

"Andrea, are you all right?" came Nana's voice.

The door was shut tight and the sausage was firmly in place.

My teeth began to chatter.

"Andrea—" Nana opened the door and poked her head in. "What's the mat—" Her toothless mouth fell open. "Oh my soul and body!" she cried. "What's happened to you?"

She hobbled across the room, her back bent over her cane, her thin hair wild and standing out from her head. "You're white as a ghost! What happened?"

I could only sit with my arms hugging my body, my teeth chattering.

"And you're drenched!" She ran a hand over my forehead. "You've got a fever! Look at the sweat pouring off you! That must have been a nasty nightmare you had."

"N-N—" I stuttered, but I could not speak.

"And how you do shake! Come on, love, it's the fire for you. No more sleeping up here. I shall fix the settee for you nice like—"

"Nana!" I blurted.

"What is it, love?"

"I saw him!" My voice came out as a strangled cry.

"Saw who? What are you talking about?"

"He was real! I wasn't dreaming! My door was wide open and he just stood there where you are now!"

Nana's face puckered into a frown as she pulled the comforter off the bed and wrapped it about me. "Come along. You've had a bad dream, that's all. What you need is some of my hot cherry cordial. You can sleep by the fire."

I tried to resist but was too confused, and so allowed myself to be led meekly out of the bedroom and down into the sitting room.

Tucking me into the easy chair and turning up the fire, my grandmother muttered, "I shall never forgive myself if you take ill. It's me had you sleeping in that fridge of a room. Daft me forgetting that nobody but a crazy English-man can sleep in such horrible cold. It's down here for you from now on. In the warm like you're used to."

As she limped off to the scullery I let my head fall back and stared blankly at the ceiling.

Although my body was dripping wet, my mouth was dry. And I contin-ued to tremble more violently than ever.

What was it? What was it I had felt up there and that even now lingered with me? It wasn't just the vision of Victor Townsend. No, it had been some-thing else . . . some special unseen horror that had filled the entire room, that had engulfed me like a killing cloud. The spectre of Victor Townsend had been startling and alarming, yes, but that other thing . . .

Something evil . . . malevolent . . .

The clock ticked softly on the mantel before me. The heat from the gas fire rose up and embraced me. I felt my body relax. I began to drift.

How had I known it was Victor Townsend? The man I saw standing over me had been no fifteen-year-old boy but an adult. And yet I had instinc-tively identified him as Victor. Could it really be my mind playing tricks, as Nana had suggested that afternoon? In my fatigue was I conjuring up vari-ous images of my own grandfather as he might have appeared in his youth?

But how did that account for the boy in the window looking exactly like the one in the photograph, even down to the clothes?

And why had I, just now in my room, been so quick to identify the "man" as Victor?

Somewhere at the back of my mind lay the answer, for I could feel it beginning to tug at me, to tease me; but I was too tired to search for it. I had not even the strength to make my brain work. It seemed to have something to do with the house itself. With the disquieting effect it had upon me. And it seemed that Victor's appearance had been a sign, a message, warning me. But of what?

Nana materialized suddenly at my side; I jumped.

"It's not good for you," she said, extending a glass to me, "this English cold. I remember during the last war the Yanks couldn't stand it. Even your father, and him coming from Canada, couldn't take it. It's a different kind of cold, you see, it gets right through your skin and to your bones. Only the English can put up with it. Here, love, hot cherry cordial."

I took it silently and sipped under her maternal eye. Satisfied that I was going to take my medicine willingly, Nana then creaked about her labours at turning the sofa into as comfortable a bed as possible. She removed the cushions, produced blankets from the sideboard, and fluffed the pillows. As I watched her I slowly drank the cordial and reflected again upon what had just happened.

Although the fear was gone, an intense curiosity remained. I let my eyes glide over the walls and furniture of this cluttered room and found myself thinking, Perhaps it was like this when *he* lived here.

Then I pictured again the melancholy face of Jennifer that had so intrigued me the night before. My great-grandmother. What had it been like for her? Had she also shed no tears upon Victor's disappearance? Had she perhaps been glad to be rid of him?

I studied the arthritic motions of Nana and realized that she must know a great deal more about the Townsends than she was willing to say. And yet it was, for some reason, a painful subject with her. Why? She never knew her father-in-law, had only heard from others about his transgressions (and what were they? I wondered now in half amusement: Gambling? Drinking? Swearing? All those shocking Victorian improprieties? Can Victor Townsend have been *so bad?*). Nana had never known him firsthand, but still she must have heard a lot from my grandfather. Yes, Nana was a storehouse of Townsend lore, and I now intended to tap it.

"There! All nice and comfy like, love. We'll keep the fire on low. Now you climb under the covers and get warm."

Now was not the time to delve into my grandmother's store of information. Not now with me so exhausted and she all in a midnight's muddle. Tomorrow, perhaps, in the light of day. I would bring up the subject and gently press it until I knew the full story of this house.

"Want me to leave the light on?" She hesitated in the doorway, wobbling on her cane. From where I lay, the blankets pulled up to my chin, Nana looked centuries old. And yet still hauntingly beautiful. "Please," I said, "I'll turn it out later."

"Right you are. Well, good night lovey, and sleep tight."

She pulled the door closed and could be heard a minute later scaling the steep stairs. After another long wait her heavy feet and cane could be heard bumping across the floor. Then there was silence overhead.

I lay on my back apprehensively. The clock ticked, the gas fire made no sound. There was no wind beyond the heavy drapes. All around was a heavy silence.

My eyes travelled again up to the ceiling and stopped at the juncture of the two walls. I lay staring at this spot for a while.

I pictured my door as I had seen it standing open in that eerie light. It *had* been open. But then, turning on the light, I had found it closed tight and with the bolster in place. That could only mean one thing: the door had been closed from the inside.

My eyes continued to stare at the point where wall met ceiling. On this level the wall separated me from the unused parlour. But overhead, on the next storeßy, the wall separated the two bedrooms. So I stared now at the ceiling as if I could see on the other side.

And I thought, Whatever closed my bedroom door is still up there.

When I awoke the next morning sunlight was streaming through the windows and filling the sitting room. From where I lay I could see patches of bright blue sky between the grey clouds, and a few sparrows sat upon the brick wall in celebration of the day. Then I saw the kitchen door standing open and heard Nana moving about. She was humming a tune and rattling plates.

How I had slept!

Drawing myself to a sitting position, I looked around at the clock. It was nearly noon.

Nana's cordial had done the trick! I felt greatly refreshed, more rested than I had in several days. The sofa had been quite comfortable and I had felt not the least bit of cold. And above all, I had had no "visitations."

I smiled at that now. Strange how differently we look at things at night and then in the day. At night all shadows are menacing, all sounds supernatural. But in the daylight we see how fanciful becomes the imagination at the darkest hours. Sunlight, dispelling both shadows and fears, also instills a sense of courage. Now I felt quite cavalier about last night's "ordeal."

However, I had not been without dreams.

Bidding my grandmother a good morning, assuring her of my best health and rest, I then made my way back upstairs to the bedroom where, unafraid and a little ashamed of my previous behaviour, I unpacked toiletries and the day's clothes, and then made my way back to the freezing bathroom.

Yes, there had been dreams. Nothing tangible, random scenes, scattered muffled phrases, vague faces fading in and out. People moving about me, looking down at me, whispering over me. And in the background, "Für Elise" being played upon a tinny piano.

But dreams, all dreams.

Coming back downstairs I felt completely rejuvenated and refreshed and prepared to face the day. Nana had hot buttered scones and a big pot of tea set out for me. I took my place and began to eat ravenously.

"When I came in this morning," Nana said, smiling, "I could have dropped a bomb near you and not wakened you, you were that deeply asleep."

"Thanks to your great nursing care, Nana."

"No more nightmares then?"

I thought about the vague dreams and was unable to recall them now. "No more nightmares."

"Now I shall not be cooking today, love, because you'll be going to your Uncle William's tonight, and your Aunt May will be fixing you a nice supper. He's anxious to see you again, your Uncle William is."

I nodded and poured my sweet tea. How odd it sounded: He would be seeing me again, but for me it would be the first time.

"You'll like your Aunt May. Welsh she is and a proper nice person. I don't 'spect you remember her, you was only two when you left for America. She and your mum were such good friends. Went everywhere together. No doubt she'll have some tales to tell you!"

This reminded me of something. Picking up another scone and smearing it with lemon curd, I casually studied my grandmother's face. She looked younger this morning, well rested. And in high spirits. I wondered if this was a good time.

"Speaking of tales, Nana," I said, not looking at her, "can you tell me anything more about the Townsends?"

"Not much to say. They came from good London stock. There's others up near Scotland I think."

"What I meant was, about my great-grandfather, Victor Townsend."

She put her cup down and stared at the tea leaves in the bottom. Her face seemed to fall inward as though she were weighing an important decision. Finally, slowly, she said, "You see, Andrea, there's some things that's best forgotten. It'll do you no good to hear the things that went on in this house because they weren't for proper folk to talk about. Now I know about them and so does your granddad, but we never told the children. William and Elsie and Ruth know nothing about them days. And neither should you."

"You mean some of the Townsends misbehaved."

Nana's eyes took on a grave look. "It's more than that. I know what you're thinking, that I'm a stuffy old Victorian lady and that I'm easily shocked by today's sins. Well, all right, I am. I think I'm a proper Christian and I *am* shocked by what's going on in the world today. But times change, don't they, and some things you have to accept. Like young people sleeping together without getting married and all the drug problems. But, Andrea, there's things that are shocking in any century, aye, horrible *unspeakable* things, and it's them that went on in this house with the Townsends."

The tone in my grandmother's voice saddened me, but nonetheless I said, "I want to know, Nana."

"Why?"

"Because . . . " I searched around for the words. Why couldn't I drop the subject and forget it as she obviously wished I would do? Why this *need* to know? "Because they're my family, too, just like you and Granddad and Elsie and William are. I want to know about all of you, and the ones in my past as well. I've come so far, I want to go home with something."

"What about the Dobsons then? Let me tell you about my side of the family."

"Those too, Nana. But *all* of them. Especially the Townsends."

"I can't—"

"I have no heritage, Nana," I said. "I have twenty-five years in Southern California and that's it. It ends there, like a movie. Is that all I am?"

She looked at me sadly.

"If I have a past, then I want to know *all* of it—the bad as well as the good. I have a right to know."

We gazed at one another across the little table and across the years, and I heard my own words echo in my mind. What on earth was I saying? What had caused me to blurt it all out like that? I had never felt that way before. I had never cared about my lineage before. Until now, I had not been interested in even the living relatives, let alone the dead ones. Why? Why now and not before, and why such a desperate need to know?

At the back of my mind I knew: It was this house.

"Aye, you do have a right, love. Only . . . "

I watched her face. The thoughts that went on behind it were clearly reflected there: her reluctance to talk about the past, her distaste with what she knew, her struggle between my right to know and yet wanting to spare me the pain of it.

Finally, releasing a long sigh, she said, "Very well, love. I'll tell you what you want to know."

We left the table and took seats before the gas fire. I did not press her. She needed time and courage to think, so I waited patiently and silently.

"What I know," came her weary voice at last, "I know from Robert, your granddad. When I married him sixty-two years ago, he lived all alone in this house. He was the only one left of the Townsends that had lived here since 1880. So you see, I never knew his family, not one of them. And not even your granddad knew them, because they all disappeared or died off before he was a lad. Robert was raised by his grandmother in this house, and just before he joined the Royal Engineers, she died. So you see, Andrea, I never knew her. Anyway, she was the one, Robert's grandmother, who told him the stories about the Townsends. Then he passed them on to me. And what he told me was this."

Nana seemed to brace herself. "That his father, Victor Townsend, was a despicable man. Some say he dabbled in the Black Arts. Some say he had direct dealings with the Devil himself. This could be true because of the things he did. And I won't tell you those, Andrea, because nothing in the world will get my lips to utter the unspeakable acts that man . . . that *demon* committed. But I'll tell you this: While he was alive, Victor Townsend made this house a living hell for everyone in it."

CHAPTER 4

*A*YE, THOSE WERE SORROWFUL TIMES. THERE WERE THREE off them, you see, the children. Victor was the oldest, then John, and then Harriet. It was in 1880 that Mr. Townsend brought his family from London to George Street. And he was a good man, was Robert's grandfather. A proper churchgoer and a strict father. And he was well respected here in Warrington. How it was he fathered the likes of Victor . . . "

Nana sat there shaking her head, her face a portrait of grief. I tried not to force her, tried to hold back, but I was ever anxious for more.

"What did Victor do, Nana?"

She raised her head as if by great effort. "Do?"

"Yes. For a living, I mean."

"Oh . . . " My grandmother placed a hand on her forehead. "Let me see. I don't rightly know. In fact, I don't think I ever knew. Perhaps your granddad knows, but I don't think he ever told me. Now John, the younger brother, worked at the steel mill I believe, as some sort of clerk."

"Was he married too?"

Nana gave me a perplexed look. "What do you mean *too?* Of course John was married. He was married to Jennifer, the one whose picture I showed you—"

"But I thought she was Victor's wife."

"Oh, Andrea, no. Jennifer was married to John. Victor never had a wife."

"But you said she was my great-grandmother."

"Andrea." My grandmother's voice became grave. "Jennifer married John Townsend and moved into this house. But somehow, one night, well . . . " She cast her eyes down. "Victor came home in one of his rages and he . . . well, he got hold of poor Jennifer, you see, and he . . . he *forced* her."

I became acutely aware of the ticking of the clock. It seemed to be whispering. I don't know how many minutes went by before my eyes focused again on Nana's face, but when they did, I could feel some small amount of sympathy for the misery reflected there.

"You see, Andrea," she said softly, "your granddad was conceived by rape."

"Nana—"

"Now John—Jennifer's husband and Victor's brother—couldn't take this, when it was learned that Jennifer was pregnant, so he left her. Both brothers disappeared, and Jennifer was left alone to have the baby by herself and to raise it on her own. She never saw or heard from John or Victor ever again. The child's grandmother, Victor and John's mother, raised the baby, and I gather from your grandfather that she was a bit dotty, if you know what I mean."

"What about the sister, Harriet? And what happened to Jennifer herself?"

"Well, I don't know what happened to Harriet, although I seem to recall something rather unusual or mysterious about the circumstances of her death. And Jennifer died before your granddad got to know her. Of a broken heart, they say."

"I see . . . "

"Not all of it you don't. You don't see the worst tragedy of it, not by a long chalk!"

The passion in my grandmother's voice startled me. Now her eyes were alive and animated. She gestured as she spoke. "You don't know how it's haunted your granddad all his life, knowing what he knew about his real father. It's made him a tormented man! He was an unhappy little boy, living alone in this house with bedridden old Mrs. Townsend, but when he grew old enough to understand what had happened, it scarred him for life. Your granddad's had to live with the burden and shame of his father, of having learned what a cruel and sadistic man his father had been. Your granddad's lived all his life with this horrible shadow over him. He never had had a happy memory, never had been loved by anyone till he met me. And, Andrea, I've heard him cry out in his sleep with nightmares or sit in that chair and cry like a baby because of the blood that ran through his veins."

Nana's eyes filled with tears. Her lips trembled. "Now you think, oh well, it happened a long time ago! But do you know what your granddad thinks? He thinks Victor Townsend was insane! And he's lived in fear all his life that the bad blood would show up again in his children! When I was pregnant with Elsie, your grandfather was like an obsessed man. He was terrified of Victor's bad blood showing up. And then your mother was born. And then William. And they all turned out all right. But then your granddad started thinking that it might show up yet in his grandchildren. He was afraid that Victor might appear in any one of you—Albert or Ann or Christine or you or Richard. That's the real tragedy, Andrea—what the past has done to your granddad. And I'm the only person's known it all these years. And now you know it. Only I wish you didn't!"

She burst into tears; I felt absolutely wretched.

"It's been horrible for your granddad," she went on, "knowing how he came to be born, that he was the result of a sadistic attack. He told me once that his mother must have hated the sight of him because he reminded her of Victor's brutality. And maybe that's why she died when he was but a baby. Maybe she couldn't bear to see him."

"Nana—"

"Yes, Victor Townsend was an evil man! He tortured everyone in this house! And that's why I don't like to look at his picture or even speak his name. And I'm as ashamed as your grandfather is to be related to him. Just as you should be!"

On an impulse I got to my feet and strode to the window. The blue sky was gone now, as were the sunshine and sparrows. Instead there was a dark angry sky overhead and raindrops spattered the panes.

Only two days before I had been expected to show some affection or sentiment for these strangers who were my relatives, and while they hugged me and kissed me and cried to see me, I was supposed to do the same. Yet I could not.

And now it was expected of me to loathe and detest one of my relatives simply because everyone else did. This, too, I found I could not do.

For some reason unknown to me, Nana's words had only moved me to pity and compassion for her and Granddad. However, no matter what she said of Victor Townsend, it seemed I could not feel hate in my heart for him.

Suddenly I spun about and stared at the old woman in the chair.

How odd! And yet true all the same. Somehow, for some reason, I could not bring myself to hate the man who had made life a hell for so many people. Why? I wondered.

Drying her eyes and quickly composing herself, my grandmother drew herself up on her bowed legs and cane and apologized for the outburst. "I've cried too many times in the past to do it now. By the time you're eighty-three years old you'll realize that crying doesn't help anything. But I'm telling you now, I won't speak any more of the subject. I've said enough, maybe too much, but at least now you know the truth."

And although I should have readily accepted this, a gnawing little doubt whispered at the back of my mind, Do I?

The drive to Warrington Hospital was different this time. For today I knew something about the man I was to visit. Yesterday I had visited a dying old man, a stranger in a bed that smelled of decay. But today I was going to visit the son of Victor Townsend. That was a different prospect.

Aunt Elsie chatted in the front seat about the weather, holding on her lap a box of chocolates for her father. Uncle Edouard, in his incomprehensible French/Lancashire accent, echoed everything she said, while I remained crunched in the small backseat, oblivious to the cold, ruminating over my long dialogue with Nana.

As we passed again through the double doors of the entrance, I felt beset by mixed emotions, A great part of me wanted nothing more to do with this business and was wishing me back home at once. Even if it meant confronting Doug again. But another, stronger part of me felt strangely drawn towards the enigma of the events in the house on George Street and towards the little old man whose life was haunted by them. Yesterday he had meant nothing to me; today I perhaps knew more about him than his own children did.

And it was for this reason that I felt a small kinship with him; the knowledge of Victor Townsend would be our bond.

We sat as we had the day before, upon the folded-out wooden chairs, and around the bed. Today Granddad was propped up, looking like an old rag doll. Although his eyes were open, they were dull and phlegmatic and it seemed doubtful at first that he saw us.

"Hullo, Dad," said Elsie as she undid the cellophane wrapper of the chocolate box. "Brought you some sweets."

Granddad's lips drew back in an imitation of a grin.

"Want one?" she said teasingly.

Granddad did not respond but merely sat grinning. Or possibly it was a grimace of pain, for how could one tell?

Aunt Elsie stuffed a chocolate between his thin lips and at once the mouth started sucking. In the end, I suppose, we are reduced to the basic instincts we are born with.

I thought of my grandfather as a baby again.

"Look who's with us!" said Elsie, her voice travelling all over the ward. "It's our Andrea come from America! You missed her yesterday, you was asleep."

His clouded eyes continued to gaze in Elsie's direction, and then, as if the information had at last registered, Granddad turned his smiling face to me. He grinned for a moment, sucking on his chocolate, and then quite suddenly, his face fell and his mouth stopped moving.

A chill shot down my spine.

The look on my grandfather's face was startling, for who could have suspected such a benign and infantile face capable of showing such . . . what? Anger? Hatred?

"You seem rude today, Dad," said Elsie and she reached out to stuff another piece of candy into his mouth.

But in a move so swift that none of us saw it coming, my grandfather's arm shot up and knocked Elsie's hand out of the way.

"Dad!"

He continued to glower darkly at me, those hazy eyes which seemed incapable of sight holding me fast. I shuddered.

"What's got into him?" said Elsie. "I've never seen him like this before."

"He must think our Andrea's someone else," said Uncle Ed, picking up the chocolate off the floor, brushing it off, popping it into his mouth.

I swallowed hard and tried to hold up beneath the malignant stare. Granddad's face was all malevolence and hostility.

Presently I found my voice and was able to murmur, "Hello, Granddad, you know it's me, don't you?"

The angry stare continued for a few seconds more, the furrow beneath his brows etched deeply. Then, like a cloud passing away from the sun, my grandfather's face melted and relaxed into its former self.

Pursing his lips and with a trembling chin, my granddad managed to say, "W-Wooth?"

"Crikey!" said Elsie. "He thinks you're your mum!" Then she leaned across the bed and shouted, "Not Ruth, Dad. It's Andrea! Your granddaughter!"

His grin returned. "Wooth? Y-you've come back have you?"

"Dad—"

"It's all right, Aunt Elsie. I'm sure in his mind Andrea is still two years old. Let him think I'm my mother. Look how he's smiling."

The fact that my heart was being wrenched and twisted I did not let on, for not even I could believe how powerfully this man was affecting me. I looked long at his worn-out face and I thought of the horrible stigma he had had to live with all his life, knowing the circumstances of his conception, and the agonized waiting to see if the evil blood of Victor Townsend would reappear in one of us.

"It's all right, Granddad," I said soothingly, patting his hand. "Everything's all right now."

My Uncle William lived in a section of Warrington known as Padgate, and his house, being quite modern, was semidetached, had large front and back lawns and, best of all, had central heating.

Our reunion was quite an occasion. This robust man with the enormous belly and florid complexion embraced me and kissed me and prattled almost as incessantly as had Aunt Elsie. His wife, May, was another large woman who also wore plain practical dresses and combed her grey hair in a random fashion. They were simple people, my Uncle William and Aunt May, middle class and unpretentious.

"It's our Andrea!" cried Aunt May as I was delivered into the kitchen where she stood over boiling pots. "You've grown since I saw you last!"

We all laughed and went through the ritual of removing our layers of clothing, then the five of us moved into the sitting room, which was considerably more modern than Nana's, and helped ourselves to tea and pastries.

"I've made a trifle for after supper," said Aunt May. "I'll 'spect you haven't had one of them in years, have you, love?" She patted my knee.

"So how was Dad today?" asked my Uncle William, his mouth full.

"Sitting up and proper talking he was, ain't that right, Ed? And ate nearly a whole box of sweets, too!"

"Dad's all right. Be home in a couple of weeks, he will. Just needed a rest." I watched my Uncle William cram a pastry into his mouth as he leaned on the television set, and I thought what a comfortable man he was. My mother's brother, with the family furrow between the eyebrows.

There was some talk of Granddad and then of my mother's foot operation and then, inevitably, of the past. While Uncle William and Aunt Elsie reminisced about their days together with my mother, Uncle Edouard picked up the London *Times*, Aunt May returned to the kitchen, and I shrank back into my corner, a disinterested observer.

It was very warm in Uncle William's house, not at all like Nana's. Here you could go out of the room and not be shocked by the chill of the hall. Feeling relaxed, I kicked off my shoes and brought my legs up under me. Then I laid my head on the back of the easy chair and idly listened to everyone talk.

My mind wandered, floated. It seemed to break free of me and soar of its own will. Thoughts came and went in flurries. I visualized the house on George Street. I reflected passingly on how harmless the house seemed when I was away from it, how childish my imagined discomfort whenever I stepped through the front door, and how surely its effect on me was only the result of its shadowy Victorian atmosphere.

I pondered the bad dream of the night before, of how real the terror had been then and how distant it seemed now. I remembered the young boy peering in the window at me. His frank curiosity of me.

Lastly I came to think of my grandfather and I relived again the chilling moments beneath his queer gaze. And I wondered, When he looked at me, what had he seen?

"Andrea."

"Yes?"

"She's been dozing. Proper tired she is."

"No, I wasn't—"

"You know," said Uncle William, "it's wonderful having you here again. I wish your mum could have come too, but it is nice having you. You'll not run off too soon now will you? What about your job?"

I tried to picture the stockbroker I worked for. Strangely, his face would not come into focus. "I had a month's vacation due to me, so I'm not losing any money. But I don't know how long I'll be staying . . . " Then I pictured Doug. His face, too, remained out of focus.

A while later we all went into the kitchen for a hearty supper of boiled veal and cabbage with roast potatoes and carrots. Uncle William served a red Spanish wine and made a brief speech about the family being all together again.

"And come the weekend," said Elsie, "we'll all go to our Albert's in Morecambe Bay. The baby's growing so, you know!"

They talked for a while of the family get-together on Sunday; of my meeting Albert and Christine, my cousins, for the first time; of us all being under one roof together, including Nana, who usually did not leave her house. On and on they went about it, planning the event that was yet five days away, while I said nothing, thinking that I should very much enjoy an afternoon away from the oppressive atmosphere of Nana's dreary house.

Uncle William turned to me and said, "Tell me, Andrea, how do you like staying in Mum's freezing house?"

They all laughed.

"Listen, William," said Aunt May, "can't you take an electric heater over there for that front bedroom? It must be miserable there for Andrea."

"No!" I said suddenly, surprising even myself. "I mean, I'm fine. Honest I am. With the hot-water bottle and all the covers I'm just fine. Really!"

What was I saying! It wasn't true. I was thoroughly miserable in that room. An electric heater would have been most welcome. And yet—I tried to remember why I was objecting to it—the heater just didn't belong there . . . that was all . . .

"Sleeping all right are you, love?" asked May in motherly concern.

"Yes, really I am."

"You know," said Uncle William, spooning a load of potatoes into his mouth, "that bedroom always was cold. But then so is the whole house. Always has been. But I never complained. After you and Ruth got married and moved out, that front bedroom was mine, and bloody freezing it was too, but I never complained. You two were always a pair of softies."

I studied my uncle over the rim of my glass. When he turned to me I smiled.

"Softies, ay?" he said with a wink.

I only laughed. "It's all right, really. The cold, I mean. But after all, it is an old house, isn't it? And you're bound to, well, hear strange things in the middle of the night. That's what really—"

"Ay? What's that? Strange things? What're you talking about?"

"Oh, you know." I dawdled my fork in my cabbage. "In the middle of the night you wake up to strange noises. Didn't that ever happen to you?"

He raised his eyebrows. "Not as I recall. That house don't make noises.

Too solidly built it is. Not like the muck that goes up these days. A hundred years ago they built them to stand firm! Naw, I was never bothered by no sounds in the night. It's *this* house creaks, ain't it, May?"

"But I mean," I went hurriedly on, "didn't you ever wonder about the house? You know, hear strange sounds or maybe . . . *see* something odd? You know, unexplainable things?"

He stared at me blankly.

"What are you saying, Andrea?" said Elsie as she reached for the wine bottle. "That it's haunted?"

Everyone laughed—William, Elsie, May, Uncle Ed only smiled and kept on eating.

"That's not what I meant," I said, even though it was exactly what I did mean. "But I was just wondering if—"

"Have *you* seen something, Andrea?" asked May.

"Of course not. But you know, in Los Angeles if a house is a hundred years old, well, it has a history. You know, a legend. There are stories about it."

"Naw, not here," said Uncle William. He picked up the bowl of veal, emptied the rest of it on to his plate, ran his spoon around it, then dropped the bowl back down with a bang. "There's too many houses that old and *older* in England. They can't all have ghosts, now can they? If it's legends you're wanting to take back to America, then you'll have to go to Penketh for that. Nothing like that round here. No time for ghosts."

Elsie regarded me across the table, her head tipped to one side. "Are you disappointed, Andrea?"

"Don't be silly! Of course not! I was only wondering, that's all."

"Americans do get their fancies about England, don't they?" said Uncle William. "We all live in haunted houses and the like. Sorry, love, ain't no ghosts within miles of here. Too cold for 'em!" He burst out laughing again and I sincerely wished I hadn't brought the subject up.

When he quieted a little he said, "There's nothing mysterious about our old house, is there, Elsie? I was born there in 1922, lived in it until I was nearly thirty, and never once heard or saw anything out of the ordinary. It's always been a nice quiet house, that one. Well built. Solid it is. Not like the new ones these days. You know, our Christine is looking to save her money to buy one of them out at . . . "

With the change of subject I decided to withdraw. Eating quietly and not really enjoying the food, I felt irritated and let down. I had actually been hoping that my weird experiences in the house were nothing new and that my relatives had encountered similar incidents in the past.

But there was nothing. Nothing at all.

After supper and before Uncle William and Aunt May made their regular visit to the hospital, I decided to telephone my mother. My relatives rallied to the idea at once and, to my great dismay, as soon as the overseas operator rang back with my call, they all clustered about me so that I had no opportunity to speak privately with my mother.

In fact, they all had to take turns saying hello to her. And when all was said and done, all the tears were shed and the receiver had been passed around many times, in the end I had said very little to her and felt the sharp disappointment of it.

I felt cheated. There was so much I had wanted to say to her, so much I had wanted to ask. But as it turned out, all I had had the chance to do was ask about her foot, tell her a little about Granddad, talk a bit about my stay with Nana, and then explain that four people were waiting in line to talk to her.

Uncle William and Aunt May dropped me off at Nana's on their way to the hospital. They stopped in long enough to see that she was all right and to tell her what a lovely dinner we had all had, and if only she had been there. And while they chatted, I mentally scolded myself for letting the house descend upon me again, for that is exactly what it had done the very moment we had stepped through the door. And I reminded myself that I should be more concerned with my granddad's well-being—after all, that was the reason I was here—and less morbidly preoccupied with the house.

At nine o'clock, as the two of us sat again before the gas fire, Nana turned on the radio to listen to her "Scottish Music Hour." It was after about five minutes of the bagpipes that it happened again.

We were both resting back and quietly listening to the music, Nana humming along with "Amazing Grace," when I noticed the clock had stopped ticking.

I stared at it.

Then, in the background, sounding as if it came from a great distance, was the playing of an ill-tuned piano—"Für Elise" again, but this time by a more practised hand and not as amateurish as it had been two nights ago.

I turned to look at my grandmother. With her head back and her face a picture of repose, she quietly hummed "Amazing Grace."

The moment seemed to last forever, as though time had been brought to a standstill and we were suspended in an instant between two realities. I stared incredulously at Nana. How could she not hear the piano!

My face grew hot. The room seemed to close in on me. Fear started to take hold of me as I realized what was happening. "Nana . . . "

She did not open her eyes.

The piano grew louder. It was very close to my ears now, coming from everywhere at once. The Scottish pipes sounded far away.

"Nana . . . "

Finally she looked up. "What is it, love?"

The second she opened her eyes, the piano stopped. I glanced at the clock. It was ticking again.

"I'm awfully tired, Nana." I ran my hands over my face. "Would you mind if I went to bed?"

"Not at all! Here's thoughtless me keeping you up." She reached for her cane and started to struggle out of her chair.

"Don't get up, Nana. No need for you to get up."

"Nonsense! I shan't sit down here while you're trying to sleep."

"What—"

"Your robe and nightgown are already there under that pillow. I didn't want you going up them cold stairs again."

I looked over at the sofa, confused. Then I saw that the cushions were off, that the blankets were spread out, and I realized what she meant. "You want me to sleep here tonight?"

"Of course! You were so nice and warm last night, no need for you ever to go back up to the front bedroom."

"Oh, but . . . " An urgency came over me which I could not fathom, a reluctance to sleep down here that was equalled by a sudden desire to go back upstairs again. And while I should have questioned this queer anxiousness to sleep in the front bedroom, I did not, but tried falteringly to explain to Nana.

"That was last night," I said. "I had had a nightmare. Tonight I'll be all right. Honest, Nana, the bedroom is—"

"Never you mind, love. It's my fault 'cause you've heard me complaining about the cost of gas rates and all my mithering about energy and power and now you can't even enjoy my little bit of a gas heater in good conscience. Well, don't you bother about the grumblings of an old lady. We shall keep the heater going for as long as you're here and that's all there is to it. Good night, love."

Helpless, I watched her hobble out of the room and close the door behind herself.

I sat down on the sofa with a thump. Now what had that been all about? I spread my hands and looked at them. What had possesed me to argue with her? My rational mind had actually agreed with Nana, that the sitting room was the best place for me to sleep. And yet . . . another, deeper part of me had felt the pull of the upstairs. It had been almost as if something were forcing me to do things against my will.

I raised my eyes and looked around the room. An ordinary enough room, filled with familiar furnishings and comfortable clutter. And yet . . . why could I not relax? Surely after two days I must be over the jet lag. Surely I was getting used to my new surroundings. And yet, oddly enough, rather than diminish as I had expected it would, the eerie feeling I had about the house had only grown.

And that piano. Obviously Nana had not heard it. Why? Where had it come from? Was it only I who could hear it? But why? Why had none of my relatives ever experienced anything unexplainable in this old house? Why only me? Had I, by coming here, somehow caused it? What was it about *me* that was conducive to stirring the old ethers of this house?

I snapped my head up to the ceiling.

What was that sound?

Slowly rising to my feet and keeping my eyes on the ceiling, I strained my ears against the night silence.

It sounded like a woman crying.

"Nana?" I whispered.

Suddenly forgetting my own personal dilemma and concerned that my grandmother was up in her bed crying, I hurried out of the sitting room and into the dark hall.

In my haste I did not notice that the clock had stopped ticking again.

CHAPTER 5

COULD BARELY HEAR THE SOBS OVER THE POUNDING OF MY heart, for the blackness of the stairwell frightened me. Yet I moved as quickly as I could. It distressed me that my grandmother was crying alone in her room. What had upset her?

After flicking on the frail hall light, I approached her door cautiously and placed my ear against it, listening. Nana's bedroom was silent. Baffled, I stepped back and looked down the hall. In the light of the one bulb I could almost see the door of the front bedroom. It was closed. The crying seemed to be coming from the other side.

Stepping gingerly, almost tiptoeing, I made my way down the hall, and as I neared the other door the crying seemed to grow louder.

Transfixed, I stood before the bedroom door and listened. All around me hung the icy night air. Except for the weeping, there was only silence; a heavy hush that smacked of things dead. It made my skin crawl. The impulse to turn and flee rose in me, surmounted me, and yet I could not move, for a force greater than my own was with me in that dim hallway, a force that now compelled me to reach out and place my hand on the doorknob.

It was hard and as cold as frost. Swinging the door silently open, I saw the interminable blackness of the bedroom and felt a cold breath waft in my face.

Drawn inside, impelled by a power I could not fight, I stretched my eyes to the darkness and saw, as I stepped in, a strange light, which came from no visible source, illuminating the centre of the room. With the periphery in darkness, it was an ethereal incandescence that was bright in the centre but which faded into a mist at the edges, like the halo-light used in movies to produce a "soft" effect. The light was focused on the bed.

I gazed at a form lying there: a small body dressed in white, her little shoulders rising and falling with sobs.

I saw a young girl, not more than twelve or thirteen years old, lying face-down across the bed. She wore an ankle-length dress of white cotton which was embellished with frills, lace, and ribbons. About her tiny waist was a large sash which was brought up in a huge bow at her back, and on her feet were small leather slippers.

From where I stood I could see the ruffled petticoats and white stockings.

With her face buried in her arms, the girl wept as if her heart would break.

I don't know how long I stood and stared, for, unafraid as I was, I was held in simple fascination. In fact, so intent did I become in the wonder of what I saw, the detail of the scene, the illusion of reality, that it was not until the child raised her head that I grew alarmed.

What would happen when she saw me?

In the next moment a most remarkable thing occurred. The girl did indeed turn her eyes to me, and although I jumped when her gaze met mine, I realized almost immediately that she did not see me. In fact, she looked right through me.

With my heart pounding wildly, I gaped dumbly at the plain face of this child, recognizing it to be an older version of the plain little girl who had stood with her two brothers on the steps in the photograph. At that time she had been five or six years old. But here she was about seven years older;

Harriet Townsend, sister of Victor and John.

To my great wonder she slowly sat up, her thin arms supporting her, the long curls falling over her shoulders. Harriet's homely little face was puffy from tears, yet she had stopped crying and seemed to be looking at something or someone behind me.

When she spoke it startled me. Although the scene had a most uncanny aura of realism about it, I had not expected it to be so complete.

"I don't care what Father says!" she said petulantly, her lower lip thrust out. "I shall stay up here and starve myself to death and he won't care!"

She continued to look steadily through me, as if listening to the unseen person, then she tossed back her head and said, "Why did Victor have to go away? He didn't, you know. He didn't have to. Father wanted him to stay here and work at the mill. But no, Victor had to have his own way. I hope he shall be desperately miserable in London! And I hope he cuts himself and dies of a poison!"

Her face twisted angrily as her companion replied. While I could not imagine who it was that spoke, it was not difficult to fill in the blanks of that half of the conversation.

"Well you can just tell Father that I shall lock myself in the wardrobe and starve myself to death. Victor promised me he would never go away."

He promised?

Harriet Townsend pierced me with a challenging glare. In the next instant, however, her defiance turned to shock and then to fear as her eyes grew wide and her mouth opened in a cry. "Don't hit me!" she pleaded, scrambling to the back of the bed. "I'm sorry! I didn't mean it! Oh please, *please* don't hit me!"

The child raised her arms in self-defence as she screamed, *"Don't do it!"*

Falling forward a step, I blurted clumsily, "Harriet—"

The overhead light flashed on. I turned around, blinking stupidly.

"What're you doing up here?"

I screwed my eyes tightly, then opened them to my grandmother, who stood in the doorway. Her face wore an odd expression.

"I—I—"

"You should be asleep," she said.

I looked over at the bed, my jaw hanging down, and saw my suitcase and its contents scattered over the eider-down comforter. The strange light was gone now, as was Harriet, and it also seemed that the harsh edge of cold in the room had softened somewhat. I looked back at my grandmother, baffled. Hadn't she seen? Hadn't she *heard*?

"My . . . my slippers," I replied lamely. "I came up for my slippers."

"I heard you say something."

"Yes." I ran my fingers through my hair. "Stupid me, I banged my shin in the dark. Oh, here we are." I bent and picked up my slippers.

As we turned out the light and closed the bedroom door, I wondered how long Nana had been standing behind me, how much she had seen or heard. When I left her at her own bedroom door, she planted a kiss on my cheek. "Good night, love. And don't stray from the heat again else you'll catch cold, you will."

As she went into her own room, my grandmother turned off the small overhead light, at once plunging the whole house into darkness. I stood at the top of the stairs, knowing they were there but unable to see them, and felt lingering traces of my mystifying encounter with Harriet. I moved slowly, as if in a dream, all the while her pathetic voice echoing in my mind.

What was it I had seen? Had it been my imagination, the product of my emotional instability and the trying effects of being in a strange house? Or had I really seen her?

When I reached the bottom step I had to grope my way in the blackness, feeling along the wall for the sitting-room door. As I did so, the very faintest sound of a piano seemed to drift on the air from far, far away. My skin prickled. Standing in that dark cold hallway I had the impression of being trapped in a vast, dank cave, and could imagine it going on for ever and ever. And from somewhere far above me, drifting down from among ancient stalactites, was Beethoven's "Für Elise," echoing and eerie.

"No . . . " I unwittingly whispered. Whatever its cause, I had not the courage to face it.

So I frantically blundered my way to the sitting-room door, and when it fell open beneath my weight I gasped with relief.

But I was not alone.

A young man stood leaning on the mantel, smiling at me, the glass in his hand containing some dark drink.

"Beastly night out," he said, gesturing for me to come close to the fire.

Standing like an idiot in the doorway, I gawked into the fireplace and saw there the logs and the jumping flames and the sparks flying. It was a real fire that roared there now; the gas heater was gone.

I looked again at the young man, his kindly face watching me in amusement. "You're wet through," he said flippantly. "Serves you right."

Stunned, I looked down at myself, at my jeans and T-shirt, and then turned slightly and looked over my shoulder. There was another young man behind me, hanging a drenched cloak on the rack in the hall and knocking his top hat against his knee.

Without thinking, I fell back against the sideboard, clutching my chest with one hand as I did so. My body became suddenly paralysed, my limbs grew heavy and unresponsive. I could hear my pulse in my ears, a rapid thumping that I was sure must be heard all over the house.

I don't know if it was terror or simple amazement (for I had become gripped by both) that nailed me to the sideboard at that moment, but when Victor Townsend passed by me just then, although he brought with him a draught of cold night air, I was too hypnotized even to shiver.

"It cleans the air, brother," he said in a resonant voice, rubbing his hands over the fire.

Transfixed, I watched John Townsend stride to the armoire, remove a glass from it, and then pour from a carafe some of the amber liquid he was drinking. The two men then toasted one another, drank the stuff, and laughed.

Stupefied, I realized that they were unaware of me.

For brothers, John and Victor were very unalike. The former was shorter and younger, I would guess twenty years old to Victor's twenty-two or so, and although not as handsome as Victor, John had a softer face, a gentler air about him that was immediately endearing.

Victor—my great-grandfather (how strange to think of him as such!)—had a mane of wild black hair and thick sideburns down to his jaw. His eyes were large and deep-set, his brows heavy with the furrow at the centre. His stature was greater than that of his younger brother, being broader of shoulder and a head taller.

However, the two were similarly dressed in a striking fashion. Indeed, they appeared to be vying with one another for the most excellence in dress. While I could not give the costumes an exact date in history, I was familiar enough with them to know that the clothes were those of the late nineteenth century, and that their dark frock coats and pin-striped pants must have marked them as men of taste and propriety.

"I see that's something you haven't lost your taste for while in London," said John as he watched Victor decant another glass.

"I've only been gone a year, brother. You talk as if you expected changes."

"I expected you at least to come home smarter. King's College has no small reputation. What are they teaching you in that medical school anyway?"

"Bedside manner."

John threw back his head and roared. "My dear brother, *you* could be teaching the Londoners on that subject! Now tell me," he leaned towards Victor, grinning secretively, "do you really enjoy cutting up corpses?"

"You are being morbid, John, and on my first night home, too."

"Very well then, we shall speak of pleasant things. Have you got to examine any young ladies yet?"

Victor shook his head and smiled. "I fear you are incorrigible, John. One does not become a physician for the prurient thrill of cadavers and naked ladies."

"Oh aye!" John waved a theatrical arm. "It's your love of mankind, your compassion for the suffering, your driving devotion to put an end to all pain and misery!"

"Something like that," murmured Victor.

For a moment the two brothers stood silently before the fire, staring into the flames, and it was then that I noticed how the room had changed. Flowered paper now covered all the walls and the carpet was a rich Persian of navy blues and bright reds. The armoire stood new and shiny in the corner, and the horsehair sofa was minus Nana's Woolworth cover. On the mantel stood a straddle-legged clock, on either side of which was a pair of Staffordshire dogs. Gas lights on the walls illuminated the room, and I could see oval portraits hung about of people unfamiliar to me.

The scene mesmerized me. Not wanting to destroy it and not knowing how fragile it was, I did not move and only barely breathed.

Although I could not see the door open, for I was afraid to turn my head, I heard the sound of someone entering the room, then I felt the accompanying cold draught.

Victor turned around and, giving us his handsomest smile, extended both hands to Harriet as she came towards him.

"Victor, I'm so happy you've come to visit!"

Brother and sister embraced and kissed, then he held her off at arm's length to look at her. "You've grown in the year!" he said.

And it was true. The young woman who stood with us now was not the same peevish child who had cried upstairs a few minutes ago. For one thing, Harriet had discarded the dress of childhood and was now wearing a long silk gown that had a high neck and tight bodice which, at the level of the hips, flared out into a heavy skirt that was hung in the front like window drapes and gathered up in the rear into a voluminous bustle. Yards of material were in this dress, yet the skirt was bound in such a way that Harriet had to take small steps to walk. Her long curls were now swept off her neck and on to her head in a pile that was held in place by pins and ribbons.

I thought her most elegant. And in the gas light, with the firelight glowing on her cheeks, Harriet seemed almost pretty.

"I'm fourteen years old now," she said proudly. "A lot's happened to me in a year."

"She still cries like she used to, though."

"John!"

Victor suppressed a smile. "Do you, Harriet, cry a lot?"

"You should have seen her the night you left, Victor. Proper dramatic she was. Threatened to lock herself in the wardrobe and starve herself to death."

Now Victor gave in to his smile. "You did that for me?"

From where I stood I could see Harriet blush. "I was hurt that you left, Victor. But now I don't care. Now I'm proud you're going to be a doctor."

John turned away, muttering, "Father should be so proud . . . "

"And I am glad you won that scholarship. Because you *are* the smartest man in Warrington, and I—"

"Warrington's a small town," said John with the decanter in his hand. "More brandy, Victor?"

Victor shook his head.

"Might I have some?" said Harriet, tossing her head back.

"And spoil that lovely face of yours? You know what Father would do to it if he caught you drinking brandy."

"Brandy!" said Victor. "You have grown up, haven't you, Harriet?"

"More than you think. I've been to the tennis courts."

"Harriet!" John cast her a disapproving look. "Father warned you about that."

"Oh, I don't play. I just watch. He hasn't forbidden my watching."

"He'll be angry with you if he finds out."

"And who's going to tell him?"

"Tennis," said Victor, raising his eyebrows. "Here in Warrington?"

"Yes, Victor. My friend Megan O'Hanrahan plays tennis. *And* she smokes cigarettes."

"She's a fast girl, that Megan," said John darkly. "You'd best stay away from her."

But Victor said, "In London it's not such a scandal for a young lady to play tennis."

"Well this isn't London!"

"Oh John, you are a stiff." Harriet seized Victor's arm and spoke rapidly. "I don't really care about the tennis or other sports, even though Claire McMasters does shoot archery out at Penketh, but do you know what I would dearly love?"

Victor regarded his little sister with amusement in his eyes, "What?"

"A bicycle!"

John spun around. "Oh, of all the—"

"One moment, sir, your sister is talking. Now why do you want a bicycle, Harriet, of all things?"

"Megan O'Hanrahan has one and—"

"And you can see her petticoats as she pedals down the street, that's what!"

Harriet's hand flew to her breast. "John!" she said breathlessly.

"It isn't decent! And not only will Father not allow his daughter to make such a display of herself, neither will I. No sister of mine—"

"Victor, speak up for me!"

"Well, I . . . " He scratched his head.

"You'll not do it and that's final. A young lady showing off what's under her frock!"

"John Townsend, how can you be so common! Of course I shall wear bloomers—"

"And Father certainly won't allow those things in this house! Let the Americans wear them if they want, they invented them. But no Townsend women are going to disgrace themselves. And certainly not by riding a bicycle."

Harriet glowered angrily at John. Then she turned to Victor. "What do you think?"

"I'm afraid I shall have to agree with John on this. Tennis is one thing but bicycling is another altogether. I think you'd best forget the idea."

"It's them Irish," said John, reaching for the brandy again and filling his glass. "She's been told to keep away from them O'Hanrahans. Bad people."

"They're good people!"

"They're Catholics is what they are!"

"They're just as God-fearing as you and Father—"

"Don't contradict me, sister!" shouted John.

Harriet stood stunned for an instant, looking from one brother to the other, then, flinging her hands up to her face, whipped about and ran crying from the room.

As she flew past me I turned, opening my mouth to speak. But she was gone too quickly and slammed the door in my face.

Angry, I turned back to the brothers, a reproach on my lips, but when I faced the fireplace again, they were gone.

I was for the moment bewildered, wondering where they had gone, and then, remembering, I let out a short nervous laugh. I had actually been about to speak to them!

Slowly and with trepidation I walked to the centre of the room. It was back to normal again with the gas heater in the place of the roaring fire, the walls plain white, and the clock ticking quietly.

Feeling my legs suddenly give way, I slumped down into an easy chair and gaped in total bewilderment at the gas fire. What on earth had all that been about? How was it possible that I should imagine such an incredible scene? So lifelike, so perfect in detail, so seemingly real!

I was in shock. My whole body felt disjointed. All strength had run out of me. My mind was numb, as if I sat in a trance.

What had I just witnessed? A trick played by my fatigued, susceptible mind? The optical illusion of a fantasy invented by Nana's stories coupled with the bizarre atmosphere of this house? Or . . .

I screwed my eyes tight against the thought.

Or . . . had I really *seen* something here? Had I been visited by ghosts or had I somehow been granted a glimpse into the past?

I looked up at the clock. Is that what it was? A brief look back into time?

I continued to stare at the clock. No, I was not being haunted in the usual sense of the word, but rather what I was witnessing seemed to be events in the past. It was as though I had stumbled upon a flaw in the mechanism of Time through which I was able to view certain happenings.

And there was something else queer about it, too. I rubbed my forehead as a mild headache started to throb behind my eyes. It was the sequence in which everything was happening. I thought back to my first evening here (had it really been only two days before?) and recalled "Für Elise" the first time I had heard it, and how it had sounded as if played by a child. Yet, later it had come from a more practised hand. Then there was Victor at the window, a boy of fifteen. Yet when I saw him at my bedside that night, he was older, although not quite as old as I had seen him just now. And then Harriet, crying upstairs on the bed but reappearing a few minutes later a year older.

Had the clock been somehow turned back to the very beginning, to 1880 when the Townsends first moved into this house, and then set in motion again to run its natural course? If so, why? Or was I really only imagining it all?

There was a theory, I had read it somewhere, that Time was really all happening at once, that past and present and future were actually all running at the same time and that it was the properties of the physical universe which kept us from seeing into other ages. It was thought that certain "sensitives" such as mediums and clairvoyants had the ability to penetrate the barriers and see the past or future. That possibly this explained *déjà vu,* or premonitions. That possibly when we are most unaware and the barriers are weakest, we accidentally stumble across and have a "flash" into the future. Or into the past . . .

Clocks and calendars are man's inventions, yet Time existed long before that. Is it, then, a cycle—returning always to the same point? Or is Time a river, with all ages flowing concomitantly at once? If all of history exists now, and the future as well, then might it not be possible to happen upon an opening somewhere, a window as it were, and glimpse the other currents that flow alongside?

If the past could truly exist now, then I had found it.

When I awoke it was still dark. I lay sprawled in the easy chair still in my clothes, with the heat from the gas fire burning my legs. I sat up abruptly, rubbing my eyes and wondering for an instant where I was. I gaped at the clock. It said four.

Then I looked around the room. My body was stiff and painful from the position in which I had slept, so that I had to move slowly. Everything was as it had been. I had merely fallen asleep thinking about the seeming visit into the past. If that was truly what it had been. Or could it have been a dream? Had I fallen asleep before the heater hours ago, and only dreamed that I had heard the sobs, had gone upstairs to find out who cried in my bedroom? But no, there were my slippers. At least that part had really happened. Then what about the rest of it? John and Victor and Harriet? Could I have imagined them?

No, it had all been too real. The three of them had stood before the fire and laughed and talked as truly as if they were living people.

Then what accounted for it?

I could only return to thinking about Time, to wondering whether I had come across some accidental opening, and although I was not convinced that this was what had really happened, I didn't know what actually had.

Not wishing to fall asleep again, I got up and walked around the room. And as I did I went over and over the questions which plagued my mind. If I can see them why can't they see me? Is it only a one-way mirror, like the kind found in police stations? And if I can see them and hear them and feel the cold draught when they enter the room, might I not also be able to reach out and touch them? And if I did, what would I feel? Would *they* feel the pressure of my fingers? And further, why did it appear that their time was moving in chronological order; was there some purpose, some *reason?*

I fell back down into the chair, overwhelmed. Yes, what was the purpose to all this? Why was I being made to see certain things, why had I no control over it? Surely now, if I tried, I could not *will* Harriet and her brothers back. And yet, when they chose to return, I should most likely not be able to avoid it.

But they seemed unaware of me. In any cases of hauntings I had ever read or heard of, it was the apparition who controlled the situation and who haunted for some reason. But this? Odd scenes here and there from the past, like clips of a movie film, all as real and solid as if I truly existed for the moment in nineteenth-century England?

Why me? shouted my mind over and over again. If there is indeed a purpose to all of this, then why me? Why not Christine or one of my other cousins? Why not William or Elsie or Nana?

Why me?

I was doubled over in the chair, my head resting on my knees when a new, chilling thought came to my mind. Sitting up abruptly, I narrowed my eyes at the ticking clock, and I thought. Everything is moving along in sequence, just as it did nearly a hundred years ago. Then that means . . . that means . . .

"No!" I flew to my feet.

Against my will Nana's words came back to mind: "Victor Townsend was a despicable man. Some say he dabbled in the Black Arts. Some said he had direct dealings with the Devil himself. I cannot utter the unspeakable acts that demon committed. While he was alive, Victor Townsend made this house a living hell for everyone in it."

"No . . . " I moaned.

"Andrea."

I rolled my head from side to side. It throbbed terribly.

"Andrea, love."

Finally I opened my eyes and focused on my grandmother's face.

"Andrea, are you all right?"

I looked at her, knowing that she once had been very lovely and very fresh, and I privately mourned the irretrievable loss. "Yes . . . I'm . . . all right."

"It's nearly ten. Do you want to get up or do you want to sleep some more?"

Feeling myself frown, I looked down the length of my body, at the nightgown I wore and at the blankets covering me, then I let my head fall to the side and I saw my clothes neatly folded on the chair.

When had I taken them off?

"Oh, Nana . . . " I moaned, rubbing my eyes. "I've got such a headache."

"Poor love. Let me get you some tablets then. Don't move."

As I watched her limp to the sideboard and draw open a top drawer, I tried to think back over last night. I recalled seeing Harriet on the bed upstairs and then her conversation with her two brothers. And I remembered pacing the floor and trying to figure it all out. But after that it was a blank. I had absolutely no memory of getting undressed and into bed.

"Here, love." Her slender, knotted hand held out two white pills for me, and with the other she extended a glass of water. "These will do you."

"What are they?"

"Something for your headache. Take them."

"Thanks, Nana."

I sat up and took the pills, wondering why I suffered this loss of memory and why my head should hurt so. Then, as my grandmother shuffled off into her scullery, I languidly gathered up my clothes and moved into the hall. The cold air met me like a slap in the face. I began to shiver as I mounted the stairs. After a night in the oven warmth of the sitting room the rest of the house felt like a deep freeze.

Halfway up the stairs I stopped.

A memory, only fleeting and barely seizable, flashed in my mind. It was a fragment of a dream I had had. Only the faintest trace of it remained, for, try though I might, struggle though I did with my memory, I could not remember the dream. Except for one shred. It had something to do with the clothes wardrobe in the front bedroom.

Holding on to the banister and shivering in my flimsy nightgown, I fought a fruitless battle with my tenacious memory. Somehow, at one point in the night, I had entertained a very strange dream. And part of that dream had had to do with the wardrobe—something unusual about the wardrobe.

I shook my head. Lost, it would not be brought back. I continued up the stairs and went into the bathroom.

Some time later, refreshed and feeling the relief of Nana's aspirins, I emerged from the cold bathroom and padded my way along the upstairs hall to the front bedroom. Here, my suitcase was sprawled out on the bed as I had left it the day before. All my toiletries, underwear, fresh change of clothes lay just as I had left them. The room had a biting morning chill about it, but as daylight filtered through the curtains, it was not the formidable room it had been the night before. Now it was simply an old bedroom. The brass bedstead was dingy and in need of polishing. Dust lay in a blanket along the unused fireplace mantel. The walls were damp with the paint peeling. The wardrobe was old and worn and showing signs of great age.

The wardrobe.

I stopped what I was doing and turned around. Eyeing the great oak piece as if this would bring back the curious dream, I studied the wardrobe for some time. One of its doors stood slightly ajar.

I thought of Harriet lying on my bed, sobbing and threatening she would lock herself in the wardrobe and starve herself to death. I also recalled my first night sleeping here when, after that first queer nightmare of waking up to the feeling of pressure on my body, I had turned to look at the mirror just as I was about to switch off the light. And for some reason I had been held by the reflection in the mirror; the image of the wardrobe, which stood across the room.

Now, in the crisp morning hours with daylight filling the room and giving me a sense of courage, I approached the wardrobe with a mixture of curiosity and apprehension.

What had the dream been about?

Reaching out, I took hold of the wardrobe door and slowly swung it open. Inside, where I had first hung them, were the blue jeans and T-shirt I had travelled in from Los Angeles in. They were just as I had left them. So I opened the other door and discovered only emptiness and a few twisted coat hangers.

Just an empty old clothes wardrobe, that was all.

I made an effort to tidy up the things on the bed, gathered a small pile of hand laundry which I expected to do in the kitchen sink, and went back downstairs to join my grandmother.

"You want to do what?" asked Nana as we finished off the last of the buttered toast and bacon.

"I want to go for a walk. I want to get outside for a while."

She glanced out of the window at the crisp blue sky. "It looks a nice day, but in these parts you can't never tell. November's always a bad month for weather, love. Could cloud up any time."

"I'll dress warmly, Nana. But I've been cooped up too long. And Uncle Ed and Aunt Elsie won't be here for a while, yet I'd like a bit of air, if you don't mind."

Although reluctant, she relented. I drew two of her cardigans over my T-shirt, stuffed my hair into a knitted hat, and draped a woollen scarf around my neck.

"Where'll you go?" she asked.

I looked out of the sitting-room window at the vast field which undulated away from the alley behind Nana's house. "Where does that go?"

"That's Newfeld Heath. Runs along one of the Mersey canals. Can't get lost if you go along there. Just go down to the end of the road, turn right on Kent Avenue, and follow it out. You'll be on the heath in five minutes. Don't be long now, will you?"

Nana walked me to the door, reminded me again of the time, and closed the door behind me.

As I stood on the front steps tucking the ends of my muffler into the collar of my sweater, a peculiar sensation swept over me. Although I stood in bright sunshine and felt an invigorating cold wind on my face, and although I gazed across the street at ordinary brick houses with their little gardens and a few cars parked out front, I was suddenly overcome with the odd notion that I didn't want to be out here after all.

I started to go down one step and, for some unknown reason, hesitated. I felt almost as if I were reluctant to go, a vague unwillingness, all of a sudden, to leave the house.

I puzzled over this. Why on earth should I hang back? Five minutes ago I couldn't get out of the house fast enough. And yet now, lingering on the step, I felt myself compelled by a gentle force to remain indoors. It was almost as if . . .

I shook my head and forced myself down the steps.

Almost as if the house didn't want me to leave.

Chiding myself for such fantastical notions, I pressed on down the path, through the creaky gate, and out on to the pavement. Absurd! The house trying to keep me there! I even forced a laugh to prove to myself how silly I was being. And so, aiming myself into the biting wind and forcing myself not to cast a glance back at Nana's house, I shook off the feeling and struck off down the street.

After a few minutes I was able to stroll down George Street and enjoy the sharp day and freedom. I turned at Kent Avenue and followed it to where the cobblestones blended into the wild growth of the heath's edge.

Newfeld Heath is a barren stretch of wasteland that runs alongside an offshoot of the Mersey for the length of a mile and is several acres wide. A rising and falling of shallow slopes, it is covered with occasional patches of emerald green grass, scars of rock and raw earth, and scattered in great profusion with spiny gorse. Treading carefully, trying to avoid catching my pants on the nettles, I struck off in the direction of the canal.

With my hands thrust into the pockets of my jeans, I breathed deeply of the glassy air and lifted my face to the sun. It amazed me how quickly my spirits rose with the brief escape from Nana's house. I desperately needed to be away from the gloom and uneasiness it seemed to fill me with, and also away from Nana; to be alone for a while with my thoughts.

Only two days and three nights had passed in my grandmother's house, and yet it seemed an eternity. I marvelled at how draining this trip was turning out to be, and how out of control I seemed to have become. I was no longer in command of myself; my emotions, my thoughts, my imagination, and even my body seemed to have got away from me.

Why? Could it really just be the effects of jet lag, which surely I must be over by now? Was it the strange environment? The new people? Culture shock? Returning to the place of my birth after so many years?

I plodded through the field and, turning inward, paid scant attention to my surroundings.

Although there had to be a rational answer to the questions, I could not help but find myself returning again and again to the matter of the house. The house itself. No matter which direction I steered my thoughts, I always came back to the notion that my grandmother's house was having a strange, unexplainable effect upon me. Even to the point of obsession. But why?

I came to a halt not far from the canal and gazed into the wind. There was a houseboat moored to the bank, bobbing on the water; laundry was strung out over the deck, fluttering. Two boys crouched at the water's edge, teasing something with a stick.

I turned and gazed back at the row of identical backyards that bordered the heath. All with rusted gates and crumbling brick walls. Which one was Nana's house? And what was there about it that made it so different from all the rest?

Not in appearance, of course, for my grandmother's house was so like every other on George Street that it was impossible to pick it out with the eye.

Rather it was the *air* of the place, the atmosphere. Almost as if it breathed, as if something dwelt there. Something unseen . . .

Shaking my head to dispel such notions, I continued my trek along the heath.

I thought of Nana. I pictured her face, its paradoxical elusiveness: one moment beautiful, the next, old and ordinary. Radiant one moment, fading the next. And I wondered at her energy, her ability to fend for herself at such an age, to be able to see to my comforts, to be able to face life and all its odds. Especially after having lived with the same man for sixty-two years and to be suddenly without him.

I hiked my shoulders against the cold wind. It felt good, invigorating. And Nana's little white pills had taken care of the headache.

What must it be like to live with the same man for sixty-two years? Nana had said to me on that first evening, "I went to my marriage bed a virgin, and he was like a stranger to me."

I thought of Doug, of our first night together, and of our last. Nana and my granddad had lived together for sixty-two years until the ambulance had taken him away. Doug and I had lived together for six months until I had decided to call it quits.

"You panic, Andi," Doug had said to me on our last night together. "You see a relationship getting too deep, too serious, and you panic. So you pull out. You call an end to it before it has the power to hurt you. You're afraid of pain."

And I had defended myself with: "Isn't everyone?"

"Sure. But how do you know there'll be pain? I love you, and I think you love me, even though you've never said it. What are you so afraid of?"

When I had boarded the jet for London four days before, I had felt certain about my decision concerning the relationship with Doug; he was right, I did not want the deep involvement that he sought. I didn't want marriage or a family. I wanted to be free and unhampered.

And that was exactly the word I had used when I had told him I wanted the relationship to end: "unhampered." Doug had said, "What about love?"

And I had said, "Love has nothing to do with this. I'm talking about freedom. I don't want to commit myself. I don't want to be tied down."

And he had said again, "What are you afraid of?"

We had ended on a bitter, unsatisfactory note. I had wanted a cool, objective parting. I had tried to make him understand my need for freedom, and all he had been able to talk about was love and fear. As if those two things had anything to do with what I was trying to tell him.

After an exciting, happy six months, we fought for the first time. It had turned out not to be the separation I had wanted. So Doug and I had parted miserably, sorrowfully, and I in a turmoil. The letters from England had seemed a godsend, an excuse to get away (all right, to *run* away) for a while. To get a better perspective on what had happened. To straighten myself out, strengthen my resolves, and take command of my emotions.

Unfortunately, that was not how things were turning out.

I stopped again on the heath and squinted against the dazzling blue sky. It was the colour of robins' eggs and spotted with puffs of clouds. How odd it was to be standing here, eight thousand miles away from home, making the acquaintance of people who were nearly as blood related to me as my parents and brother. And how odd to think that I had been born here; that I had *started* here.

"You have no beginning and no destiny," Doug had said that last night, the familiar smile gone from his face to be replaced by something I had never seen before. "You have no roots and you're afraid to cultivate any. No past, no future, Andi. You're as plastic and hollow as the city you live in."

And that was how it had ended. Where was my old self-sufficiency now! Where was the strength and commitment to myself that I had always been able to rely on before this? I had brought an end to other relationships in the past and had always got over them. Why did this one seem determined to linger?

I felt my cheeks smart against the harsh wind as I stared again at the backs of the row of houses bordering the heath, one of them Nana's. For some reason, Doug's words about not wanting to start a family triggered the memory of something Nana had said to me two nights before, something about Granddad always being afraid that Victor Townsend's "bad blood" would show up in one of his grandchildren.

I shivered a little, flapped my arms about myself, and turned back to

Kent Avenue. I could see now, having got away from it for a while and having been able to spend some time alone with my thoughts, that the crazy feeling I had about Nana's house was only the product of my overworked mind. Glimpses into the past! Absurd—they had been dreams; I had fallen asleep and not been aware of it. After a few more days in that house I knew I would be as comfortable with it as were my relatives and the hallucinations would cease.

Unfortunately, I was proven wrong the moment I walked through the door.

At once the gloom fell over me, enshrouded me, drew me inside and made me tremble with a greater cold than before. "Nana . . . " I tried calling out, but my voice failed me. I leaned against the front door, gazing down the shadowy hall, and thought, Oh no . . .

After a long minute passed, I saw the sitting-room door open, golden light spill on the worn carpet, and heard my grandmother's voice. "Back, love? Thought I heard the door. Come on then, Elsie and Ed'll be here soon to take you to hospital."

Discouraged that I had not, after all, rid myself of the overpowering atmosphere of this place, I followed Nana into the sitting room, pulled off my woollens, and went to stand by the heater.

"Must be cold out," said my grandmother as she shuffled towards the kitchen. "Your face looks like rhubarb. You shall want something warm inside you before you go out again. I'll get my cherry cordial out and pour you a nice glass."

"You know, Nana," I called after her, "I think I'd prefer a bit of brandy, if you don't mind."

She called back, "Sorry, love, don't have no brandy."

"But of course you do!" I shook my head at the tragedy of old-age senility and forgetfulness and went over to the armoire.

I saw there the old china set and the shelf of leather-bound books. And then I remembered.

The brandy had existed in *their* time.

I spun around and watched Nana hobble through the kitchen door. A flush rose to my cheeks making them feel hot. The absurdity of what I had just done overwhelmed me with a sense of horror.

When Nana came out again I was still standing by the armoire, my face, I was certain, a study in shock. But she did not see this, for she handed me the glass of warmed cordial and turned away from me, I stared after her in profound amazement.

For one fleeting instant I had confused dreams with reality.

When Aunt Elsie and Uncle Ed finally arrived, I was relieved, for they represented the present and sanity. I had to get out of this house again and away from whatever it was that was influencing me so.

As we put on our coats at the front door, Aunt Elsie said, "Bundle up good, Andrea. There's a bad spell coming. Looks like rain on the horizon. I think we're in for a gale."

My grandfather was sitting up, his eyes wide open, and he appeared a little more alert than usual. He smiled when we walked in.

"Hullo, Dad," said Elsie, taking her usual spot. "Got a treat for you today. Look at this." She pulled a green and gold can out of her bag. "Treacle! For your afternoon butties!"

My grandfather grinned happily.

Uncle Ed, always soft-spoken, said quietly, "Feeling better today are you?"

Granddad nodded, as if he had understood. Then, surprisingly, he turned to me.

I felt ill at ease beneath that hooded gaze, for his eyes were so foggy and his expression so enigmatic that it was impossible to know what he was feeling. Perhaps he had turned in my direction because he had heard the sound of my chair. Or perhaps it was merely his habit to look first this way, then that. But whatever, when he spoke to me I could not mask my surprise. "Wooth? You've come back have you?"

"Yes, Granddad, I'm here." Gingerly I reached out for his hand, brown-spotted and covered with thick veins, and patted it.

"Wooth? You've come back have you?"

Now Elsie leaned across the bed and shouted, "It's Andrea, Dad! Ruth's back in Los Angeles!"

He nodded and grinned childlike. "Aye, I know. It's our Wooth all right. Put wood in th'hole, would you?"

I blinked and sat up. "What, Granddad?"

"Put wood in th'hole, would you?" he repeated, still smiling.

I looked to Aunt Elsie. She said, "He wants the door closed." She got up and shut it. "Always had a thing about open doors, he has."

"Is that what he said?"

Before she could reply, the sister came by and, standing at the foot of the bed, regarded my grandfather with professional disapproval. "Won't walk for us, he won't," she said to Elsie and Ed. "He just refuses to get up and walk for us. Don't you, Mr. Townsend!"

Granddad merely kept his eyes on me and nodded.

"Sister's talking to you, Dad, not Andrea!" shouted Elsie.

Now he turned his head and looked at his daughter. His grin remained fixed, his eyes clouded.

"She says you won't walk for them. Doctor wants you to walk. How can you go home to Mum if you don't walk?"

Granddad nodded to her as he had done to me, so that Elsie turned to the sister and shrugged. "He's not with us today, is he?"

"Oh well," said the nurse noncommittally. "He has his days. He's best late at night, because then he talks up a storm and we can't keep him quiet."

Elsie's face took on a look of concern. "Is he, you know, coherent? Does he make sense, Sister?"

"Well, I don't rightly know, do I? It could be to you, it isn't to me. He talks to people that aren't here."

I pricked my ears up at this and turned my attention to the nurse. She was an older woman wearing a navy blue uniform with a white apron pinned to the front. Her grey head was bare and she had a nervous tic on the right side of her face. She spoke in the same Lancashire accent.

"Do you know to whom he talks," I asked suddenly.

My aunt said, "This is my niece from America. Andrea. She's my sister's daughter. When she heard that her granddad was ill she flew right over to be with him."

"Can you tell me to whom he talks, Sister?"

"I really don't rightly know who it is. Could be anyone I suppose. Don't make no sense."

"Has he mentioned any names?"

"Andrea," said Elsie. "What are you on about?"

I looked at my aunt with borderline impatience. "Nothing, Aunt Elsie. I thought maybe . . . that he might have mentioned my mother's name. Maybe he has said something to her, you know, thinking she was here. And I could go home and tell her he sent her a message"—I waved my hands helplessly—"you know."

"No women," said the sister suddenly. "He's never mentioned any women's names. Just a man. He talks at night to a man."

"Has he . . . " I swallowed hard. "Have you ever heard a name?"

"Let me think. He can carry on a conversation, you know. And most of it is about the horse races. He thinks he's placing a bet, you know. Or he's ordering a pint of ale. Names . . . now let me see." She rubbed the cheek with the tic.

I had moved to the edge of my chair.

Finally, she snapped her fingers and said, "Aye, there was one I remember. Just the other night it was, too. And last night as well, now that I recall. He was talking to someone named Victor. That was it. Victor."

I slid back in the chair.

"Victor!" said Aunt Elsie. "Granddad never knew anyone by that name. He must've made it up!"

"Oh aye," said the sister as she started to walk away. "I'm sure he did. They all do in here, you know. Make up unseen visitors."

As she moved down the line of beds to inspect each of her patients, I watched the Sister's back and thought, He's seen Victor too.

CHAPTER 6

THAT EVENING BY THE GAS FIRE WAS INTERMINABLE, FOR I was afflicted with an impatience I could not comprehend. It seemed as if the revelations of the day were all boiling about in my soul and building up to some climax which I dreaded. The elusive memory of the wardrobe had continued to taunt me all day, despite the fact that I had tried to toss it off as the by-product of some queer, unredeemable dream. And then the incident with the brandy, seemingly small and insignificant now, had also continued to prey upon my consciousness as a nagging reminder that I had, for one moment, slipped between time frames. And lastly there had been the news of Granddad's nocturnal talks with his father. Perhaps this had been the greatest blow of all.

Sitting now before the gas fire and listening to the rhythmic click of Nana's knitting needles, I recalled the conversation in the car driving back from the hospital.

"Fancy Dad making up a visitor!" Elsie had said to Uncle Ed and me. "It's like a child inventing an invisible playmate."

I had sat with my forehead on the cold window, my head banging against it as the Renault bounced over the cobblestones. "I don't think it's an invention, Aunt Elsie," I had heard my voice say from far away.

"Whatever do you mean?"

"I think maybe Granddad is imagining his father is visiting him."

"His father!" Elsie's apple red face screwed up for a minute. "Crikey! I think you're right! Wasn't that the name of Dad's father? Victor? Victor Townsend! Aye, now I remember." She twisted her great hulk in the seat to look at me. "But Dad never knew his father, Andrea. It seems to me he ran off before Dad was born."

I forced a shrug. My eyes rebounded off each building and structure we passed, staring but unseeing. "Maybe he's given him a face and form so he can talk to him."

While my surmise had convinced Aunt Elsie, who was astonished that her father should be fantasizing about his own dad at this point in his life, it did not convince me. Considering what had happened to me in the last three days, I could not entirely dismiss the idea that Granddad had somehow really seen Victor.

This was the painful part. So easy it had been that morning on the heath to laugh at my "dreams" and my melodrama of the night before, so simple it had been to chalk it all up as just one of those things that happens when you're jet-lagged and culture-shocked, it came as a very unsettling thought now that I might have been right in the first place—that I had really glimpsed the past.

If not, then was it only a coincidence that my grandfather should happen to "see" Victor Townsend when I also did?

After a quiet tea of scones and ham sandwiches, Nana had taken out her knitting and I had retrieved some stationery from my suitcase, ostensibly to write some letters home. Yet I had not been able to concentrate on anything other than the growing mystery of this house, so that by nine o'clock I was quite restive.

All I could wonder was, Will anything happen tonight?

"Do you know any good stories, Andrea?" asked Nana quite unexpectedly.

I looked up from my blank stationery. "Do I know what?"

"Stories. You know, funny ones. Jokes." She turned to me and peered at me over the rims of her glasses. Her hands did not stop their work. "Do you know any good jokes?"

"Oh . . . well . . . " I cast my eyes about the room. "I can't think off-hand . . . "

"You know, I can never remember a joke five minutes after I've heard it." She looked down at her knitting and worked as she talked. I tried to keep my eyes on her and feign interest. "Your Uncle William was always a good one for telling stories, ever since he was a lad. Must have got it from my side of the family, 'cause I can't say as the Townsends had much of a sense of humour. It's hard to laugh when you're unhappy all the time, I 'spect."

It was an effort to keep my eyes on Nana. While my mind fought to wander down other avenues of thought, I had to struggle to pay attention to Nana and the present. She spoke slowly and in time with the click-clack of her needles. Her hands fluttered like birds over the yarn, darting in and out, stopping only now and again to pull more length from the ball.

"Your mum always said your brother inherited my family's sense of humour. It's a funny thing about family likenesses, isn't it? Look at you, Andrea. Got a lot of your granddad in your face, you have. Oh, you can't see it now because he's so old. But when he was younger, well, I could see right off that you were going to take after him. A lot of the Townsend likeness in you, there is."

As she spoke, I looked up at the clock on the mantel. It had stopped ticking. I held myself rigid, grasping the arms of my chair until my fingers dug deep into the stuffing.

"Thank goodness that's all you inherited from the Townsends," she went on.

The sound of her voice came to me in a muffled form, as though cotton were stuffed in my ears. Although I clung desperately to the arms of the chair, I felt the room tip and turn about me, Nana swimming before my eyes. Her voice grew fainter and fainter until I could only see her lips move but not hear what she said. A cold draught blew into the room, shadows danced on the walls. I gaped incredulously at my nana, sitting in her chair and chatting away as she knitted, while the room twisted and moved about and grew increasingly colder.

"No . . . " I whispered.

The chill wind increased as I saw vague shapes now emerge from the walls and move about me, fading in and out of my vision like silhouettes on a carousel. They grew large and shrank down, they came close to my face and drew back, and all the while the sitting room swung about me in some macabre dance.

I had a vision of myself being caught at the centre of a great whirlpool, for everything spun about me and it was as if I was being sucked down to the centre. I grew dizzy and nauseated, with fresh perspiration breaking out on my forehead. The room tilted and lurched. I clung to the easy chair like a person drowning, and still I tumbled down and ever down to the bottom of the abyss.

As the vertigo increased and I grew dizzier, the dark forms drew nearer to me and clustered about my chair, hovering and waiting. I tried to speak, to call out to my grandmother, but she was far away from me now—a tiny little woman knitting in a miniature chair at the far end of this enormous room—and I knew she wouldn't be able to hear.

Finally, as the silhouettes came so near that I thought they would touch me, they all blended together in a blackness that was like a curtain and they closed over me.

When I opened my eyes I saw that the room was still. I looked around, blinking. Everything was the way it had been, nothing was changed. Next to me was Nana, knitting quietly and murmuring to herself. Before us was the familiar gas fire. And on the mantel ticked the clock. It was only a few minutes past nine.

"Have you seen much of it?" she asked without looking up.

"Much of . . . what . . . " I put my hand to my forehead and wiped away the sweat. My T-shirt was wet through.

"The Queen's Jubilee. Have you had much of it on American television?" Nana looked up. "I should love to hear your impressions—I say, what's wrong? Feeling poorly?"

"No, Nana . . . I just . . . I was nodding. I was falling asleep and I guess I didn't hear you."

"That's all right, love. Time enough for chatter tomorrow. It's time we were getting on to bed."

As she struggled to her feet I gazed imploringly at my grandmother, trying to find some way to tell her what had happened, to speak my fears to her. But my tongue would not obey, and so I simply sat and stared dumbly at her. She bundled her knitting in the bag, hung it over the chair, and came to give me a sloppy kiss on the cheek.

"God love you," she murmured against my face. "And bless you for coming here."

"Good night, Nana," I said feebly.

"Good night, love. You know how to turn up the gas if you need it, don't you?"

"Yes." I stood and followed her to the door, closing it behind her and making certain it was secure. Then I sank against the door and leaned there, pressing my face against the wood.

What had happened just a minute ago? What had caused such a sickening upheaval? It was as if I had been caught in some bizarre vortex of Time, as though "they" had started to come back but somehow, possibly by the presence of Nana, had been thwarted and the clash had created a cataclysm. It had been as if a dam had suddenly been thrust into a river causing the current to backwash and swirl in eddies.

I clutched my stomach with the nausea that the spinning had caused, and I wondered if my weak legs would be able to carry me back to the chair. Now that the chill was gone from the room I felt hotter than before, flushed and burning as if I had a fever. I turned from the door, thinking I would turn down the gas heater, but found myself standing before John Townsend.

Gasping, I fell back against the door. He did not move. Standing in the centre of the room, John was holding a glass of brandy and casting frequent glances towards the clock. He appeared impatient as though waiting for someone.

And what year is this now? I wondered, feeling the extraordinary heat from the roaring fire reach my face. The logs were piled high, brilliant and glowing, while giant flames leaped up into the chimney. John's face reflected the fire's glow, which harshened his otherwise soft and gentle features. His hair, not as dark as Victor's, now glinted like polished chestnuts, and his warm brown eyes turned to gold.

I stared in amazement, surprised that I should feel no fear, curious about what I was going to witness this time. The room was the same as it had been the night before, with no changes that I could see. There were the same Victorian knickknacks about, the armoire and other furniture looking new, and the wallpaper still bright.

When John lifted his head all of a sudden and looked directly at me, my heart gave a leap, but I did not move. "Where have you been?" he asked angrily.

I turned my head to the side and was startled to see Harriet standing there. With my back pressed against the door, it could not have opened or closed. And yet there was Harriet standing next to me. She was as real as if she were alive today, for I was able in that minute to give her close study and could have sworn that a living, breathing, flesh-and-blood woman stood there. She was slightly older than when I had seen her last—fifteen or possibly even sixteen now—and her dress was different, having changed from tight sleeves to ones which puffed out above the elbow. Styles were changing, my relatives were growing older, and time was passing.

"The postman was just here," she said next to me, her voice as clear and solid as if she indeed stood there. "We've a letter from Victor."

From where I stood I could see a peculiar agitation in her face and in the movement of her hands, although I suspected John was unaware of it. Harriet held her back uncommonly rigid and her gestures were mechanical, and she spoke as if she were trying to exercise control over her voice.

"Victor? Let me have it."

"It's addressed to Father."

"I shall read it first. Come now, Harriet."

She stepped forward and extended the letter to him. As she did so, I happened to notice the quick movement of Harriet's other hand, a furtive gesture on the other side of her skirt, and it seemed to me that she twisted her body away from her brother just a little, as if trying to hide something.

Then I saw it. There was a second letter, clutched protectively in her other hand and which she now, with John looking away, tucked into a hidden pocket in her skirt.

"What does he say?" she asked loudly.

John read silently for a few minutes, then handed the letter to Harriet. "Here, read it for yourself. Have you been writing to him, Harriet?"

"Of course I have. None of *you* will." She took the letter, all traces of her former apprehension gone, and read it eagerly. "Oh, John!" she cried in dismay. "He wants to go to Edinburgh!"

"It's Lister," said her brother, turning to the fire. "That upstart."

"Mr. Lister is a fine surgeon, John. He attended upon the Queen when she had that operation on her arm, you remember. He's not an upstart."

"Ten years ago, London was ready to throw him out on his ear, *you* will remember, for his vivisectionist views and his insult to the Royal College of Surgeons. Why, he as good as accused King's College of being medieval!"

"I don't know about that, John, but it appears from this letter that Mr. Lister has convinced our Victor he should go up to Scotland."

"*And* he's an atheist."

Harriet read further, shaking her head. "Mr. Lister is a Quaker. Not being a member of the Church of England does not make one an atheist. But look here, Victor is mentioning experiments. He's talking about *research*." She looked up at John, her face horrified. "I thought he wanted to be a doctor, not a scientist!"

"These days it's hard to tell the difference. I tell you, Harriet, our Victor doesn't know his own mind. I think he's been poisoned by all that carbolic spray!"

"Oh, could it be?" She looked down at the letter again. "He says he already has an appointment and that he will be earning good money."

John folded his arms contemptuously and leaned on the mantel. "It's about time. Your brother has been living off the Crown for three years now, while I have been slaving away at the mill, may it rot. Victor has always had delusions of superiority, you know. He quite fancies himself another Louis Pasteur."

"Would that be so bad, John, if he could find a cure for another disease? Perhaps cholera!"

"Now you are defending him, sister. Please make up your mind; do you want him to go or do you want him to come home?"

She dropped her hand in defeat, the letter crumpling in her fingers, and a sigh escaped her throat. "I don't know. I had hoped he would come back to Warrington and set up practice here. But if he'll be happier in Scotland—"

"Who can be happy in that godforsaken country?"

Harriet suddenly turned around as if she had heard a sound. "I think the photographer is here. I'll tell Mother."

I watched Harriet rush from the sitting room and disappear into the scullery, from which she emerged a moment later with another woman behind her. Mrs.. Townsend, Victor's mother, was a large bosomy woman who moved like a steam engine. Her dress, obviously years older than Harriet's, was a black bombazine with high collar, dropped shoulders, and an enormous bustle at the rear. Seeing her in this voluminous dress that was more cumbersome than Harriet's and that took up a great deal of the sitting room, I found myself curiously thinking of it as old-fashioned. Her feet could not be seen, which enhanced the train locomotive effect, and she walked with her large bosom thrust forward. The face of the woman was hard and plain with no attractive features or artifices to improve it. Her long thick hair, twisted on top of her head, was capped with a little white hat, giving her the impression of a tall Queen Victoria.

A clattering noise at my side caused me to turn and see the entrance of the photographer. A mole-like man with bushy side whiskers and oiled-down hair, he struggled with several clumsy boxes, grunting and groaning into the sitting room.

"You are a punctual man, Mr. Cameron," said Mrs.. Townsend in an officious voice. "Mr. Townsend will be down presently."

"Shan't take me a minute to set up, madam. Home portraits is my business so I'm quite practised in rapid erection."

I saw John wince and turn away.

Together we all watched Mr. Cameron, with darty little rodent gestures, assemble his equipment in the centre of the sitting room. In fascination, I saw his accordion-like camera emerge from its box and be afixed atop the tripod. A black cloth fell from its back and halfway to the floor. A second box revealed wooden cassettes, metal plates, and bottles containing various labelled compounds. Mr. Cameron, with the help of John, pulled the sofa away from the wall, then went to work adjusting his camera to height and distance from that spot.

"Now if you will please, sir, madam, mistress, take your positions behind the settee. That poster will make a lovely backdrop. From the Great Exhibition is it?"

"I hear Mr. Townsend coming now," said the mother, pushing her great size into the small space behind the couch.

I turned in time to see Victor's father materialize on our side of the door, still buttoning his stiff collar into place. Also a person of great size, Mr. Townsend created a most formidable impression, dressed as he was all in black, with a black cravat tied under the starched collar and his black hair plastered down with oil. Two characteristics dominated his face: the large handlebar moustache that stood out from his cheeks as if made from wood, and the deep furrow between his eyebrows. Without a doubt this was Victor's father, an impressively handsome man with a most commanding bearing. He was Granddad's grandfather, my great-great-grandfather.

"Let's get about it then," he boomed in a thick accent that I could barely understand. He spoke like a Cockney, although Mrs.. Townsend did not, and I suspected this was due to his London upbringing.

The family assembled against the wall, Harriet and John in front of the mother and father—but staggered so that everyone could be seen—and beneath the poster on the wall. This colourful oversized handbill was an advertisement for "Wylde's Great Globe," which, according to the ad, was a "wonder of the modern age" and, being sixty feet in diameter and boasting of many exhibition rooms, required several hours for viewing. Although there was no date on it, I suspected it was a souvenir from happy times past.

Mr. Cameron worked quickly and deftly at his adjustments, dodging in and out of the black cloth, sliding the bellows camera back and forth until, satisfied with sharpness, he locked it in place. Then, sliding two plates back to back in the camera, he took one last look under the cloth and said, "I shall turn out the lights now. No one is to move. Stay just as you are please. No moving now . . . "

Sprinkling out a precise amount of magnesium powder on to the metal hod which he held in one hand, Mr. Cameron then turned down the gas lights until the room was almost totally dark. In the bit of light that crept through the curtains I could see him lift the cover off the lens, slide the wooden cassette out of the camera, and then, in a smooth rapid movement, strike a match and ignite the powder. There was a bright flash like lightning, then a dense, acrid white smoke filled the air. As the Townsends coughed a little, Mr. Cameron quickly replaced the lens cover, slid the wooden cassette back over the copper plate, and then turned the gas lights back up.

The four people behind the couch used sleeves and handkerchiefs to wipe the scattered dust off their faces while Mr. Cameron turned the cassette around and dropped more powder on to the hod.

"One more time, ladies and gentlemen, just to be certain. I think you all blinked on that one. Remember, please try to keep your eyes open when the flash goes off."

He repeated the process, and after all was done, Harriet noticed with dismay that one lock of her hair had fallen down and had been hanging over one ear.

"Shall I take more, Mr. Townsend?" asked the nervous little photographer.

"You're already stealing from us for this one, Mr. Cameron. I shall not perpetrate your crime further."

"But Father—" whined Harriet.

"Listen to Mr. Townsend," said the mother, moving away from the wall. "If the first one doesn't come out, then the second will have to do. Curl or no curl. We are not rich people, Harriet."

Hearing this and watching the family dissemble as Mr. Cameron packed up his equipment, I wondered why they had elected to have the portrait taken now instead of waiting until Victor's next visit so that the entire family would be in it. From their behaviour, it would seem they didn't want Victor in the picture . . .

They left me now, fading out like a movie scene, until I was alone once again in my own sitting room and before the gas heater. I was left feeling drained, as if I had been under a great strain, so that I plopped down in the easy chair. The clock on the mantel read ten minutes past nine.

I sat up. That was impossible! I had spent at least half an hour with the Townsends, if not longer! And yet according to this clock—"my" time—Nana had only just left.

I pressed my fists into my eyes and groaned out loud. What was happening to me? Had I only fallen asleep here in this chair, had a rapid dream, and awakened to think it had really happened? I searched about in my memory for some clue. It seemed to me that dream experts said the average dream lasted about twenty seconds, even though to the sleeper it may seem like a long time. Can this have been what happened to me then? Had Nana's talk and her old photographs somehow created a fertile spot in the area of my imagination? Is that all this was—dreams?

I let my hands drop, watching them fall into my lap. There must be some way I could find out for sure! I had to know if I was merely suffering from illusions or if it was all real! But how?

I stared down at my hands, going over in my mind what I had just witnessed. The ferret-like Mr. Cameron, the steam-engine mother, the moustached father. And the pungent smell of the burned powder. And as I went over it all, something about it seemed to stick in my mind like a thorn: one word—"photograph." The family had had their picture taken.

Of course! There was my answer. The Townsend photo album Nana had spoken of. Was it possible that the family portrait I had just seen taken by Mr. Cameron was in there? And if it was . . .

Suddenly the desire to find that album became a frantic one. I *had* to see it. Some of my answers should lie there, in the faded brown photographs of times long past and people long dead.

If the group portrait of the Townsends taken behind the sofa was in that album, then I would know for certain that I had indeed found a window into the past.

At first I was reluctant to go through Nana's sideboard drawers, for I knew I was trespassing upon her privacy, but as my desperation increased, I overcame this feeling and drove madly through her things like a person possessed.

After fifteen minutes of rifling through sewing boxes, pairs of gloves, racks of old silverware, and mountains of hoarded trinkets that were the sum total of Nana's existence, I sat on the floor before the sideboard in despair. The album was not there.

After a moment of fretting, my legs crossed and my fingers twisting at themselves, an idea came to me. But it was a chilling one, a thought which I did not at all welcome. Raising my eyes to the wall behind the sofa, I stared intently at it as if able to see the room on the other side. And as I did so, Nana's words rang again in my ears: "The parlour hasn't been used in ever so many years. At least twenty or twenty-five. Not since our William got married and moved out. No need for it now, can't heat it, so we use it for storage."

Feeling my scalp prickle, I slowly came to my feet. Only last night, after coming downstairs from finding Harriet on my bed, I had stumbled about in the dark hallway and had heard the piano play "Für Elise" again. And it had been coming from the parlour. Was that where it always came from, each time it intruded upon the "Scottish Music Hour"? And if so, who was it that played?

I swallowed hard for courage and wiped my hands down my jeans. Fearful though I was, my need to find that album was greater, so I slowly walked to the door and quietly drew it open.

The hallway, the same bottomless cavern and filled with arctic air, gaped before me. My eyes grew wide, straining. I had the odd sensation of stepping into a long tunnel that had no end. Behind me was the warmth and light and security of the sitting room, while ahead of me lay a menacing blackness filled with an unearthly cold. Yet the pull of the next room was greater than my own fear; the Townsend album would have my answers. I had to know.

It was strange that I should be afraid, and I realized it even then, blindly feeling my way along the damp wall, for so far none of what had happened had harmed me. Indeed, the two scenes with the family in the sitting room had only been cheerful and pleasant and I had felt no threat to myself. So why was it that now, approaching the parlour door, I should feel the crawl of terror over my skin, a gripping, sinking feeling deep in my bowels that I should not pursue this further? Why should I be afraid now when I wasn't moments before, watching the family portrait being taken? It was as though the air about me were evil, as though I were entering upon a realm that was far removed from John and Harriet and their roaring fire. I felt as though the hellish tragedies that had taken place in this house all those years ago were now contained in this spot, and that I foolishly entered it.

The sensation was a familiar one. I had felt it two nights before when I had found Victor standing over my bed. It had been the air then, a terrifying aura that had emanated from the darkness as though some evil horrors lurked there. This was the same feeling now, as I left the safety of the sitting room and delivered myself into the dark catacomb of the hallway. It was almost as though something were waiting for me.

CHAPTER 7

Y HANDS FOUND THE PARLOUR DOOR AND I PAUSED BEFORE pushing it open. Looking over my shoulder, I saw the door to the sitting room open by only a slit—hadn't I left it standing wide open?—and a peculiar trick of the eye, like an optical illusion, made it appear very far away. An uncommon dryness filled my mouth and throat while trickles of sweat ran down my back. My hand rested on the icy doorknob, untouched in so many years.

My heart pounded in a rhythm against my rib cage, as if saying, What will you find on the other side?

And my mind, terrified, but unable to turn back, replied, We must find that album.

I don't remember turning the knob or pushing open the door, but in the next instant it stood open. I saw the same endless night before me and smelled the air of age and decay. It was a musty atmosphere, reminiscent of a dank cellar, and there was something else, too. It smelled of death and oblivion.

Before I stepped in I glanced back at the sitting room. The door was all the way closed now so that no light filtered out. Although this should have alarmed me (for I *had* left the door wide open), it did not, for I had no thought now for anything except that album. Similarly, my body had no will of its own. The same unseen power that impelled me to find the book now drew me into the parlour.

When my teeth started to chatter the sound startled me. But realizing what it was, I held my ground and tried to look around the parlour. It had no edges, no walls, no end. It went on for ever and ever, the eternal region of night and nothing and hopelessness.

Whatever dwelt in here was unhappy.

Without thinking, I reached up and brushed the light switch. Miraculously the overhead bulb burst into life, baring before me the interior of a room that had stood unused and neglected for countless years. White sheets thick with dust were draped over bulky furniture, the legs of chairs and tables seen underneath. A bare wooden floor, scuffed; an old boarded-up fireplace; mildewed draperies over the window. And to my left, an antique roll-top desk buried in layers of dust.

This last I approached cautiously, fearful that my presence might upset the fragile balance of the room. I had the uncanny sensation of being watched, although the window was hidden and there were no pictures about. Chiding myself for such an overactive imagination, I firmly grasped the edge of the roll-top and, with great effort, managed to raise it. A clamorous noise came up from its hidden mechanisms, the dust-choked slats rattling and groaning against my hand. It would go only halfway and no farther.

Bending at the waist, I peered under the roll-top and saw a desk littered with old papers, books, boxes, and general rubbish. There were pigeon holes, most of them empty, some stuffed with yellow envelopes. The odour of mould met me, causing me to gag. I saw nothing that could be a photograph album.

But there were drawers. One long one across the centre, three deep ones going down the side to the floor. The first would not move under my hand, and my fingers were too cold and painful to fight it. The next drawer slid easily but it was empty. The third was full of old Christmas and birthday wrappings, tangled ribbons, and a rusted pair of scissors. I struggled with the last drawer, sensing the futility of my search and wondering where I would turn after this, when it finally came open under my force, revealing, on top of a stack of crumbling newspapers, a family photo album.

Coming out of the parlour to find the sitting-room door standing wide open, as I had originally left it, I was too excited about the album to give it any thought. More imaginings is what it was, just as the menacing air of the parlour had been my own fabrication. For surely, I thought upon turning out the light in the parlour and closing the door behind me, it had all been nothing more than the product of an overactive imagination stimulated by the eerie setting.

Once inside the sitting room with the door firmly shut behind me, I realized for the first time how desperate had been my need to find this album for, clasping it now to my breast, I felt all the strength go out of my legs. Here was the permanent record of the Townsend story. Here would be my answer.

Making myself comfortable in the easy chair before the fire, with my feet up on the ottoman, I made almost a ritual of preparing myself, making sure everything was just right, and of slowly opening the book.

Mildew had made the first few pages inseparable, and a creeping rot had turned paper and photographs into a rancid-smelling pulp. The pages crumbled as I turned them, making my heart churn with the horror of such pointless destruction. How many pictures had been ruined, how much Townsend history had succumbed to the ravages of the years? But as I gingerly worked my way to the centre of the album, I found to my joy that the interior was in a fair state of preservation. Oval portraits, faded and cracked, bared to me the faces of yet older Townsends: women in crinolines and Civil War coiffures; men in starched collars that stood up, their hair brushed forward in the Romantic fashion. I was even further back in time now, gazing possibly upon the faces of Victor's grandparents, unfamiliar people with no recognizable traits. All strangers to me, these ancestors whose distant passions had been the genesis of my own creation. I was a little in awe of them as I stared down at those blank expressions, at those hollow eyes, and tried to delve the stiff façades for some trace of personality underneath. In a small way, no matter how diluted now, I was nourished by the same blood that had nourished these.

And then I saw it.

So intent had I become in perusing the portraits of my ancestors (barely making out such dates as 1868 and 1855) that I had for the moment forgotten the purpose of my going through this album. When I came to it, so much did it shock me and slap me back to sensibility that I stopped breathing and gaped in amazement at the picture.

There were Mr. and Mrs.. Townsend in the back, "Wylde's Great Globe" poster on the wall above their heads, John and Harriet in front. There was the same black bombazine dress of the mother; the father's handsome moustache; John's gentle face with a hint of a smile. And Harriet, one curl dangling haphazardly over one ear.

When I heard myself gasp I brought my head up. But I was still alone in the room, still back in my own time and sitting before the gas heater. And yet, I now knew beyond a doubt that a short while before I had not been in my own time but had somehow slipped back to another age.

The date under the photograph, in a careful Spencerian hand, was July 1890.

How was it possible?

I carelessly let the album slide out of my lap and on to the floor. A headache began to drum behind my eyes, a nagging, sickening thud much like the one I had awakened to that morning. Letting a moan escape my lips, I suffered more from the futility of my questions than from the pain in my head.

How was it possible?

And yet, possible it must be, for it had happened. The photograph in the album was the same one I had seen Mr. Cameron take just an hour ago.

There was Harriet with her tenacious curl, and there was her dark skirt with a secret letter hidden in its left-hand pocket.

The photo was a testimony to one instant in time, freezing it and recording it for future generations. And yet I had witnessed that same moment, had almost been a part of it, as it had really happened—fluid and moving, peopled with flesh and blood and voice.

I had smelled the smoke of the magnesium flash!

There must be a reason for it. The Townsends were moving along in time towards their inescapable destinies, just as we all must, and for some reason I was being forced to watch. Was there then some story to it as the scenes unfolded before my eyes?

If this were so, then was I truly going to be forced to endure the horrors that were soon to take place in this house—those unspeakable acts which had turned George Street into the Townsends' private hell?

The throbbing of my head increased with each unanswerable question. I massaged my temples, unable to put my mind at rest.

What was the solution then? If there were no answers, no reasons for why this should be happening to me, or to what end, then would not the simple solution be to leave Nana's house and not come back?

It was in the very deepest regions of my soul that I knew the answer. Only that afternoon, as I had stepped out of the house to go for a walk on the heath, I had sensed its reluctance, its *unwillingness* to let me go. Then, I had dismissed it as imagination. Now I knew the truth. I could not leave the house on George Street.

It would not let me go.

Nana's hand was on my shoulder again, her face puckered in worry. I blinked idiotically at her, wondering when she had come in and why I hadn't heard her.

"It's getting on to noon," she said in concern. "I've kept quiet this morning so you could sleep, but you started making noises. And your face doesn't look at all well. Andrea, can you hear me?"

I lolled my head about, wincing beneath the pain, and saw through the haze that I was in my nightgown and lying under the covers on the sofa. It was unbearably warm in the room. "Yes, Nana, I'm . . . all right. But I have . . . " My hand came up and flopped down on my forehead. I felt drugged. "Another headache."

"Poor love. It's the damp, it is. I'll get you some more tablets. And there's no going to hospital today."

"Oh, Nana . . . " I raised up on my elbows. "I want to go."

My grandmother turned away from me and hobbled across the room. Going directly to the window behind the little dining table, she reached up and with a grunt yanked the curtains open. "Now look at that, will you?"

I stared at the window, mystified. It looked as if someone had gone over it with thick white paint. "What is it . . . ?"

"It's that awful Glasgow fog. They had it yesterday—I heard about it on the wireless. But now it's moved down to us. We're quite socked in, love, there'll be no going nowhere today."

"Fog . . . "

"Like clockwork you can count on it. Glasgow gets it the day before, then it comes down to us. Now I'm going to fix you some hot tea, that's what you want, and a good lot of food in your stomach. Not used to the damp, you're not. And there's a storm building up in the north. That's what's making the air so heavy."

After gulping down three of Nana's white pills, I gathered my things and made a dash upstairs for the bathroom. Regardless of the freezing cold, I drew myself a hot bath, filling it with some of Nana's rich oils, and brought my dirty laundry in with me. It seemed a sensible arrangement as Nana had no facilities for laundry and I was running out of a fresh change. Soaking myself in the steaming water and trying to keep my entire body submerged, I swished my clothes about and ruminated further over the night's events.

A new idea came to me this time, and I gave it a great deal of consideration. Although I had the feeling—a really nebulous sort of premonition—that the house did not want me to leave, I wondered nonetheless what would happen if I tried.

Obviously it was allowing me to visit my grandfather, for I believe he figured into the purpose somehow. But I recalled a subconscious restlessness at Uncle William's house—a small nagging desire to be getting back to this place—and then the pull it had exerted upon me when I had stepped out to go to the heath. Apparently the house had been working on me even then, planting in my mind a reluctance to leave.

But, I wondered now as I wallowed in the luxurious bath, what would happen if I gathered all my strength and determination and tried to break away? Would it let me go?

Indeed, how would it stop me?

Nonsensical musings, I told myself as I roughly towelled down in the raw air of the bathroom. Such ridiculous thoughts, thinking of myself as a prisoner of this house. Of course I could leave. And any time I wanted. It's just that it wouldn't be fair to leave Nana right now. And I couldn't go back to L.A. after only four days. It was only proper that I should stay awhile longer, keep Nana company, visit my grandfather, and renew the old bloodlines across the ocean.

I would leave when I was ready to leave.

The food, though delicious, was unappetizing to me, yet I forced myself to eat. Nana's careful scrutiny was upon me as I forked batter-dipped fish and crunchy fried potatoes into my mouth.

"Is your hair dry yet, love?"

I stuck a finger under the towel that wrapped my head and felt around. "Feels like it."

"Why don't you sit before the heater and get it good and dry. I don't want you catching cold. I'm sure Elsie and Ed won't be by today, they never go out when the fog's this bad."

I looked again at the windows, not believing my eyes. If there was a yard out there, if there were brick walls and a green gate and skeletal rose bushes, they could in no way be seen. Never before had I seen fog so thick, so dense, and so white. It was like cotton wool.

"When will it lift?"

"By tonight, I 'spect. Now get on with you to the fire!"

I languidly brushed my hair before the warmth of the heater, not wanting to get too close, for I found the room already too warm for comfort. But
Nana was concerned about my health, and since I had just come out of the
bath, I had to agree with her. My eyes were held in the blue gas flames as I
brushed, thinking dreamily about the four people I had observed here the
night before.

Hearing Nana back in the scullery washing our dishes (she refused to
allow me admittance), I picked up the Townsend album and opened it up
to that page.

Looking at it, I was struck again with the same queer feeling I had had
last night, the weird sensation of seeing the result of Mr. Cameron's art. How
strange to have witnessed the actual scene of this photograph's birth! How
bizarre to think that this picture, now yellowed and brittle, had sat in this
album for so many decades, passing through each day from 1890 until now,
while only a few hours ago I had looked upon the event of its creation.

I marvelled at the tricks of Time. The intricacies and eddies and currents of the great river of Time were an enigma to me. Somewhere I recalled
reading, "Time goes you say? Ah no! Alas, Time stays and we go." Was this
the explanation? That rather than Time being in motion, it is *we* who fly by
while Time stands still?

And if one of us were to find a way to stand still for just an instant, we
would be able to look back . . .

"Wherever did you find that?"

My head jerked up. "What?"

Nana eased her weary body into the chair, supporting herself on the
cane until the last possible minute. Did she still exist, *right now,* as a younger
version of herself in some other time frame? Or was it only the dead we
could look back on? Was it possible to find the window to our own past and
view ourselves as we were when young?

"I found it in the parlour."

"The parlour!"

And if I were watching the lives of Harriet and John and Victor unfold
as they once had, would I also be on hand for the birth of my own grandfa-

ther? When Jenny enters the picture, as I was certain she soon would, and Victor "forces" her, would I then a short while later see my grandfather as a tiny baby?

"I hope you don't think I was snooping, Nana, but you mentioned this album the other night and I was so curious. I thought it might be *in* the parlour—"

"It's the Townsends'. I haven't looked at that in ever so many years. Why, not since before your mum was born. Here, let me look."

I handed it over, continuing my latest train of thought. Would I truly see my grandfather as he was as a baby, or were these glimpses into the past reserved only for those dead?

I watched Nana's brown-spotted hands fumble with the ancient pages, seeing corners and edges fall off beneath her fingers. She paused a moment before the sitting-room portrait, first looking through her glasses and then over them. Then she went on to the others, only a few of which she said were recognizable to her.

"There's none of your great-grandfather and great-grandmother," she said, handing it back to me. "None of the Victor and Jennifer I told you about."

"Yes, I know." I cradled the album in my lap. "I wonder why."

"Hoo! That's no wonder, considering what *he* did to *her* and how unhappy it made her. But enough of that. I don't want no more talk of the Townsends. I won't have your granddad's most painful memory brought up in this house."

I had to raise an eyebrow at this. What would Nana do if she knew that not only was the subject being brought up, but it was actually being *relived* here in this house?

But then I smiled ruefully when, resuming again the brushing of my long damp hair, I remembered that the very event to which Nana had just referred—what *he* did to *her*—was going to be taking place soon.

Nana fell asleep with knitting in her lap. I had a book in my hands, one which she had placed there earlier in the hopes that I would start reading it, but the book remained unopened, for I too began to feel the morphic effects of the afternoon. The blanket of fog against our window, the cumbersome warmth of the room, the heavy meal we had just eaten, plus my strain of the night before all joined together now to envelop me in a sweet drowsiness. I let my head fall back and closed my eyes.

The ticking of the clock whispered softly against my ears. When it stopped I was not alarmed. I simply lifted my head and opened my eyes.

There was Victor Townsend.

I looked over at my grandmother. Her chin was resting on her chest, her lips fluttering in and out with each breath. Then I looked back at Victor. I was struck again by his stature and by his handsome countenance. How could he appear so real to me? How was it that this apparition from the past could have such substance, such solidity, as though he were a real, living, breathing man? I could examine every detail of him, from the fine cut of his dark frock coat to the thick black lashes of his heavy eyes. I gazed admiringly at his square shoulders and straight back, lingered over his head of untamed hair, and, lastly, looked long into his rugged face, which seemed etched with sadness and dejection.

Victor was leaning against the mantel, brooding into the fire in moody reflection. He seemed weighed down by his thoughts, troubled by what he saw in the flames, so that I had to fight the urge to speak to him and ask him what was wrong.

And then I wondered, What if I *did* try to speak? Would he hear me?

I had no opportunity to put this to the test as, in the next moment, Victor lifted his head and stared at a spot behind me. I felt a cold draught, then heard the clicking shut of the sitting-room door. Someone had just joined us.

I remained fixed in my chair, afraid of what my movement might do, afraid of losing this moment with Victor Townsend. When his father appeared from behind the chair and was suddenly standing at my side, I held my breath.

Both men regarded one another for a few grave moments, each deliberating his next words, each wearing that mask of unhappiness that told me this was a remorseful moment for them both.

Finally, it was Victor who spoke. "I have come to say goodbye, sir, and to ask your blessing."

The elder Townsend, mastering his emotions by clenching his fists at his sides, seemed in the grip of some powerful passion. I looked up at him in wonder, seeing him tower over me and yet be unaware of me, his heavy jaw set firmly, his lips pressed bloodless.

I looked back at the son. Victor hung upon his father's reply. His whole stance was one of expectation, of hope. What went on behind those dark eyes? Was Victor's struggle as desperate as that of his father? They seemed to me as two combatants stubbornly locked in a clash of wills that need never be. If only one of them would let down an inch of his pride, if only one of them would—

"You dare to ask my blessing after you have gone against my wishes?" Mr. Townsend's voice was remarkably strained and tight, as though he might choke any moment.

But Victor stood firm. As his eyes penetrated the gaze of his father, I felt an incredible paroxysm wash over me, an emotion of such intensity that it fell upon me like a tangible thing. This passion, arising from both Victor and his father, was filling the room and descending upon me like a heavy cloud. And it overwhelmed me in a tide of love and worship and devotion and disappointment and rejection. These two men, intensely proud and both suffering the agonies of their love for one another, were filling me with their private conflict. I wanted to cry out, to tell them that their obstinacy was childish, that their affection for one another was all that mattered, and that if only one of them would humble himself for just a moment they needn't endure this anguish.

But I could not interfere, for what was happening *had already happened.* I was witnessing an event that took place almost a hundred years ago. I could not change it. I was being allowed to observe, but I would not be permitted to interfere.

"I'm sorry you don't understand, sir," said Victor finally, his voice betraying the strains of defeat. "I wish to go to the Royal Infirmary and teach and do research as Mr. Lister once did, for I feel that is where the need is and where my calling lies."

"Your calling is here!" cried Mr. Townsend. "With your family and in your own home. Will you go off and save the lives of Scots when your own people need you?"

"There are doctors enough in Warrington, sir, and when I receive my degree I shall have to go straight—"

"You can go straight there now, my man, and you can go straight to hell, too, for my money! What son of mine is this that doesn't care a thr'pence for the welfare of his own family! Young John has stayed and is the Lord's blessing to me. He alone obeyed his father's wish."

"I have my own life to live now, sir," said Victor with great control.

"Aye, and to do it you have to turn your back on your own family. I fought from the very start against your becoming one of them leeches. But now that you're going to be one, you might as well bring yourself home and be with them that loves you. But I shan't go begging you, no, my man, and I shan't have words with you no more! There'll be hell to pay when it comes time to reckon what you've done, cutting up corpses and sticking your nose in—"

"Goodbye then, sir." Victor held out a hand, his face drained of colour and looking harsh in the fire's glow.

The elder Townsend hung suspended for a moment longer, torn between love and pride, and then, without another word, turned on his heel and stormed out.

I stared at Victor. He stood as if made of stone, his hand still extended, his pallor heightened by the contrast of his black hair and eyes, and I wanted to utter some words of comfort.

When he finally faded from my vision and the roaring fire was replaced again by the gas heater, I couldn't keep myself from covering my face with my hands.

Nana awoke with a start. "Ay? Ay, what?"

I twisted away from her, wiping my eyes.

"Ay? Oh, I must have dozed off. Look at the time. It's getting on, isn't it? Can't be sitting here sleeping else I shan't sleep tonight. Now look, I've dropped me knitting and got it tangled."

Choking back the tears and fortifying myself with the knowledge that

Victor was no longer suffering the rejection of the father he so desperately loved, I faced my grandmother and tried to smile.

"How's the book?" she asked.

"Just fine." My voice wavered. "I guess I dozed off, too." I looked at the clock. Only a minute had passed in the time it had taken for Victor and his father to have their confrontation. I listened to the familiar ticking, as the clock seemed to whisper, "Passing, passing, passing," and I realized that when I had my "spells" with the past, the time of the present was for an instant suspended. Knowing now that the cessation of the ticking was also the signal that the past was about to come forth, I realized also that this was the bridge between the two ages. First the clock ticking today's time, then a brief silence in which the framework of Time was altered, and then the ticking of yesterday's time. It was as though the clock had to pause, like shifting gears, before carrying on in another age.

And yet Time in the present seemed to stand still. It moved sluggishly while the past unravelled before my eyes at a normal rate. Or was it that *I* had slowed down and was watching the rapid run-off of yesterday's events?

It didn't matter. It was a puzzle that could never be solved, and its solution could bring me no advantage. Whatever was going on in this house, whatever mysterious plan I had been dragged into, it must run its course, regardless of why, or how, or to what end.

CHAPTER 8

Uncle William and Aunt May decided to brave the fog and drop in for a short visit. This cheered Nana, who had grown a little glum towards late afternoon, fretting about Granddad's not having a visit from anyone today. But William and May, undaunted by the lack of visibility, were determined to make it to the hospital this evening.

"Do you want to come with us, Andrea?"

I nodded vigorously, swallowing my cheese sandwich and washing it down with warm unsterilized milk. I needed to get out of the house for a while. I had to get away from Nana and whatever forces were at work here. I needed fresh air and a change of scene and the company of other people.

For the first time, I appreciated my relatives.

"Well, I don't know, Andrea," said Nana as she pressed a hand against my forehead. "I think you're coming down with a cold."

"I feel fine!"

"Had a headache all day, she has, and yesterday too. I think it's the damp."

Aunt May also took liberties with my forehead. "Feels all right to me. Would you like to come with us, love?"

"Yes, very much."

"All right then," said Nana with a sigh. "But be sure to bundle up good and proper like. Said on the wireless there's a storm coming."

"I'll go down and get the car heater running," said Uncle William, throwing his heavy coat and muffler on, which made him look like an Alaskan Toklat. "Don't come out till you're ready and I'll have the car door open for you. You shan't feel a bit of cold."

But the trouble was, I was getting used to the cold by now and didn't need all the wrappings Nana was insisting I put on. In fact, the sitting room had felt stuffy to me all day and I had frequently felt like getting up and opening the door. Nonetheless, under my grandmother's maternal ministrations, I suffered her motherly concerns and allowed myself to be stuffed into a sweater, coat, wool hat, wool muffler, and wool mittens. Feeling suffocated, I was anxious to get out into the fog.

I was stopped at the front door.

The very second my foot started to step over the threshold, the vertigo hit me so hard that I had to quickly grasp the doorframe in order not to fall over.

"What is it, love?" I heard my Aunt May's voice come from far away.

The foggy street tilted and churned before my eyes, reaching up to me and falling away. Far off in the distance stood my tiny Uncle William, now looking like a gopher on his hind legs, standing next to a miniature Renault. It was as though I were looking at him through a concave lens. Aunt May was at my side, and I saw her lips working soundlessly. The floor moved beneath my feet like an earthquake; I grabbed both sides of the door to keep upright, seeing the terraced houses spin about me, and felt my stomach fly up to my throat as if I were on a speeding merry-go-round.

When the wooden floor met the back of my skull like a hammer, the dizziness stopped and I gazed stupidly up at the ceiling.

"My soul and body!" I heard Nana cry. "She's passed out!"

Three bewildered faces converged over me, like a football huddle, and in the next instant I was being raised off the floor. With his beefy arms about me in a bear hug, Uncle William dragged me to my feet, where I hung in his embrace like a rag doll. Nana and Aunt May spent a great deal of energy flapping their arms and crying "Oh dear!" over and over again, while I was dragged backwards away from the front door and down the hall.

I was steered into the sitting room, dropped into an easy chair, and at once had my outer layers roughly stripped off me.

When I was completely lucid again, I saw that I was sitting before the gas fire, its flame set at its highest, a heavy quilt around my legs, and a cup of hot tea in my hands. And there were the three bewildered faces again, all gaping at me expectantly.

"I'm all right now," I said feebly. "It was the rush. You know, hurrying with everything and running to the car—"

"Nonsense!" said Nana, slapping my arm. "It's the flu you've got and no more about it! Now drink your tea, there's a love."

"Are you really all right, Andrea?" said my Aunt May. "We can fetch the doctor for you—"

"No! I'm . . . all right, really I am. It was the excitement. It's hot in here!" I tried to toss off the quilt, but Nana fought me off and tucked it back around.

"You're feverish!" she snapped.

But Aunt May placed a hand on my forehead and cheeks and said, "She's not, Mum. You know, she's cool. Now what do you make of that, William?"

My uncle hiked his massive shoulders. "People have cold skin when they faint, don't they? So it's not the flu. It's something else."

"She's got the chills!" my nana persevered. "And she's not going out of this house!"

I sank deeper into the easy chair and stared sadly into the dregs of my tea cup. Nana had no idea how true her words were. I was *not* going out of this house because this house wouldn't let me. I was its prisoner. Whatever power was at work here was not done with me yet, and while I had been allowed three visits so far with my grandfather, tonight I could not go. Maybe tomorrow . . .

This last I must have said out loud, for Uncle William now spoke up. "We'll see about that, love, if you're better. Right now I think Mum is right. What you need is hot tea and a good night's sleep. We'll be getting on then, May, before the visiting hour is over."

"But what if she isn't all right? They've not got a telephone, Will!"

"Then we'll stop in after seeing Granddad. If our Andrea wants the doctor then, she'll tell us, won't you, love?"

I nodded weakly.

After they left, Nana turned to the sofa and dragged the blanket off it, throwing it over my chest and shoulders. I was beginning to swelter so that I thought I would scream, and although I was touched by her concern for my welfare, I was impatient for Nana to leave me alone and for the next "spell" to happen. If only there was a way I could command their appearance. If only I could *will* them here and get it over with. But I could not. Just as I could not *avoid* seeing them if I wished.

The evening hours dragged on. Nana knitted contentedly, looking at me now and then and feeling my forehead, and when Uncle William and Aunt May returned, I seized the opportunity to be rid of my blankets.

Nana poured them some tea as they reported their visit with Granddad. "Proper lively he was tonight. Had a good talk with him we did. Of course, none of it made any sense . . . "

I went about the sitting room and gathered up the clothes I had washed that morning. Thanks to the gas heater and Nana's idea of hanging them around the sitting room, they were all dry so I prepared to take them upstairs.

"Here, here!" cried Nana. "Where do you think you're going?"

"My clothes are dry. I just want to take them up—"

"Oh no! William will take them up for you. Now you stay here by the fire."

"But, Nana—"

"Andrea, love," said May gently, "you *did* have a fainting spell earlier on."

"But I'm all right now." I clutched my folded jeans and T-shirts close to me, protectively.

"Here now," said Uncle William. "If the lass is okay, then let her go. It's only up the stairs. Do her good to move around a bit."

"Well . . . " Nana reluctantly conceded.

Before she could change her mind, I hurried to the door and heard, just as I opened it, Nana say to Uncle William, "So tell me what the doctor has said about when Robert can come home."

My uncle leaned forward to reply. He opened his mouth but no sound came out.

I looked at the clock. It was silent.

Holding myself rigid against the door, I waited for the appearance of the others. I looked around the room, expecting to see Nana's Woolworth covers disappear and the roaring fire show up in the place of the gas heater. But nothing changed.

Where were they?

Nana and William and his wife sat over their tea cups at the table, bent in a conversational attitude, but not speaking or moving.

Frantically I looked back at the clock. It was still silent.

Still nothing happened.

"Where are you?" I whispered.

Finally I wildly flung the door open and darted into the hall. Tripping on the first stair, I fell forward and dropped my clothes. "Wait . . . " I whispered. "Wait for me!" I hastily gathered up my things and scrambled up the stairs, falling twice on the way.

Once at the top, I leaned against the wall, breathing heavily. Although my breath came out as steam I did not feel the cold. I knew the air of the upstairs hall must be cruelly bitter, yet I did not feel it.

I fumbled about in the dark and managed to turn on the overhead light. With a bit of illumination I was able to see the door of the front bedroom standing ajar. I regarded it with apprehension and determination.

"Yes . . . " I whispered, walking slowly towards it.

When I reached the threshold I stopped and looked in. There was nothing but cold empty darkness. No evil. No unseen forces. No hidden horrors. Just a dark room.

So I switched on the light.

Nothing was out of the ordinary. Everything was as I had left it that morning after my bath. The bed, the curtains, my toiletries on the chair, my clothes in the wardrobe.

I stopped.

The wardrobe.

There was something wrong with the wardrobe.

Not knowing why, I walked slowly to it, unable to take my eyes off its oak-wood grain, its dull finish, its small brass fixtures. And as I drew myself up before it, I had the most uncanny feeling of having done this before.

Then the horror began. I sensed the change in the room. I didn't have to see anything to know that a shift was taking place. Something was entering, something that hadn't been there just a second before, something that was now joining me. It was the same evil atmosphere of the night before, seeping out from the crevices of the wardrobe like some foul stench, swirling up to my nostrils, filling me with a gripping terror that was as palpable as the dreadful cold of the room. It was the air of graves and crypts. It wound itself about me, causing me to shudder not from cold but in fear.

Now I wanted to run.

Held fast as I was before the wardrobe, I wanted to break away and run and flee from the satanic power that had this house in its grip.

My eyes grew wider and wider until they felt as if they were coming out of their sockets. I gaped at the wardrobe before me. I listened. My body was taut. I trembled uncontrollably. Yet I could not run.

There was a sound inside the wardrobe.

"Oh God . . . " I whimpered. "Please . . . "

Something moved inside the wardrobe.

Then I felt my arm start to rise.

"N-no . . . "

I stared in horror as my hand reached out for the brass knob. It took hold. My hand, under the command of another presence in the room, seized the brass knob.

And I knew. Whatever was on the other side, I was going to let it out . . .

"Please God . . . " I moaned. I felt tears run down my cheeks.

My hand started to turn the knob.

"*Andrea!*"

My hand suddenly dropped limply at my side; it throbbed painfully. At the same time, as if the bonds which had held me in that spot had been suddenly severed, I staggered back and fell against the bed. Sprawling over my suitcase, I saw great drops of sweat tumble from my forehead and on to my arms.

"Andrea!" came Uncle William's voice again. He was standing at the foot of the stairs calling up. "Are you all right?"

"Yes . . . " I said in a bare whisper. I cleared my throat and tried again. "Yes, Uncle William! Be right down."

"We're going now, love!"

"All right. Coming."

Somehow I found the strength to push myself up from the bed and sway on my own two feet. Whatever had had momentary possession of my body had robbed it of all strength. I looked down at my T-shirt. It clung to me.

Trying to gather up my wits, I hastily pulled off my soaked shirt and dragged a dry one over my head. Now I moved quickly. Leaving my newly dried clothes where they lay, I dashed out of the bedroom, flicking out the light and slamming the door behind me. Then I ran recklessly down the stairs and met my aunt and uncle in the hallway, just buttoning up their coats.

"If the fog's gone tomorrow maybe we'll see you. That's if that big storm from the north doesn't come our way." Aunt May talked as she wound a muffler around her face. "Listen, Andrea, if you think you'd like to come over to our place, you know, to watch telly or to use our phone or whatever, you're welcome. How you can stand this cold draughty house I'll never know."

"Oh . . . it's all right, really . . . " I thought of the telephone and then of my mother. Suddenly, I had no desire to talk to her.

After William and May left I locked the front door and pushed the sausage in place. Then I followed Nana into the sitting room. At once the stifling heat of the room overcame me. I looked down at the gas heater. It was impossible, and yet Nana had turned it down to its lowest possible setting. Just the barest ripple of blue could be seen on the coils. And yet outside Uncle William had said the temperature was twenty-six degrees!

"Getting chilly in here," said Nana, rubbing her hands and heading for the heater.

"No," I said quickly. "It's fine in here."

"What? It's downright cold, and I've got four cardigans on. Look at you, a thin little shirt with hardly no sleeves. How could you have stood it upstairs the whole time you were gone?"

Upstairs. The wardrobe. The horrible fear . . .

"Nana . . . "

"Yes, love?"

"I . . . "

Her eyes were on me, the pupils wide and clouded, bushy eyebrows hanging over. The lines on her face seemed to have multiplied since the last time I looked; she seemed to have aged a hundred years. "How is Granddad?" I asked finally.

"Oh, not so good, love. Don't know what's wrong with him. The doctor has a word for it. He calls it a *vascular* condition. Says all his veins and arteries have gone bad. That's why he can't walk no more and why his mind is muddled. They can't say if he's ever going to get well or if we'll ever see him home again."

"I'm sorry." And I truly was. The loneliness and worry were taking their toll on my grandmother. I could not believe how much she had aged in just the few days I had been here.

"Well, you see, love, your granddad and I have never been separated in sixty-two years. Well, not since the Great War. Not even a day, mind you, and now it's been a few weeks, I feel so lost without him."

She felt about her many pockets for a handkerchief and, finding one, blew her nose into it. "Well, it's late, love, and I'm tired. Shall we go to bed?"

"Oh yes, Nana."

After she kissed me good night and I had kicked the bolster against the foot of the door, I returned to my easy chair and turned off the gas heater. Then I sat back to think awhile.

For one minute there I had been ready to tell Nana everything, to spill out all that I had seen, all my fears, and my suspicions. But then, in the next moment, I had seen the sadness in her eyes and the creases of fatigue on her face and I could not bear to add to her suffering.

But there was yet another reason for my having decided at the last minute not to tell Nana about what was happening, and it was this: Although I had been afraid up in the bedroom just now and had experienced a terror I should not like to meet again, I was nonetheless becoming anxious to see more and more of my long-dead relatives. The need to know their story was growing within me, as well as a mounting curiosity to see how it would end. And fear of breaking the "spell" by telling Nana or anyone had kept me silent. It all seemed so fragile to me that I harboured the fear of spoiling it all by speaking of it to another person. It seemed as though I had been initiated into a secret fraternity, that I was privy to esoterica that no outsiders had any right knowing. I was actually becoming afraid of upsetting the events that had been set in motion and thereby never again seeing John or Harriet or Victor. And I did want to see them again.

I needed to see them again.

Now I laughed at this thought. For I was being caught up in their emotions, was being forced to feel their passions and to witness their happiness and their sorrow. Indeed, with Victor and his father I had not so much *seen* their conflict as I had *felt* it. The dead Townsends were transmitting their feelings to me so that I, too, felt what they felt. How could I not start to feel a kinship with them, a bond which I could never have with anyone else? It was something special. Something not of this world and not of this life. And I was beginning to cherish it. Just as I was beginning to cherish the Townsends, regardless of what they might do in days to come.

And will I still be fond of Victor, I wondered sadly, after I have witnessed his terrible crimes?

I would not think of it. Not now. Not with his image still fresh in my mind as if he actually stood before me.

My heart gave a leap.

Victor Townsend *was* standing before me.

Standing spread-legged before the fireplace with both hands behind his back, my great-grandfather rocked a little on his heels as he spoke to the person in the chair beside me. "I had to chance it, John, I had to come home one more time before going on to Edinburgh. I shall receive my certificate in five months and then I shall go straight from London to Edinburgh. And who knows when next we will see one another?"

"You risk having Father walk in and throw you out."

"Yes, I know. But he rarely gets home from the pub before eight, so I shall have a few last moments with my family."

"Mother won't see you either."

"Yes, I know." Victor peered darkly at the rug. "She would like to, but she's afraid of Father."

"We're all afraid of him, Victor, except you. Do you think I wouldn't have liked to go off to London and become a gentleman like you? You even speak bloody proper now, did you know that? Wouldn't know you were a Lancashire lad! But really, Victor, you were the only one with courage to go against him. And I admire you for that."

I watched John's profile as he spoke. There was a shadow of sadness in his eyes as he watched his brother wistfully. "Aye, I admire you. I'm not pleased with my clerk's job at the mill. But I shall have to be, shan't I? Father would throw me out if I were to defy him and I have nowhere to go. Whereas you, you sod, you had to win that blinking scholarship!"

Victor brought his head up and laughed. There was light in his eyes and it elated me to see his beautiful smile. "Brother, you are every bit as happy with your eight pound a week and you know it. And besides, you shall inherit from Father, not I, I have been disconnected from the Townsend name."

"But you can fight it. England has laws of primogeniture . . . "

Victor shook his head. "I should never do that and you know it. The house will be yours, John, I don't want it. All I want is my microscope and my following of devoted students. And Scotland is where I shall find them."

The door flew open just then and a gust of cold air brought Harriet in. And behind her, untying the strings of her bonnet from beneath her chin, was Jennifer.

Unthinkingly, I sat up.

The two girls hurried in, closed the door behind them, and then Harriet ran forward, flinging her arms around Victor. "John said you were coming!" she cried breathlessly. "Oh thank you for coming, Victor! Thank you for being so brave!"

He suffered her embrace with a laugh, watching in amusement as his young sister lavished him with kisses and praise, talking very rapidly. His eyes danced merrily; creases appeared at the corners. The furrow between his brows smoothed out and almost disappeared.

And then it happened.

Victor glanced away from his sister and over to the other girl, and his face froze. The sparkle faded from his eyes to be immediately replaced by another, more intense light. He stared at her as if stunned, ignoring now Harriet's chatter and John's occasional repartee, and Jennifer, having looked at Victor in the process of lifting her bonnet off her head, had also stopped short. They stared at one another across the room.

I was the only one who saw it, for Harriet and John were engaged in a rapid-fire exchange about the O'Hanrahans' new horseless carriage, the first in Warrington. I was the only witness to the miracle that took place that day back in 1890, the only one who saw how Victor and Jennifer became the unwitting victims of a destiny from which neither could escape.

Is this what is meant by love at first sight? Surely that is what I felt as I watched the two stare unmovingly at one another. I *felt* the sudden turbulence of Victor's soul, was caught up in it. The unexpected desire that swept over his body engulfed mine as well. What Victor experienced in the first few moments of seeing Jennifer, I also felt.

And Jennifer. What was it that had gripped her suddenly? Looking at her startled expression, I discovered there also a wellspring of intensity and passion, a sudden surging of emotion that had not been there a moment before. And I sensed also confusion and dismay, for these feelings were new to her and they alarmed her.

Finally Victor spoke. "My sister has forgotten her manners," he said softly. "It appears I must introduce myself. Victor Townsend," and he gave a little bow.

Harriet spun around. "Soon to be Dr. Townsend! Oh, Victor, forgive me! I was to excited to see you that I forgot I had brought Jenny home. Victor, this is Jennifer Adams. She lives on Marina Avenue off the green."

He stepped forward and took her gloved hand. I felt the explosion. It came from both of them.

They were beautiful people, he so handsome and striking, she so lovely and small, it was only right that this love should have been born between them. And yet, knowing what I knew about the future that lay ahead of them, it also saddened me. It seemed unfair to me, having this foisted on them when they were not seeking it, for I saw them now as victims, the two of them, and no matter what would take place within these walls in their rapidly approaching future, I could only pray that their brief time together would be spent in happiness.

John now stood and offered Jennifer his chair. He stood straight and stiff before her and behaved in his most gentlemanly manner. From their attitude I guessed that the two already knew one another. Harriet took Jenny's cloak and removed it from the room with her own. Victor continued to stand and stare at her, his face now dark and troubled. Jennifer ran anxious hands down her skirt, a simple garment with less yardage than Harriet's and a modest bustle, and graciously took a seat before the fire. I saw in her downcast eyes bewilderment and perplexity. My heart went out to her, knowing what she felt.

"Anyway," said Harriet, coming back into the room, "it's quite a remarkable affair, isn't it, Jenny? Makes an awful racket and puffs out horrible fumes. *But it moves by itself.*"

Now Victor, visibly struggling with himself, shook his head and frowned at his sister. He pulled his mind from wherever it had strayed and said, "Whatever are you going on about?"

"The O'Hanrahans' horseless carriage! Jenny and I have been to see it today. It moves by itself, Victor!"

"The internal combustion engine," said Victor quietly, allowing his eyes to stray to the young woman in the chair beside me. I had the impression he was trying to reassure himself that she was indeed there, that he had not imagined her. "It was bound to come sooner or later. This is a modern age, Harriet, all sorts of new things are coming into being."

"The O'Hanrahans even have a telephone now! And they say electricity is here to stay. Why can't we have electricity?"

John shrugged and leaned against the fireplace. "That horseless carriage won't stay, I'll wager that. Too costly, too noisy, too much trouble to keep, and it fouls the air. It's simply a new toy, a gadget, but it won't replace the horse. The O'Hanrahans have more money than they know what to do with. And besides, you've been warned about that lot."

"Oh, John—"

"Harriet," said Victor impulsively, "you made me forget. I've brought you a present." He produced a small package which he had been holding behind his back.

"Victor! Oh thank you!" Harriet carefully undid the outer wrap and lifted the lid of the little box. Her eyes grew wide in amazement. "What is it?"

"It's a watch that you wear around your wrist."

John leaned forward to examine it. "What the devil . . . why, it's no more than a pocket watch!"

"Yet it is worn on the arm. It was made for a lady, you see, since she does not have a watch pocket in her dress. Here, Harriet, give me your hand."

I watched as Victor very carefully placed the tiny watch below his sister's sleeve and then fastened the strap in place. "There you go now, just like the fashionable ladies in London."

Harriet beamed like a child. Bringing it up to her ear, she listened for a moment, then with a squeal threw her arms around Victor.

"Certainly I never get such attention," said John teasingly, although I thought I detected a trace of resentment in his voice.

Now I saw Jennifer staring into the fire, her little hands folded in her lap. The deep waves of her brown hair caught the fire's glow in highlights of gold and copper. There was a heaviness to her eyes that moved me, a depth of longing and of bewilderment. Her profile fascinated me, the delicate sweep of her nose, the little rosebud lips, the small pointed chin. Jennifer was even more beautiful than in her photograph, and it gave me great pride to know that she was my great-grandmother.

This last thought also startled me, for so real was she at this moment, and so close, her small bosom rising and falling gently in a kind of sleepy respiration, that I thought if I should reach out now I could touch her.

And what would happen if I did? These people from the past were unaware of my presence, and yet they seemed so real to me. So real . . .

"I must show Mother!" exclaimed Harriet, running to the door. "She'll never have heard of a wrist watch!"

There was a gust of wind, the opening and closing of the door, and then only the crackling of the fire against a background of silence.

I looked up at Victor. There was a tempest in his eyes, a storm that raged within his soul, twisting his face into a scowl. And I felt him ask himself,

Why did this happen?

It touched me so that I wanted to cry out to him and embrace him as Harriet was privileged to do. Yet I could not. Having to be satisfied to sit and look on, I observed the torment of Victor's questioning soul.

And I *felt* it as well. I could not protect myself against the passions of these people. I had no defences with which to fight them. From all sides I was besieged by a myriad of human feelings: Jennifer, nervously examining the strange effect Victor had on her; John wrestling with his jealousy at his brother's being the centre of attention; and Victor, having fallen in love with a girl he had known only a few minutes, demanding of God, Why?

"It's dark out," said John suddenly. "And Father will want the fires on upstairs. If you will excuse me . . . "

He smiled down at Jennifer, but she only gazed back blankly. John swept past me and out of the sitting room so that I was ultimately left alone with my great-grandparents.

The silence was at first awkward, Jenny twisting her fingers and watching the fire, with Victor standing before her, his eyes deep in reflection. I wished they would speak, voice their feelings, reveal what was in their hearts before the others came back.

As if in answer to my mental pleadings, Jenny now lifted her head and said, "Harriet says you are to go to Edinburgh in a few months, Mr. Townsend."

He turned his dark scowl to Jennifer and at once it faded away to be replaced by a look of puzzlement. And through his mind, briefly, there flashed the thought, All those women in London, how many? Faceless, nameless, they had counted at one time; had been important for a day, a week; had been good for a diversion. But this, this is something new . . . "Yes, I shall. Immediately upon receiving my medical certificate I shall remove myself to the Royal Infirmary."

"And will you be gone long?" Her voice was shy, coming out like a whisper. From my place at her side I could see the anxious fluttering of her heart.

"It is indefinite, Miss Adams. Perhaps I shall not come back at all."

Her eyes flew open. "Oh! How unfortunate, sir, for . . . your family!"

"I've no desire to live in Warrington. My ambition is to find cures for diseases. There is a great deal of research being done in Scotland now, and with a letter from Mr. Lister I shall meet the right men."

"It is most admirable, I am sure."

Now she bent her head and took to staring again at her hands.

As Victor towered over her, marvelling at her smallness, at her vulnerability, I felt again a surge of desire sweep over him. He trembled slightly. "How long have you been in Warrington. Miss Adams?"

She spoke without looking up. "A year, Mr. Townsend. We come from Prestatyn in Wales—"

"Yes, I rather thought—"

"My father has secured a good post at the mill. He's a manager, you see . . ."

Now Jennifer, her voice dying away, raised her eyes to Victor, adoration thinly veiling her face. I felt her love for him swell, causing her to shudder as if wrestling with a physical thing. Jenny's lips were slightly parted, the unspoken word trapped there, and her wide, questioning eyes were like those of a doe.

And I heard her mind whisper, How can this be so . . . ?

In a low voice Victor said, "It pleases me to have made your acquaintance, Miss Adams, although it is unfortunate that it should come at so late a time."

She gave a little gasp.

"If perhaps we had met a year ago," he said evenly, "then . . . "

"Yes, Mr. Townsend?" she whispered.

This man who was an imposing tower of strength now weakened considerably. "Then possibly we could have become friends."

"And are we not now? I have known Harriet for a year. We spend a good deal of time together. And she has spoken a lot about you. I feel as if I know you already, Mr. Townsend, and that we haven't just met."

His lips jerked in a smile. "You must come to Edinburgh sometime."

Jenny let her eyes drop again and her shoulders slumped forward. "Scotland is very far away, I fear I should never—"

"Jennifer, if I may call you that! Possibly I can return to Warrington someday for a visit. Will you be here?"

Startled by the urgency in his voice, Jenny regarded Victor in mild alarm. "My father has no intention of moving again. I am sure Warrington is our permanent home. But will you come back? *Can* you come back?"

Angrily, twisted by his passion, Victor turned away from her and, placing both hands on the mantelpiece, said in a strangled voice, "I can never come back. For as long as this is my father's house, I can never come back. He no longer calls me his son. If you are indeed Harriet's friend, as you say, and if she does speak of me, then you must know the story, you must know of the war that wages between my father and me—"

"Yes, she—"

"Then you must know that even now I should not be here, for it would anger him anew and he would throw me out were he to find me. Even now . . . " His voice grew tight, uncontrollable. "He will be home any minute and I must leave. I am sorry that, having only just met you, I must so abruptly and rudely leave you. Yet it is not my wish. I must go away to a foreign land without an embrace from my mother or the blessing of my father. I have only my brother and sister and whatever friendship awaits me in Scotland. I must leave my friends in London and those I once knew here. For the sake of my ambition, I must enter into my new life as a man totally alone."

He spun around, anger and futility in his glare. Why now? cried his soul. Why did I have to look upon this girl and feel the love for her that I do? How can it be? What torture has been visited upon me?

"Victor . . . " I said all of a sudden, my heart racing in time with his own.

"We cannot be friends, Jennifer," he went on, "because you and I will never see one another again. I can never come back to this house."

I flew to my feet and reached out a hand. "Victor, listen!"

But my fingers met only empty space and I was back in Nana's old sitting room again.

CHAPTER 9

*S*HE FOUND ME STANDING BY THE WINDOW STARING OUT AT A grey wet morning. I had been up since dawn, having slept but a few hours and even then I had been visited by strange, unsettling dreams. I suppose I startled her, standing there in the cold dark room, for she exclaimed, "Andrea! I didn't expect to see you up!" There was the click of the switch and then light flooded the room.

"Why's it so cold in here?"

I heard her shuffle across the room, her cane sounding like a third foot clomping on the floor. Then she cried out, "The gas is off! Andrea, love, did you know that the gas had gone out?"

"Yes, Nana," I said quietly. "I turned it off."

"You what? It's like an ice box in here! Whatever did you do that for?"

I did not reply but remained with my eyes fixed on the moss-covered walls and brittle rose bushes heavy with dew. And I listened as my grandmother hobbled to the sideboard, opened a drawer, withdrew some matches, hobbled back, and lit the fire. It made the faintest roaring sound, if you listened carefully, but it was not like the roar and crackle of the real fires that had once burned there.

"Ain't you feeling well, love? Standing there in that bit of a shirt with nothing round you. Come on, let's have some tea then."

She manoeuvred her awkward body through the cluttered room and went into the scullery. I held my place by the window. The bleak morning outside was a mirror reflection of my mood.

"Fog's lifted!" Nana sang out from the scullery. "Any sign of sunshine?"

I shook my head.

"Ay?" She appeared around the door. "Any sun yet, love?"

"No, Nana. Cloudy."

"Aye, it would be. I 'spect that big storm will be upon us before too long. It never fails. Always lots of rain this time of year, you know . . . " She rattled pans and plates, her voice coming from a great distance. "But the summer this year was right beautiful. We had a heat wave. Two whole weeks of seventy degrees! Thought I should pass out with it! But you see, now we've got the winter and we're paying for it. By Christmas we might have snow. We don't usually. But this year, well, I can feel it in my bones . . . "

I tuned out her prattle. Another voice, cynical, whispered in my head, If we didn't have weather, ninety percent of all conversations wouldn't get started.

Finally I pulled away from the window and moved aimlessly about the room. I was possibly depressed, although I could not be certain, for I had never felt this way before. It was an odd state of mind that gripped me now, a combination of a little sadness, a little anxiety, and a little restlessness. And yet, even then the mood was not the sum total of these, for there was a great part of me that was this morning utterly void and blank, as though no condition dwelled there at all.

Coming to rest before the mantelpiece, I stared at the clock. That's what it was. I was filled with an *absence*. It was as though emotions and feelings had been drained out of me, leaving in their stead a grey bleakness. If only I had been depressed. At least that would have been a positive condition, a *having* of something rather than a losing of something. No, I was not depressed or sad or troubled. I was simply blank.

Where had my soul gone?

"Andrea!" shrieked Nana.

I felt her fingers dig into the flesh of my upper arm and then I flew backward until I crashed against the sideboard. I stared dazedly at Nana.

"Andrea, you almost set yourself *on fire!*" she wailed, puffing from the exertion of knocking me away.

Stupidly I looked down at my jeans. The cuffs and pant legs were singed brown. There was the smell of burning in the air. Nana lumbered up to me and, with great effort, bent down to lift a pant leg.

My skin was bright red.

"You've burnt yourself," she wheezed. "Another minute and these pants would have burst into flames. Andrea, love, what's the matter?" She placed a shaky hand on my cheek. "Another headache?"

"Nana . . ." I twisted my face away. Now I could feel the pain of my scorched legs, the sensitivity as the jeans rubbed against them. It frightened me.

"It's my fault. I set the gas on high and you didn't know it. It's been on low all the time you've been here and I didn't tell you I'd put it on high. Crikey . . . "

I was finally able to focus on Nana's face. The age of it, the dilapidated state of it made me want to cry.

Why couldn't we stay the way we were in youth, just as John and Victor and Harriet and Jennifer were still so young and beautiful? How had they managed to find eternal life? How had they found the key to suspending time? Why did we have to suffer this ignominy?

"Poor love," cooed my grandmother, wiping the tears off my face. "You're not at all well. Come on, let's put some butter on them legs."

She started to lead me to the heater but I hung back. "It's all right, love, I've turned it down."

"No . . . I'm warm enough, I'll sit here on the sofa."

I sat on its edge, as far as possible from the heat, and absently watched my grandmother apply her old-fashioned first aid to my burns. I felt like crying. After that one foolish moment of trying to reach Victor, I had sat up all night waiting for them to return.

And they had not come back.

"Are you sure you're up to it?" Aunt Elsie said, her eyes roaming my face in concern. "You know, Mum is right, you don't look at all well. You've gone white, Andrea."

"I'm okay, really." Well, my shins hurt terribly, I was uncomfortable with the heat of the room, there was a cold emptiness where my heart should have been, and I was beginning to feel the effects of so little sleep the night before. So what else could I say to my aunt than "I'm okay, really"?

"You can go to the hospital tomorrow, not today," said Nana.

I gave this a moment's thought, although I was not really thinking but *feeling* the house to see what it wanted me to do. However, as I could learn nothing from it, I decided to try. If it wanted to stop me, it would.

"I'd like to go today, Nana. Granddad will think I've gone back home without saying goodbye to him."

"It's all right, Mum," said Elsie. "Just a short ride in the car and then an hour in the hospital. I don't think it will do her any harm. Only today be sure you take your time getting ready."

So I wordlessly suffered the ritual of buttoning and bundling up, and then, reaching the threshold of the front door, hesitated a moment. I stepped over, put my foot on the cold cement, and knew that today I was going to see my grandfather.

Although I rode along in silence, my aunt did not. A regular commentary on the high points of Warrington was rattled off for my benefit: there was the steel mill and the city hall and the motorway to Manchester and the new Marks and Spencer's and the old Woolworth where "your mum and I worked during the war."

I tried to smile and nod politely, but in truth I was impatient with her inane ramblings. For my living relatives I seemed to bear nothing more than mild tolerance. It was my dead ones I wanted to be with.

Granddad was in a stupor again and totally uncommunicative. But I did not mind, being content to sit by his side and gaze at the face of Victor's son.

While Aunt Elsie and Uncle Edouard continued their charade of having a conversation with the recumbent old man, I merely took hold of his wasted, fleshless hand and held it for the duration of one hour. For me this was an homage to the Townsends, and it brought me, ironically, a sense of peace.

We returned afterward to a heavy dinner of beef and Yorkshire pudding, complete with roast potatoes, carrots, and slabs of bread and butter. I ate sparingly, listening all the while to Aunt Elsie report to my grandmother the latest news about Warrington: who was getting married, who was pregnant, who was getting divorced. Typical of small towns, Warrington offered no privacy to anyone.

And yet, I thought with a wry smile, I am harbouring the greatest secret of all.

At one point during the dinner I studied my talkative aunt and considered briefly telling her about my experiences in the house. But only briefly, for I quickly saw how ruinous such a step would be. Elsie would decry my claims and in her earthy, pragmatic way would insist it's the weather that was making me see things. And suppose I did tell her. Might that not break the spell? What if my telling another person would shatter the fragile bridge I had found to the past?

"I've had good news!" she said suddenly, slamming a chunky hand on the table. "And I'd forgot to tell you. Ann called me from Amsterdam this morning to say she'll be at our Albert's this Sunday."

"Oh, how lovely!" My grandmother beamed at me. "Won't that be nice for our Andrea to meet her cousins?"

"It'll be good, I think," said Elsie, "being with someone her own age for a change."

I quickly looked away. How old had Victor been last night? Twenty-five, twenty-six? And John, slightly less?

"You'll like our Albert's. He's got a lovely cottage at Morecambe Bay. P'rhaps we can see the Illuminations . . . "

As she talked on I thought ruefully, It would be nice to go, I suppose. But what if the house won't let me?

My aunt and uncle stayed only a short while longer and then started packing up to go home. I remained seated, favouring now my shins, which felt as if they'd been badly sunburned, while my grandmother saw the two of them to the front door. I listened to them move down the hall, murmur awhile at the other end, then the door slammed shut and Nana locked it. When she came back into the sitting room I was staring once again out of the window.

"Thinking about your granddad are you?" she asked softly, standing next to me.

I lifted up my eyes. Although I said "Yes" to my grandmother, I had in truth been thinking about *them*.

The evening dragged on and on. My legs were in unbearable pain now and could not tolerate anything touching them. I had rolled up my pant legs to my knees and sat as far away from the fire as I could. Nana's butter, smeared over my shins, reflected the light.

When I saw Harriet, seated in my easy chair and bent intently over something in her lap, I saw that Nana had fallen asleep and dozed peacefully in her own chair. There was a roaring fire in front of her, bright wallpaper on the walls, the Edwardian vases, the papier-mâché tables, all the Victorian accoutrements surrounded her, and yet she slept blissfully unaware. How odd it was to see her there, actually a part of the scene, and yet not at all. And if she were to awake suddenly, would it all disappear?

I leaned forward to see what it was Harriet was busy about, and saw on her lap a book, a few sheets of paper and an envelope, and in her hand a pen. She appeared to be writing a letter.

Her clothes were different now and I saw her breasts straining against the fabric of the blouse, an indication of her final entry into womanhood. The outfit intrigued me. So unlike the frilly, bustled dresses of the other times, Harriet's costume tonight was comprised of knickerbockers, woollen stockings, flat-heeled shoes, a rather masculine jacket, and, atop her coiffure, something like a sailor hat. She appeared dressed for outdoors.

I leaned forward as far as I could without disturbing the friability of the scene. It was indeed a letter she wrote in her lap, but I could not get close enough to discover to whom. I wondered for a moment if it might be to Victor, and then I remembered the letter she had so secretly stuffed in her skirt pocket the night Mr. Cameron had taken their portrait. Did Harriet have a secret friend with whom she corresponded?

Presently, her gestures gave me the answer. Glancing at the clock too many times and over her shoulder all too frequently, plus the rapidity with which she scratched out the letter, indicated that her task was a forbidden one and that she feared to be caught at if. A boyfriend, I wondered . . .

Then the aromas reached my nose, the sweet smell of duck roasting on an open spit. The tang of rice pudding bubbling on top of a stove. The scent of gravy, of corn, of hot bread. I looked over at the scullery door. Dimly seen in the "halo" light of the scene, I could not tell if I was looking at today's door, or if it was the door of Harriet's time. Whatever, Nana and I had nothing cooking in the kitchen. All was cold and closed up for us. So it must have been Harriet's supper that was filling the house with delicious smells. It must have been Mrs. Townsend in the kitchen, preparing the family's evening meal.

And yet I could smell it . . .

Another mystery. How was this possible? But then, how could I see them and hear them in the first place? So far, all of my senses except one were being invaded by the past, and I wondered if that, too, would eventually succumb. That at one point I would be able to reach out and touch . . .

But I would not try it now. I was too rapt in my study of Harriet to chance losing her by one thoughtless move. No, I would remain perfectly still while she wrote her letter.

And yet . . .

Another thought came to me now. I had spoken to Victor last night, I had spoken to him twice, and the first time . . . the *first time* he had not disappeared. He had gone right on talking to Jennifer. It was only the second time, when I had stood up and tried to touch him, that the scene had dissolved.

Might it not be possible, then, to communicate with them? Might he simply not have heard me, speaking as he had been so urgently to Jennifer? I could try again. I wouldn't move at all, just speak. I would say something to Harriet, quietly, casually, unobtrusively.

She was writing so peacefully, the air was so still. All we could hear was the crackle of the fire and the tick of the clock on the mantel. The clock of yesterday. Possibly, possibly I could utter a word and she could hear me. How I would have loved to have her hear me.

I took another look around the room. I was mildly disappointed that Victor wasn't here, and yet I really could not expect him, for he had said he was going off to Scotland and had sworn he would never come back. Did that mean I would never see him again? I doubted that. For he had an appointment with Fate within these walls and in the not too distant future. So he was coming back, I just did not know when.

Could I speak to her now? *Dare* I speak to her now?

I ran my tongue over my lips. My mouth was sticky dry.

I murmured "Harriet" as gently as I could. She did not look up. So I said a little louder, "Harriet."

Still no reaction.

"Harriet, can you hear me?"

When she finally lifted her head my heart gave a leap, but then I saw that it was only a gesture of meditation, that she was mulling over her next words, and I saw my efforts were in vain. Harriet would never be able to hear me. It was too insane.

I tried one last time. "Harriet, please listen to me."

Then I glanced over at my grandmother. Her eyes were wide open and she was staring at me.

I gave out a cry and my hand flew to my throat. "Nana! You startled me!"

"Who were you talking to?" she asked, regarding me in a strange way.

I looked at the other chair. It was empty. The gas heater was back. "N-no one, Nana. I thought you were asleep."

"I heard you talking to someone. I *saw* you. Someone named Harriet."

"No, Nana, I was only . . . " My words died away and all I could do was spread my hands in helplessness. "I guess I was just thinking out loud."

Now Nana turned her head and gave a long look at the empty easy chair before the gas heater. Her face was a mask, as unreadable and expressionless as that of a statue. She stared at the chair for the longest time, then she said slowly and carefully, "Have you seen things in this house, Andrea?"

Her words pierced me to the core as certainly as if she had shot me with a gun. Our eyes met across the room and held fast, and I wondered, What does she know?

Finally turning away from her gaze, I said quietly, "I was only thinking out loud, Nana. Harriet is my best friend back in L.A. Whenever I have a problem I always talk it out with her." Now I let out a short nervous laugh. "Gosh, Nana, don't you ever talk to yourself?"

The harsh look melted from her face and was replaced with concern. "Poor lovey, it's not going well for you here at all, is it? You left Los Angeles in such a hurry, took one of those jet planes, and here you are on the other side of the world. I once read an article in the *Manchester Guardian* about something scientists call biological rhythms, I think. And that's what your problem is, love, your rhythms are all off. And I'll wager it's got to your bowels, hasn't it?"

"Oh . . . "

"And I've got just the thing. Just you see if this doesn't work." She pushed up on the arms of the chair and hoisted herself to her feet with a grunt. With the help of the cane, my grandmother trundled to the sideboard—that endless source of supply—and reached in to withdraw an unlabelled bottle of white liquid. "Does me the trick every time," she said, puffing next into the scullery. When she came out she had a large spoon in her hand, and it was into this that she poured a dollop of the white stuff.

"Here, love." She thrust the spoon to my face.

"What is it, Nana?"

"It's medicine! The doctor give it to me a fortnight ago. All bunged up I was. Did the job proper overnight. Haven't been irregular since."

"But, Nana, I'm not—"

"Come on now, there's a love." With a smile she made a jabbing motion in the air with the spoon. A sickly sweet scent went up my nose. Closing my eyes, I opened my mouth like a child and took the entire spoon at once. It made me gag.

"Oh, Nana . . . " I put my hand to my throat, gagging. "That's awful!"

"Do the trick it will."

I pulled a face at the horrible aftertaste in my mouth. The sweetness had only been a cover-up for something underneath, something chalky and bitter, with a trace of something else . . . something unidentifiable.

"Between your burnt legs and your bound-up bowels, it's you should be in hospital, not your granddad." Nana replaced the cap on the bottle and then stowed it back in its hiding place. "Now then," she said, obviously pleased with her achievement. "No use us falling asleep in the sitting room. Might as well get on to bed. Want to sleep in the front bedroom tonight, love, in case you have to visit the toilet in a hurry? I can put two hot-water bottles in the bed for you."

Recalling my experience of yesterday with the clothes wardrobe, the horror of it still a vivid memory, I decided to stay down in the sitting room.

"I can run up real fast if I have to, Nana. And besides, down here I can have the heat . . . "

"Very well, love, suit yourself. Good night, then." She kissed both my cheeks and gave me a surprisingly strong hug. Then Nana went out of the sitting room and closed the door firmly behind her. When I heard her clambering up the stairs, I got up and turned off the gas.

I was surprised to discover I had fallen asleep. Surprised and alarmed, for I awoke with no memory of having removed my clothes and putting on my nightgown, or of crawling under the blankets on the sofa. And yet this was how I woke up, my eyes suddenly snapping open and gaping into the darkness. I wondered for the moment where I was, and then, remembering, felt the weight of the covers on my tender legs. Throwing back the blankets and sitting up on the couch, I realized what it was that had disturbed my sleep.

"Für Elise" was playing faintly.

The night was a curse, for with the cloudy sky there was not the barest bit of moon or starlight, so that I was plunged totally into darkness. Stumbling against the furniture, banging my painful shins, I groped my way to the window and drew open the curtain. Nothing. The world without was as dark as the world within. I carefully made my way back across the room towards the door, anxious to learn who played "Für Elise," and eventually reached the light switch.

Jennifer and Harriet startled me, standing as they were on either side of the fireplace.

I held my breath. Once again I marvelled at my lack of fear, that these sudden unheralded visits from the past no longer frightened me. It was as though a vague instinct at the base of my brain whispered assurances to me.

Not too much time had passed in their era, I noticed, for the two had changed only slightly. I placed them at the same age, around seventeen, and obviously young women who were conscious of changing fashion. The bustle was completely gone now and the skirt was tighter around the hips. They wore high-necked white blouses and little jackets with sleeves that puffed out at the shoulders. Both wore their hair in a knot atop the head, and both anxiously stared at the door I was leaning against.

As the fire crackled and as the clock of their year ticked away the minutes, I also noticed that "Für Elise" had stopped.

The two girls appeared worried, anxious about something. Constantly checking the time by her wrist watch, an affectation I am sure she cultivated in order to draw attention to her status symbol, Harriet puckered her colourless lips and every so often ran a darting tongue over them. Despite her tiny waist and small features, Victor and John's sister was still very homely. Indeed, the emergence into womanhood had not rescued her from the plainness that had marked her childhood but rather now seemed to magnify the fact all the more. Her eyebrows were just a bit too thick, her jaw a trace too heavy, and her nose disproportionately small for her face. And Harriet had the furrow, too, which, rather than give character and confidence to her face, only made her seem masculine. None of this was helped by the presence of Jenny who, with her continually budding loveliness, like a rose continually opening to ever more delightful proportions, actually eclipsed Harriet to the point of making one feel sorry for the Townsend girl.

I could not keep my eyes off Jenny. Just as that first night when Nana had showed me Jenny's photograph and I had at once been attracted to it, so did I now stare at this incredibly beautiful girl with a mixture of admiration and envy. I could not think of her as an apparition from the past, as some sort of freak out of Time, for my senses told me that I was in the presence of a living person, a woman who emanated an intensity in her very stance. There was agitation in her soft brown eyes; they fluttered about the room like butterflies. Her hands, as if in sympathy with her eyes, clasped and un-clasped, twined and untwined, and fidgeted with the cuffs of her sleeves. Jenny's thin eyebrows, so delicately arched, did not remain still, occasionally rising up to crease her smooth forehead.

Finally, after a painful wait, Harriet turned to Jenny and whispered, "I hear them coming."

Catching the apprehension of the girls and transferring it to my own pounding heart, I stepped away from the door, pressed myself against the wall, and turned wide-stretched eyes to the two men who now materialized in the sitting room.

It must have been raining, for John was quite wet and came in knocking droplets off his pant legs. He rushed to the fire, rubbing his hands, and mur-mured something which I did not hear. My attention was not for John but for his companion, Victor, who now stood so close to me that I could smell the dampness of his clothes and see the rain upon his hair.

And seeing him this close, I sucked in my breath. He was a different man.

Victor Townsend had altered considerably. He was years older. Al-though still only twenty-five or twenty-six, he had the face of a man who had seen too much of the world to leave room for flippancy. The smooth-ness and softness of youth were gone. His jaw, now clean shaven and ab-sent of the former sideburns, was square and tight, as if he harboured some grim secret. His eyes had become deep-set, as though they wished to look in rather than out, and were cloaked in shadows earned in the sickly lights and poisonous miasmas of a London hospital. His black wavy hair, curled at the ends, grew now below his ears and just off the shoulders, haphazardly, combed like some ancient prophet's who had come to reject the material values for those spiritual. There was something almost exotic about him now, distant and austere, as he stood so still that he could not be seen to breathe. And I wondered what had happened to cause such a drastic change.

He and Jenny stared at one another across the room, and I saw in her gaze the shock and dismay at his transformation.

What had Victor seen in those London hospitals? How often had he held death in his fingers, or tasted of profound loss, or suffered the frustration of a man who was supposed to save lives but in the end could only stand helplessly by? There were years now on Victor's face, but they showed not in lines or sagging or the usual evidences of age, for his square handsome face had none of these. His wisdom and maturity, so contradictory in the features of one so young, showed themselves in the grim set of his lips, the dour way they curved down at the corners, as though he had given up smiling. It was a tragic bitterness cloaked in melancholy. Not the look of the disillusioned but of the cynical. Victor Townsend had lost one patient too many.

I saw now that Harriet had taken a step towards her brother and, having seen the way he and Jenny looked at one another, stopped. Her hands were partly outstretched, her mouth open. She stood like someone who had just gazed upon the Gorgon.

And while John continued to rub his hands over the fire and stamp the moisture out of his boots, oblivious of the tableau behind his back, Victor continued to hold Jenny with his gaze. As I looked on, a bare few inches away from him, I saw how sharply delineated was his face in the glare of the fire, a study in chiaroscuro, and I saw how he aged with each passing minute.

It was then, as I studied him so intently, trying to probe the impenetrable veil which hardened and saddened his gaze and which protected his inner weakness from a world of death and defeat, that I felt something move within me . . .

"Mr. Townsend," whispered Jenny at last. She remained by the fire, afraid to move. "Welcome home."

"Thank you," he said in a deeper voice than I had known him to have.

Victor appeared also fearful of moving, as if afraid to spoil the dreamlike aura of the moment. He seemed to be filling his eyes with Jenny, devouring her with his shadowed, dispirited gaze, like a man who is starved or has known no warmth or who longs to come home but doesn't know the way.

Finally, conscious at last of the silence, John turned around and stretched out his arms. "What? No fanfare? Why so solemn? This is an occasion for rejoicing! The prodigal son has returned!"

I detected a strain of bitterness here covered up by forced joviality and wondered if the others noticed.

"Oh Victor!" cried Harriet, running to him now and flinging her arms about him. "Oh you *are* home! You *have* come home! I thought I had been dreaming!"

He shook his head and blinked down at her like a man coming out of a deep sleep. "Aye, Harriet, I'm home."

"And to stay? Please say it's to stay!"

Harriet pressed her head against his chest so that Victor looked over her again to Jenny as he said softly, "I've come home to stay."

"I knew it!" cried his sister. "When Father told me, I didn't believe him." She stepped back, wiping tears off her cheeks. "He showed me your letter, telling him you'd given up the Edinburgh appointment to come back here, and still I didn't believe it. It was like an answer to my prayers. To my most ardent longings. I knew you wouldn't go off to Scotland and forget us!"

Harriet whipped around. "John, where's the sherry you promised?"

"Ah!" He snapped his fingers. "In the parlour."

"And the glasses. I shall get the glasses. We shall celebrate all evening."

Harriet pushed past me and through the door, leaving a stream of lavender cologne in her wake, and John exited right behind her. For one small moment, Victor and Jenny were alone.

Still they continued to stare as if the mere sight of one another were enough for the time being, sating their yearnings with their eyes. Then Jenny spoke and she said trepidly, "I was quite surprised, Mr. Townsend, when Harriet told me the news. So sudden it was and so unexpected. I didn't know what to think."

An uncomfortable smile jerked Victor's mouth. "Nor did I know what to do. For it was after I met you that I suffered my first doubts about going to Scotland."

Her hand went to her breast. "Me? But what had I—"

"In these past five months, since the night of our first meeting, I have found a restlessness within me that cannot be contained and I knew that I should be unhappy in Scotland. Jenny, how I feared you might not still be here when I returned! And then it would have been for naught."

I saw the colour run from Jenny's face, leaving her with a strange pallor and a stricken expression. Before she could speak, John and Harriet were suddenly in the room again bearing a tray of glasses and a sherry bottle. Filling each and distributing them (I almost held my hand out), John then proposed a toast.

"To our distinguished brother, Dr. Victor Townsend, long and prosperous may his years be among us."

They all four drained the small glasses and then John proceeded to refill them. Watching the sweet drink tumble into her glass and glint in the fire's glow, Jenny said, "Where will you be setting up practice, Mr. Townsend?"

Striding now away from the door to join the threesome by the fire, Victor said, "Why are you still calling me by my surname, Jenny? Surely we are friends and can call one another by our Christian names."

"Rightly so, brother," said John, raising his glass again in a toast. "After all, Jennifer is now one of the family, in fact your sister by law, so of course Christian names are in order."

Victor looked at his brother for the first time since coming into the room. "I beg your pardon?"

"Surely you received my letter! Do you mean to tell me that you don't know?" John reached out and dropped a heavy hand on his brother's shoulder. "Good heavens, man, I was wondering why you didn't congratulate me at the train station! Jennifer and I were married two months ago!"

How strange that I should have felt the effect of those words as Victor did, seeing the room tilt for an instant, hearing the voices draw suddenly far away, seeing the sparkling glasses rise high in the firelight. How strange that I, too, should feel the impact he felt, a blow that made my mind reel, just as it did his, and to discover within my breast yet deeper pains and darker disappointments than I had thought possible.

I recalled the desperation of the hospital wards, the blood and the sickness, the senseless suffering, the malnutritioned children, the destitute mothers, those who came to die on the steps of the hospital for want of anywhere to go and for lack of a cure by the physicians within. And I thought of the lonely evenings, alone in a cramped room, sitting in the darkness late into the night with only the vision of Jennifer Adams for solace sitting there and wondering, Is it possible to be so deeply in love with her and yet not know her at all? I recalled the agonized wrestling with the decision, the lure of Scotland and its rewards against the need to see Jennifer Adams again, to love her . . .

A cold breath blew through my soul. I saw blackness and grief there, bitter failure, dejection, depression. Oblivion.

"Oh Victor," we heard Harriet say in a high, strained voice, "you didn't receive the letter? We sent it off two months ago. You mean you didn't know at all?"

We focused our eyes on Victor's younger sister, trying to remember how we were supposed to act in such a situation, what the proper conduct should be, and Victor managed to find the voice to say, "No. I received no letter . . . I didn't know."

How he found the courage to raise his eyes to Jenny I will never know. And the effort it took to find his voice and make it sound calm must have been colossal. "Then forgive me for being late with my congratulations."

We saw a strange vision rise up and swim before our eyes. It was the image of a man making a fool of himself by protesting his love to a woman who had just married his brother. And in the background, dismal and grey, the gates and walls of the Royal Infirmary in Edinburgh closed forever.

"I never received the letter," he said in a thick voice. "The college is not famous for its postal efficiency. But forgive me, I did not drink the toast." Bringing the glass to his lips, Victor tossed his head back and emptied the glass. Then he let his eyes fall again on Jennifer. More years were added now, a new veneer of cynicism and disappointment, one more blighted hope. The shadows about his eyes darkened, his face took on a haunted, hunted look, the face of a man who knew too many of the answers.

My heart went out to him. Victor stood in the centre of the room, still taller and of greater stature than his three companions, yet he was also diminished, his shoulders sloping forward, his hands dangling uselessly at his side. The sorrow he felt now, the burden of disappointment fell over me as well; I suffered once more the passions of my great-grandfather. How he could have stood it at all was beyond me, and yet stand it he did and with surprising composure. Only he and I knew the turmoil of his soul at that moment, only Victor and I saw the rancour there, for he managed himself at once and was able to present to his family the mask they wanted to see. And he took refuge behind it.

"Again I congratulate you both. So sudden it was, for it has only been five months since I was here last. And you weren't engaged then, were you?"

I marvelled at the lightness in his voice, at the seeming ease with which he spoke. Victor now went to the sherry bottle and poured himself a third, full glass.

"No, brother, we were not engaged then, but shortly after." John held out a glass to Victor. "Right to the top if you will, thank you. So you see, brother, you are not the only master of surprise in this family."

I didn't care for the way John smiled as he said this, nor did I appreciate the metallic quality to his voice. That John was jealous of Victor was obvious to me, if not to the others, and that he believed he had scored a victory over his brother was equally apparent.

"Victor," said Jennifer now in a stronger voice, "we thought you were never coming back. We had no idea."

He looked again at her, his brooding eyes veiling his thoughts. "I did not know myself until a fortnight ago. You might say I made the decision on the spur of the moment."

"Snap judgements are so unlike you, brother."

"If only we had known . . . " said Jennifer, trying to communicate with her eyes what she dared not put in words.

"And if you had known. What then?" Victor drained his third glass and set it down with a bang. "You would have postponed the ceremony until my arrival, is that it? How very thoughtful of you. And how inconsiderate of me not to have forewarned you all of my plans sooner. But then, how could I?"

"Oh, we *are* glad to have you back, Victor!" said Harriet, seizing his hand and squeezing it. I saw the light that shone in her eyes when she looked up at him, how Harriet worshipped her older brother and was blind to what had just transpired. "Father was so pleased when the letter came! You should have seen him. Why, he smiled, Victor. Father actually *smiled*. And he is so proud of you now. After all, graduating with honours from King's College—"

"Thank you for your praise, little sister," he said now, trying to hide the bitter edge to his voice with an attempt at warmth. "It's good to know I'm welcomed back."

"And Mother cried all night after she read your letter! Proper hysterical, she was! She's gone out for a goose now, Victor. We're to have a special supper tonight in your honour."

As Harriet continued to chatter on and as John took a seat before the fire with a fresh glass of sherry, his body tired from a day's work at the mill and the wine relaxing him by degrees, Victor and Jenny turned to look at one another one last time.

And my great-grandfather realized the grotesque error he had made.

CHAPTER 10

HE REST OF THE NIGHT REMAINS IN MY MEMORY AS A nightmare. Victor had come home expecting to find Jenny waiting for him and had brought with him the dreams he had woven around a love that was doomed from its very birth. Feeling both foolish and angry, Victor was nonetheless able to hide his feelings from his family and the fact that he had come home expecting to live in this house again, so he put forth the pretence that he had arranged for a room at the Horse's Head Inn. While I knew better, seeing in Victor's heart as the others couldn't and seeing there the burning shame over his foolish deed and the fierce pride that kept him from showing it, John and Harriet and Jenny accepted this and believed him when he said he had to go out now and see that his bags were transported from the station to the inn. Although the three of them wanted him to wait until after supper to move into his hotel room, Victor pressed the point of using the last of the daylight and a rather lame observation that he thought the rain was light just now.

Only I knew, as he strode into the hall to vigorously throw his cloak about his shoulders, that my great-grandfather was setting out into a crushing storm to search for accommodations, that he did not have anywhere to go, and that a warm room with a fire did not await him at the end of a short walk. And only I knew why he had to go out into the driving rain just now, why he had to throw himself into the elements and vent the fury of his soul into the tempest outside. He was too angry, too twisted with frustration to be able to sit in this tight little room any longer, and pretend. The charade was over.

As we watched him go, John offering to hail him a hansom but Victor refusing, Harriet admonishing him to be home in time for supper, and Jenny remaining silently stupefied by the fireplace, Victor plopped a top hat on his head and made towards the front door. Taking hold of the knob, he paused to cast one last dark glance over his shoulder, and it caused me to shiver, for in that last fleeting look I saw an evil foreboding of times to come.

In four years Victor Townsend had learned pessimism and mistrust. The weight of his experience had moulded a man who would never think to look for the rainbow after a rain had finished. And tonight the ultimate blow had been struck. For the sake of a girl he hardly knew, driven by a passion he could not contain, Victor had blindly and stupidly cast fortune to the wind. The cruel defeat had come from his own hand, having so unthinkingly invented a bright future for himself without stopping to consider how tenuous were the factors involved. The news of Jenny's marriage came as a fatal wound, striking him in the one last reserve of love and tenderness he had. But now that that, too, was smitten, it would scar over and leave Victor Townsend bereft of solace, with nothing to comfort him but bitter recrimination.

Once the shock subsided, after Victor had marched proudly out into the storm, I was left alone again to weep in my solitude and privately mourn the tragedy of my great-grandfather. And, being alone in that cold dark house, moving among furniture he had known, I was beset by a legion of thoughts and ideas. My mind ran around in circles like a tethered animal, coming to no conclusions, and leaving me in the end drained and exhausted.

Late into the night and into early morning I reflected upon many things. For foremost in my mind was the enigma of Victor's effect on me and how violently I empathized with him.

Earlier on, when the "visit" had just begun, I had stood staring at Victor. I had filled my eyes with him as he had filled his with Jenny, and as I had studied each detail of his face—the cynical mouth, the large handsome nose, the dark encircled eyes—I had felt something move within me. I do not intend this as metaphorical, for there was, as I took in the sad, too-wise countenance of Victor Townsend, a palpable movement inside my body, deep down in the lower, mythological regions where it is, I suppose, that true passions are born. It was here and not in my heart that I was first aroused by this cryptic, unreachable man, here in the darkest most secret part of me where something stirred to life for the first time, as though it had always been there, asleep, I unaware of its existence, and now it was awake. But it was not too long after this that I experienced the involvement of my heart, as if it responded in its tender, sentimental way to my initial, primeval spark.

I had stood there and studied Victor, so close that I needed but barely lift a hand to touch him, and I had fallen in love with him.

How was this possible? Here was the major riddle that led my mind through maze after maze, drawing no closer to a conclusion but only confusing me all the more. How was it possible that I could fall in love with a man nearly a hundred years dead? Was it because to me, in these moments when the Universe slipped between two time spheres, Victor was a living man and therefore as real to me as my Uncle Ed or Uncle William?

How could I be so moved by him, feel so helplessly drawn to him? Was it because I was being made in some unexplainable way to feel everything he felt, to suffer his secret joys and woes? There could be no answers, for the questions themselves stemmed from circumstances that existed outside the realm of logic and understanding. Just as these glimpses into the past bore no unravelling, did not lend themselves to reason, so should my involvement in Victor's passions now be just as beyond any hope of explanation. I had accepted the sojourns into the past and learned that I could neither fathom nor fight them, so now should I also accept my newly born love.

And yet it was difficult to do so. For one thing, a love such as this did not sit comfortably with me, being a stranger to deep love and unaccustomed to dealing with it. Bearing for Victor strange new endearments, ones which almost embarrassed and frightened me, I was caused to search the experience of my soul to see if I had ever before encountered such an emotion, and finding nothing of that sort led me to wonder why.

The truth of this, the truth of something I suppose I had really always known but had shied from, had been buried beneath my busy life and my surface existence, now caused me to shrink away from it. The profoundness and enormity of how I now felt for Victor made me afraid to go any deeper into my soul, for I knew what I would find there.

Nothing. Absolutely nothing.

The truth was, confronting it at last in that biting cold hour before dawn when many truths come to light, that I had never before in my life been in love. Not even with Doug.

And so I lay in the chilly darkness of my grandmother's sitting room, alone with my conscience and with the memory of what had taken place here nearly a century ago, turning inward and examining myself for the first time. It was a clumsy new experience for me as I had never before encountered the necessity to look inward. My past had been one of convenient friendships, of surface pleasures, and glancing emotions. I had had many boyfriends in my twenty-seven years and only one of them now, as the eastern sky over Warrington grew milky with dawn, could I recall to memory: Doug, whom I had so heartlessly wronged. The rest I saw only as a gross commodity. But in detail, each as an individual for whom I had felt some passing devotion, they would not come back. The truth was I had always run from the more intense emotions, had always shirked the responsibility of being truly committal to someone and was now faced with an inevitability over which I had no control.

There was the crux. Control. In the past it had always been my game we played, I had always been the leader, using rules of my own invention. These were tools of defence, these were what went into the building of safe walls which protected me from the pain of loving. Of course, my little mechanisms of defence had also worked to keep out the ecstasies, so that in sparing myself anguish I had also robbed myself of rapture. And I had always thought, A fair price to pay.

But this time I was not in control. I was as much the victim and the puppet as anyone could be, feeling the clash of my emotions against the faltering strength of my reason. How calm and untroubled my life had been, how predictable, how manageable it had been. Each facet of my life I had deftly and easily manipulated, drawing all rewards to my own hands, using devices that both protected and profited me.

And how empty it all had been.

I cried again, many times over, thinking of Victor, of the pain he had felt to hear of Jenny's marriage, of the hollow realization that he had so stupidly thrown away his future and his own happiness for a groundless dream. And I cried also for myself, recalling the empty days and the nights which had been filled in parody of love. How convenient it had all been. How tranquil. And how utterly bleak.

Between my tears I was able to smile at the irony of how it took a family of dead people to breathe life into my dormant soul and awaken my sleeping passions. For what is a person who is absent of feeling? When you subtract love and hate and jealousy and all the range of emotions which give purpose to a person's existence, then all you have left is a shell. And that is exactly what I had been before stepping my first foot into Nana's house—a cold barren lifeless shell. I had lived with and for myself in a world so small that little room had remained for anyone else. Even those friendships which I had cultivated and so highly prized had not exacted any portion from me.

I also began to think, as morning wore on and the cloudy sky emerged from night, about my brother Richard, who had in childhood been my closest friend and companion but who was now a total stranger to me. I had allowed the passage of time and the inconvenience of miles to separate us to the point where I no longer gave him the most passing of thoughts. A card at Christmas, a letter once a year if I felt like it, and that was the relationship between my brother and myself. How different we were from Harriet and Victor, she who adored her older brother to the point of blindness and he who looked down at his little sister in loving warmth and a feeling of protection.

Richard, five years my senior, had once been such a brother to me, and I had worshipped him to distraction. But then he had heard the call of adventure and frontiers and had sailed off to Australia, and I had found a comfortable niche for myself in a large brokerage firm where I could extend or limit my boundaries as I wished.

Lying on Nana's sofa and thinking again about the way Harriet acted around Victor, recalling the way she had cried when he went off to London and how avidly she had welcomed his return, memories sprang up from some hidden source and flooded my mind as if they spilled through a broken dam. Richard and myself as children: he always protecting me and standing up for me and teaching me the ways of the world and entertaining me for hours with stories of adventure and mystery. I lay there and let the memories roll by, long forgotten ones, insignificant days out of my childhood that now filled me with a sweet nostalgia and a regret that I had kept them buried for so long.

Christmas mornings opening presents. Richard gallantly killing a spider in my bed. The two of us marching off to church every Sunday morning. He helping me with my homework. Richard sharing his last piece of candy. How I had stood behind him, this tall invincible soldier! How I had looked up at him with pride in my eyes that could have matched Harriet's when she regarded Victor. Where had all this gone? Why had I forgotten these simple, commonplace little memories that now seemed so precious to me?

I was overwhelmed with a desire to talk to him again, just as we had done when I was in junior high school and Richard was going into the Air Force. We had sat on my bed that day with the door closed and Richard had spoken to me in a low, adult voice, telling me that he had to go away and that I was going to be on my own from now on and that I would have to fend for myself. In a way that I admired him for, considering the delicacy of the subject and that this was the time before the liberalization of so many things, Richard had gone on to give me some idea of the things that awaited me in life and had uttered grave warnings about the pitfalls. He had used words unfamiliar to me, had painted pictures that baffled me. But in time, as I grew up and entered adulthood and Richard sailed off to Australia, I had discovered that all he had told me was true, and that his advice had been to good purpose.

I suppose that, in the end, Richard really had been with me in my older years, that he had truly been standing at my side even when I was most convinced that I was alone in life, for the words he had given me with which to arm myself against the world had never left. I realized now, as I heard Nana stir about upstairs, that I had in some childish way blamed Richard for my lonely adolescence, that I had placed too much store in him and that with his leaving I had rejected him. And I had thought my growing-up years to be lonely ones where I had had to stand alone. But I realized now that this had not been true, that I had been unfair to my brother, thinking that he should have stayed behind and lived my life, for with his words echoing every day in my ears, the memory of that last talk in my bedroom, I had been able to go through life with open eyes and with a better understanding of things.

Richard *had* been with me after all.

I insisted that I go with Aunt Elsie and Uncle Ed to the hospital and I also sensed that the house was going to let me. There was a need growing within me to see my grandfather, to try to find some way to communicate to him what I had learned about his father. Granddad could not die without knowing that he had been wrong about his dad, that he had lived all his life a painful lie, for Victor Townsend had been a noble, beautiful man and deserving of our love.

This is what I thought on the afternoon of my seventh day in Nana's house, still under the effects of the "visit" of the night before. It was not until later that I witnessed evidence to the contrary, incidents that could only support the horror stories Granddad had lived with, scenes that shook my confidence and set cruel doubts within me. I was soon to learn that the Victor Townsend I so far knew was not the same man I was to encounter later on. That rapidly things were going to change.

And that the true horror of the house on George Street was about to emerge.

Granddad slept through our entire visit and never once stirred. While Elsie and Ed carried on their usual one-sided conversation, pretending that he could hear and that he might at any minute respond, I toyed with the idea of also talking to him. It was possible he could hear me and understand me. The difficulty, however, lay in the presence of my two relatives, whom I did not wish to be part of it. What I had to say to my grandfather I had to say in private, and there was no way I could be alone with him for even a minute. He lay on the pillow, an emaciated old man with flaky skin and a perpetual pall of stagnancy over him. Yet he was Victor's son. And he had, in his eighty-three years, borne only hatred and shame for his father's memory.

I had to change that.

My opportunity never came and then it was time to go home. As Uncle Ed folded up the wooden chairs and replaced them one by one on the stack in the corner, and as Aunt Elsie chatted on the other side of the door with the Sister, I stood staring down at my grandfather and felt the urgency of my need to speak to him. When Elsie stuck her head through the door, Uncle Ed and I joined her, and exchanged a few words with Sisters as we replaced our coats and hats. Walking through the double doors and out into the gathering gloom, I stopped suddenly and exclaimed that I had left my gloves by Granddad's bed.

"I'll just run back and get them!" I said, already turning back to the doors.

"Ed'll get them for you, love, you get in the car."

"Won't take me a minute, Elsie. Get the heater going for me." And I turned and dashed in before she could protest another moment. Not stopping to remove even my hat, I hurried back into the ward where Granddad lay and paused by the window. Elsie was climbing into the Renault and closing the door after her.

Then I looked back down at my grandfather. The ward today was exceptionally quiet; most of the visitors had gone and the sisters and nurses were taking a rest before preparing their patients' dinners. So I quickly sat on the edge of the bed and desperately searched for the proper words to say. Uncertain, I bent forward and, with my mouth as close as possible to his ear without touching it, I murmured, "Granddad, it's me, Andrea. Can you hear me? It's me, Andrea, and I've come all the way from Los Angeles to be with you. Granddad? Can you hear me?"

I glanced over at his chest. The respiration did not change. Nor did his face or the uncanny stillness of his eyelids. So I went on: "You were wrong, Granddad, about your father. You've been wrong about him all your life. You were told lies. He's a good man. Victor Townsend was a good and great man. Granddad . . . "

My throat closed over my voice and refused to open. Anxiously I glanced about the ward and then out of the window. Aunt Elsie was getting out of the car. Hurriedly I said, "Granddad, I hope you can hear me because I'm telling you the truth. I know the truth about your father, and he was not a man to be ashamed of. Oh please, Granddad, *please hear me*! Victor Townsend was a dear, kind man dedicated to saving people's lives, and the horrible things in life gave him great pain. Granddad . . . "

Hearing my aunt's booming voice on the other side of the door, I quickly slid off the bed and on to the floor where, on all fours, I pretended to search for my gloves.

"Andrea," Aunt Elsie said, coming around the bed.

"Here they are!" I cried, having pulled them out of my bag and coming up with them. "They must have fallen off my lap and under the bed. I guess I kicked them when I folded my chair. Sorry."

"Maybe I should sew a long string to them both that you can wear under your coats so you won't lose them again."

I laughed and linked my hand through her arm. "If my own head wasn't screwed on tight . . . " I said, and we pushed our way through the door.

I tried, as we did so, to catch one last glimpse of my grandfather, but the door swung shut in my face.

"How's your bowels today?" asked Nana as we ate our six o'clock tea. We dined on buttered scones and thick ham sandwiches and cold milk and watched the rain begin to fall in the garden. I was growing anxious again for my next interlude with the Townsends and had a hard time concentrating.

They were becoming an obsession with me. The need to see them again was intensifying, while the real world became less and less important. It was 1891 I longed to visit, and it was John and Harriet and Victor and Jennifer I wanted to see. Even if I could never be a part of them, even if I must be forever relegated to the periphery of their world, this was what I wanted—not reality. My living relatives were a hindrance to me, for as long as they were around the dead ones would not appear. It would not be until Nana went up to bed or was asleep in the easy chair that I would see the Townsends again, and I wished there were some way I could sever myself from Nana's tedious evening company.

While I did not question this state of affairs at the time, I did later on, when I began to grow alarmed. For at the time all I knew was that I was desperately in love with Victor Townsend and could not rest until I saw him again. I did not question the reasons for what was happening, I did not try to probe the motive for this parade of events, I was too wrapped up in the Townsend story to wonder at the purpose of it all. Yet a time would soon come when I would question this strange obsession I had, when I would begin to think of myself as a sacrificial animal and that I had become trapped in some enormously grotesque practical joke in Time.

"How's your bowels?" repeated Nana.

"Hm?" I swallowed the last of my milk and brought my eyes away from the window. "Oh, just fine, Nana."

"Want some more medicine?"

"No! Oh . . . no thank you. It did the trick."

Medicine . . . medicine . . . white stuff. When had I taken it? Had it only been last night? Had only twenty-four hours passed since my transformation from a hollow shell into a *living* human being? A living breathing woman. A woman who had stumbled upon an untapped wellspring of love and feeling and passion. Yes, I loved Victor Townsend. And I also desired him.

This last thought, suddenly springing up new and previously not considered, now startled me. Yes, it was true. I not only loved the man but I also *wanted* him. Thinking about him brought a weakness to my legs; recalling his nearness, the quality of his voice, the deep brooding eyes brought mysterious stirrings in my abdomen, for he affected me not only spiritually but physically as well. Victor Townsend was an uncommonly handsome man, and his face was etched with a strength of character and reflections of an inner melancholy that mesmerized me with the mere thought of him.

How unfair that I should never know his touch! The injustice of craving the physical excitement of a man who was dead. Although Victor appeared before me in seeming flesh and blood, I could never know him as I truly wanted to except in dreams and fantasies.

I found myself wondering what his kiss would be like . . .

This, too, startled me. As quickly as it entered my mind, the image made my heart skip a beat. My cup of steaming tea stopped halfway to my mouth. I stared at my grandmother as if it had been she rather than my rambling thoughts that had spoken the idea.

I desired my own great-grandfather!

What an incomprehensible idea! What was I to make of it? Could it be called incest? After all, he had been dead at least eighty years, if not longer. And he truly did not exist. What I saw when I gazed upon Victor Townsend was not really him but some bizarre quirk of the workings of Time, so that it was really no more than being in love with a photograph or a man fabricated from my own fantasies.

And I did fantasize about him. I had thought about Victor all day. I had thought about him in many ways, many aspects, but most of all I had wondered what it must be like to be the lover of so intense a man. His very looks had vanquished me. What would his touch do?

I brought the cup to my lips and drank the sweet tea. Why did Nana have to pour so much sugar into the tea? Why ruin a perfectly delightful treat?

It could not be avoided. I was in love with my own great-grandfather. And it was a futile love, for I had no hope of ever knowing him. I had no hope of him ever seeing me or savouring his kiss or sharing intimacies. The Victor Townsend I saw and the one who held me in his arms in my imagination were two different men. And they were both dead.

"How's your legs now? Shall I rub some cream on them?"

I stared at my grandmother. She had no idea the nature of my preoccupation, no inkling of what had made her granddaughter so quiet all day. I wanted to blurt out to her now what I had said to Granddad, that Victor

Townsend was a man to be loved and not despised, that I had seen him, and that he continued to exist somehow, some way under this very roof. Yet I could not. Nana would not understand. And what if, by telling her the story, I lost him altogether?

This was something I would not think about. The end. The final chapter of the story. For I wanted my interludes with Victor to go on for ever and ever, just as he and Jennifer now lived forever and continued to experience over again those nights of 1890. I never wanted to leave this house, never wanted to go back to Los Angeles again, for then I would lose the precious treasure I had found.

For the first time in my life I felt alive.

"They're still painful, Nana."

"Come on then, love."

We moved to our easy chairs before the gas heater and I wished there was some way I could reduce the heat. For some reason my body was becoming highly sensitive to warmth and seemed to be gravitating towards colder areas. I seemed to be subconsciously drawn to the cold, whereas before I had been repelled by it. Why this should be, I did not question. That morning, when Nana had come into the sitting room and had found me lying fully clothed on the sofa, she had exclaimed, "The gas is off again! It's freezing in here! Andrea, aren't you cold?"

And the truth of it had been: I wasn't. Even in just a T-shirt and jeans and with the house a good forty degrees I did not feel the cold. And then later, when she had turned the gas to its highest, I had felt stifled and smothered by the heat. Now, sitting before the low flame with my legs bared for her ministrations, I loathed the warmth and wished there were some way to get the room cooler.

As Nana applied the cream, gently and with care, I moved my eyes to the window over the little table and saw how dark the sky had grown. A fierce rain now pelted the windows, a storm such as I had never seen before, with grumblings of thunder far in the distance and occasional flashes of lightning. The rain came down in incredible torrents, sounding like a far-off waterfall, and the thunder, when it drew near, was like the blasting of cannons.

I found myself enjoying the rain and I had difficulty taking my eyes off it. When, a short while later and complaining of pains in her arthritic joints because of the damp, Nana announced she was going to sit in bed and read, I could barely mask my excitement.

In a short while I would see Victor again.

CHAPTER 11

I WAS SITTING ON THE COUCH AND LISTENING TO THE STEADY
rain when the clock over the fireplace stopped ticking. My eyes
shot to the dial, seeing that it was just midnight, and I shuddered
slightly as I sensed the room about me start to change. There were no physical sensations involved other than a brief chill, otherwise it was simply like
the fading out of one movie scene into another. I stared at the two easy chairs
and saw the gradual, almost invisible alteration from their present condition
into that of the past. Blending from Nana's flowery Woolworth covers into a
nondescript blur, the two chairs emerged in a shimmer of bright green velvet and in exactly the same place as before. Almost new, with the upholstery
barely marred and the stuffing still firm and with shape, the two dilapidated
chairs that had received the backsides of so many Townsends over the years
now appeared before me just as they had looked in the days of 1890. And
one of them was occupied.

It was Harriet again, writing once more in the solitude of the sitting
room her secret letters. I watched as her hand moved rapidly over the statio-

nery cradled in her lap, how her eyes darted up now and again to the clock, how she stopped once in a while, stared at the door as if she heard a sound, and then returned to her hasty writing.

I wondered who Harriet's secret correspondent was, why she wrote in such haste, why she seemed afraid of being caught. If I thought I could have read the words on that page without disturbing the fragility of the moment, I would have got up and stood beside her. But I was afraid of any movement I might make. As it was, I held my body rigid and barely breathed.

The scene was soft and warm and quiet, with only the sound of her pen scratching the paper. There were embers in the fireplace and the fall of a heavy rain could be heard on the other side of the drapes. I wondered where the rest of the family was. Looking up at the Victorian clock over the fireplace, I saw that it was also midnight in Harriet's time, which would mean the household was asleep. Mr. and Mrs. Townsend would be in the back bedroom, where Nana now slept. So I assumed that John and his new bride had taken residence in the front bedroom, where I imagined Jennifer's gowns now took up half the space in the clothes wardrobe. That meant that Harriet must have some sort of temporary arrangement in either this room or the parlour, pending the departure of the newlyweds. It could not be long, I decided, before John and Jenny would find a house of their own.

When it occurred to me that this was a rather farfetched assumption—that John and Jenny still lived here and had not yet moved out—I realized that I must be somehow receiving thoughts from Harriet's mind. Possibly that is what she was writing in her letter, a complaint (for this was the impression I received from her mind); she was venting her displeasure to someone through the medium of ink and paper. While I could not exactly read her mind, see what her precise thoughts were, I was able to sense the general drift of her thoughts, just as I had been able to do with Victor and his father and then, later, with Jennifer.

I watched Harriet intently. Then, after a moment, with the fountain pen moving rapidly across the paper and with the midnight hour ticking away in 1891, I saw her gradually fade from my sight until she and the green chairs were gone to be replaced once again by the dreary familiar ones of my time.

The brevity of the scene disappointed me. But even sharper was the let-down of not having seen Victor. But then, he did not live here now and so must rarely be present.

Then where *was* he? I wondered. Had he found a flat for himself somewhere, or a room in a private house, or was he still at the Horse's Head Inn? There had been nothing about Harriet's brief appearance that gave me any indication of how much time had passed since Victor's returning home. I had no way of knowing what had taken place in the meantime, if he was still even in Warrington.

One other thing puzzled me. What had been the purpose of my seeing Harriet just now and for so brief a time?

I had no opportunity to ponder this any further, for in the next instant a strangled scream tore the air, I flew to my feet. The sound had come so suddenly and so unexpectedly that I had no way of discerning its direction. It had seemed to fill the house at once.

Then there was a crash, as of a piece of furniture falling to the floor. My eyes shot to the ceiling. It was coming from upstairs. There was the sound of feet, as though two people were struggling, there were more crashes, and then another scream. A woman's scream.

Without another thought I dashed out of the sitting room and into the hallway. I looked up at the blackness that filled the stairway and I strained to listen.

More scuffling sounds, as of two people locked in combat, filtered down from somewhere above. Then I heard a slap and another crash. A woman cried out, her voice sharp with terror.

I wasted no time. Although unable to see even my hand in front of my face, I started to scramble up the stairs. So steep were they and so deep the blackness that I fell frequently and ended by crawling the last of the stairs on my hands and knees. When I reached the top I fought my way to my feet and fell against the wall, breathing heavily.

The dark and the silence were ominous.

My hand felt about the wall for the light switch and, finding it, managed to flick it on. But nothing happened. The darkness remained. Frantically I snapped the switch up and down, my eyes stupidly searching the obscure ceiling for the bulb. But no light came on. All about me there remained an interminable inkiness that filled me with dread and pressed me to the wall.

As I stood thus, too frightened to venture forth, I heard again the muffled sounds of a struggle, although now they were nearer and louder. A man and a woman fought desperately with one another at the end of the hall, sounding as if they were on the other side of the bedroom door. More thuds, angry growls, and an occasional slap followed by a sharp cry. Words were uttered but I could not make them out.

The darkness was formidable and I had the impression of standing at the mouth of an immense cavern. Although I was gripped with a fear that turned my arms and legs to ice, I became overpowered with the need to walk forward. I had to see what was happening on the other side of the door. A will other than my own took possession of my body, propelling me forward like a sleepwalker, so that I made my way slowly down the hall and heard the sounds draw nearer and nearer.

Then I stopped just inches from the door. I reached out blindly and felt my hand touch the hard cold wood. On the other side, the voices were now distinct.

"Oh please no . . . " whimpered Harriet. "Please, I'm sorry . . . don't do it . . . "

I squeezed my eyes tight and slapped my hands against my ears trying to keep out the pathetic sounds. But the voice of the man penetrated my feeble defence. "You'll not be marrying no papist!" he growled. "You'll not go against my will!"

I looked about the darkness in confusion, my hand resting again on the door as I tried to comprehend what was happening. That the first voice was Harriet's was doubtless, yet the voice of the man remained unidentifiable. It had the resonance of the Townsend men and was spoken in an accent that was what I took to be a mingling of Lancashire and London. It could have been Harriet's father, for he had come to Warrington as an adult after having grown up in London. But I could not be sure, unaccustomed to the subtleties of English dialects as I was. It could have been John, merely speaking slowly and properly to make himself clearly understood. Or . . .

It could have been Victor . . .

"But I love him," whined Harriet.

There was another slap and another scream. The suspense was unbearable and yet I could not move. It was as though I were being forced to hear their conflict without being allowed to interfere.

"You'll not see Sean O'Hanrahan again and that's all there is to it. Been warned about them O'Hanrahans, you have. And if I catch you writing any more of these letters, by God, girl, you'll wish yourself dead."

Now I heard a peculiar scuffling sound, like something being dragged across the floor. There were heavy footsteps and the puffing sounds of some-one exerting himself. Harriet whimpered pitifully. But no more violence was heard, no more slaps or crashes and screams. Just the scuffling, then a brief silence, and then the sound of a door clicking shut, with a key turning in the lock.

Suddenly, the door to the bedroom swung open under my hand and a cold wind blew into my face. There was a strange light in the room, like the one I had first seen shining on Harriet as she had cried petulantly on my bed. Its glow now, however, did not centre on the bed, but upon the clothes wardrobe, like a guiding beacon in the night.

I stared at it with wide-stretched eyes, recognizing the familiar taste of horror and the crawl of gooseflesh along my arms. I did not want to go in. I wanted to turn and run, fall down the stairs and scream and run out into the night. The lurking shadows of the bedroom, the malevolence of the air, the unearthly draught filled me with a sense of the supernatural. On the other side of the door existed a realm not of this world. And I was being drawn into it.

Almost trancelike, yet with every atom of my brain alert and silently screaming, I walked to the clothes wardrobe, and when I came to a rest before it, I saw how new it looked, how polished the wood and distinct the grain. It was the clothes wardrobe of times past, and it contained, I knew, not my old blue jeans and T-shirts but the grisly handiwork of a tyrant long dead.

I could not control my hand as it reached out to touch the door. A mis-erable sweat sprouted all over my body and started to run down in rivulets of ice. My breath came short; I felt the agonized fluttering of my heart. Never before had I known such fear, such acute terror.

There was something inside the wardrobe.

For some reason I dropped my gaze to my feet and saw near them, on the bright carpet of 1891, a few crimson spots of fresh blood. They seemed to lead up to the wardrobe in a little trail, with one last drop staining the bottom of the wardrobe as though it had leaked out just as the door was being shut.

Had Harriet been locked in here by one of the brutal Townsend men? Or was I now reliving the moment of another event, an altogether different occurrence?

How many times before had I felt the uncanny lure of the wardrobe, even on my first night here, and how were these incidents related?

Was it possible that it was not Harriet trapped on the inside now, but someone else? Or . . . *something* else?

While my body began to tremble violently I still had no control. I had to reach out and open the door of the wardrobe. I had to see what was inside.

And as my hand raised up against my will—*as though someone else had control of my body*—and as I felt nausea rise in my throat to choke me, I also thought, I am being forced *to set this thing free.*

My hand, though it shook uncontrollably, managed to grasp the key that sat in the little brass lock and I saw how white my fingers were as they held it tight. Then, fight it though I did, my hand slowly turned the key to the right until I heard a click.

And the wardrobe door started to creak open.

My senses swam with dizziness and nausea. A cold clammy hand reached up to my face and felt the rain of perspiration there. My hand, feeling as though it belonged to someone else, as though it were disembodied, ran across my forehead and then along the back of my neck. The wardrobe, with its door inching open, started to twist and turn before my eyes. The floor lurched beneath my feet and the eerie light that had been shining on this spot now began to fade.

As the boundaries of the dark moved in on me I managed to glimpse a patch of white on the other side of the wardrobe door, and then the blackness fell altogether across my eyes.

⚜

When I came to I was lying on the bedroom floor with a small painful lump on the back of my head. Blinking in a daze, I looked straight ahead and saw that the light in the hallway was on, that the single bulb was burning brightly and that it shed enough illumination into the bedroom to reveal my surroundings. Looming above me, dull and wormy, was the clothes wardrobe, one door standing open to display a few hangers and some blue jeans. The carpet beneath my nose was old and faded and smelted musty.

How long I had lain there after fainting I could not tell, but as I tried to get up, I saw how painful and stiff my joints were. With a sizable headache and a thumping at the back of my head, I groped my way out of the bedroom and down the hall. At the head of the stairs I paused to listen for any sound from Nana's room, but all was quiet again, and I thanked God that I hadn't awakened her. Deciding to leave the upstairs light on, I then made my way slowly down the stairs and entered with great relief the light and familiarity of the sitting room.

I knew where Nana kept her special headache tablets in the sideboard, so I helped myself to three of them and, getting a glass of water from the scullery, took them quickly and then returned to the sitting room. I locked the scullery door securely, knocked the sausage into place with my foot, and went to sit on the couch.

According to the clock, my ordeal had taken three hours, which meant that I had been unconscious for at least two, if not more. And the residual effect was a sickly one, my whole body aching and throbbing in protest of what had happened.

And just what had happened? I tried to recall the conversation, if you could call it that, I had overheard in the front bedroom. One of the Townsend men bullying Harriet. Although it had been more than mere bullying. It had been a terrorizing, possibly torturing. And why? Because she had had the bad luck to fall in love with someone he didn't approve of?

I bent forward and cradled my head in my hands. Oh, the agony of loving someone who must be forever forbidden to you!

I rocked back and forth in this position for some time, listening to the heavy rain beyond the window and bemoaning the fate of poor Harriet. Such an innocent thing, I thought, so childlike and naive. What was going to become of her, I wondered; what further unhappiness was I going to be witness to? First Victor and now Harriet. Could it be, then, that there truly were certain horrors that had existed in this house at one time and that Nana had been right? Was the evil only now beginning, a foreshadowing of things to come?

I gently lay down on the sofa, keeping my head on its side and not knowing which was worse, the bump on the back or the tender burns on my shins, and I lay staring far into the night It was just like the previous night with my mind alive and swirling with thoughts and the blessing of sleep too far away to be had. If I could have begged for relief I would have, but knowing that the house on George Street had no intention of letting me go until it was done with me, I lay on the sofa at its mercy, agonizingly awaiting the next appearance.

Sleep must have come at one point, for my grandmother awoke me the next morning, pulling apart the curtains and exclaiming on the heavy rain. Once again, as with previous mornings, I was in my nightgown with the covers pulled over me and my clothes folded neatly on the chair.

"You were nice and quiet last night, love," she said in a voice that was laced with fatigue. "You must have slept well. Now me, I had a restless night The rain always makes me arthritis flare up."

I slowly sat up, wincing with the small pain at the back of my skull.

"How's your legs this morning?" Nana was going around the room as if waking it up for the day; drawing the curtains, opening the scullery door, setting out the place mats on the little table, and lastly checking the heater. At the sight of it she cried, "It's gone off again! What's the matter with the blooming thing! I shall have to have the gas man out to look at it. Never happened before, this going out all the time."

Still saying nothing, I moved in a fog, gathering up my things and going towards the door. As I started to go out into the hall, I heard my grandmother say, "There'll be no visiting the hospital today. The rain's too bad."

Too numb to reply, I slipped out into the hall and hurried up the stairs.

In the bathroom, where the air was so cold that I saw in the mirror my lips had turned blue, I doused myself with freezing water and slowly towelled myself dry. Unlike previous mornings, the cold did not affect me now. I had got used to it.

When I was finished in the bathroom, I stood outside the door and stared down the length of the hall at the front bedroom. Its door was closed and stood in dim shadow. Memory of the night's terror gripped me again, made me draw my arms about me and shiver even though I wasn't cold. Just hours before, on the other side of that door, one of the Townsend men had inflicted some awful punishment on Harriet.

With wooden feet and a heaviness of heart, I made my way down the hall. Far below me, coming subliminally through the floorboards, was Nana's voice humming a gay tune. She lived in a different time. I came to a halt before the door and swallowed hard, running a dry tongue over my lips. I stared at the door for some time, straining to hear any sounds that might possibly be on the other side, and then finally seized the knob and turned it.

Inside, the bedroom was quite normal.

Although raining heavily outside, a watery morning poured through the half-open curtains to shed enough light into the room to dispel its sinister aspects. There was my suitcase, the bed, the small nightstand, the faded rug, and the clothes wardrobe. To this last I strode with a mechanical step and stood before the open doors, looking in.

My blue jeans hung where I had left them. And two T-shirts. On the floor of the wardrobe were a few clumps of fluff, evidence of years of unuse. Nothing more. No clues as to what might have been stuffed in here late one night in 1891. No way of knowing what it had been or how long it had been trapped in here.

Suddenly anxious to be out of that bedroom and downstairs in my grandmother's company, I spun around, dropped my things on to the bed, and dashed out of the room. With a resounding bang I slammed the door and fled down the stairs.

At the bottom, I found the parlour door standing open.

I froze in the middle of the little hallway, staring at the open door. My nerves grew taut, stretching to the limit of their endurance like rubber bands about to snap. What year are we in now? screamed my mind.

Indecision made me falter. While I preferred the familiarity and comfort of Nana's sitting room, I knew that if the past were living again in the parlour I must see it. My ears caught the chill air of the hall, reaching out for the slightest sound. When I heard something, my heart skipped a beat.

Taking a deep breath, I took a few tentative steps into the dark parlour. There were sounds of someone (or some*thing*) moving about inside.

I lingered in the doorway, my hand reaching out to rest on the jamb. I tried to see into the darkness and found there, vague and undefinable, a shape moving within. Tilting my head to one side, I tried to examine the air around me, sending out invisible feelers to try to discern in which time frame I stood.

And as I stood poised in the doorway, my eyes straining with the abysmal blackness, a white face suddenly appeared.

I sucked in a gasp and fell back.

"Too cold for you here, love," said my grandmother as she pushed past me, closing the parlour door behind her. "You'll want to be in the sitting room by the fire. There's a love."

"What were you doing in there, Nana?"

She hobbled ahead of me into the sitting room, her head eclipsed by the curve of her old back. "Just tidying up a bit, love. Tea's ready and I'll have the drop scones out in a jif."

As Nana disappeared into the scullery I took my usual seat at the table by the window and stared morosely at the unappetizing display. There was a big pot of steaming sweet tea, a tub of butter, pots of various flavoured jams, a box of granulated sugar, and the usual unlabelled bottle of warm unsterilized milk. I turned my eyes from the fare, feeling my stomach writhe in nausea, and looked at the torrential rain falling against the window.

Nana's little yard could hardly be seen through the downpour. The brick wall at the rear with its rusted green gate was just a hazy backdrop to the waterfall that obliterated the window panes. The dead rose bushes could almost be seen through the rain, bending away from the storm, their grey stick branches heavy with water. It was a miserable dreary world out there, cold and watery and all the colour of dull metal. Streams of water ran down the window like iron bars and I had the brief notion of being a prisoner in a cell.

"Nice and hot, there's a love."

I watched Nana as she approached the table with a platter of drop scones, still sizzling from the pan. The thick aroma hit my nose like a slap and I had to avert my head. Food was deplorable to me this morning. Not even the tea was an enticement.

"What's the matter, love, don't you feel well?"

"I guess it's like you said, Nana, I must have a touch of the flu. No, I don't feel well at all." I rested my chin in my hands and kept my eyes on the storm outside.

What in God's name had been in the wardrobe last night?

"You're pale, you are. Best drink your tea, love. Do you a world of good. Here, plenty of sugar in it and a dash of milk. Good and hot now." She pressed the cup into my hand. "You know I usually have some iced buns of a Saturday, but I haven't got down to the green to get some. P'rhaps tomorrow. Here now, love, you're not drinking."

I sipped the tea to assuage my grandmother, but it did nothing for my stomach. In fact, my whole body revolted at the idea of eating or drinking anything. Looking out of the window, I felt as if the same rain were falling in my soul.

We sat in silence for a few minutes, Nana buttering a scone and heaving it into her mouth. I listened to the tick of the clock, watched the storm rage without, and waited for the interminable time to pass.

A knock at the front door roused me. Watching Nana scuffle on her cane out of the room, I tried a few more sips of tea, felt my stomach churn, and pushed the cup away from me. Out in the hallway rang the voices of my Aunt Elsie and Uncle Ed.

"Blasted weather!" exclaimed my aunt as she blew in shaking like a dog. She began at once to peel off gloves, raincoat, overcoat, woollen hat, and rain boots. Then she lumbered to the heater and stood with her back to it, hiking up her skirt.

"Hullo, love," she said to me. "How's it going this morning?"

"Hi, Elsie . . . "

"Goodness, you are pale! Didn't you sleep well? Is it too cold for you at night? Look at you, barely a thing on!"

I looked down at my T-shirt, then up at Elsie, who wore a woollen jumper over a turtleneck sweater, and a heavy cardigan over all that. Even then she shivered and rubbed her hands.

"No, I'm not cold."

"Heater's been going off," said Nana, coming into the room behind Uncle Ed. "Got to get the gas man out. Here, have some tea. Got plenty. Oh, Andrea, you've hardly touched yours!"

"This is my second cup, Nana," I lied. "I poured myself another when you went to the door."

She patted my hand. "There's a love."

"She don't look too well, Mum," said Elsie, joining us at the table. Uncle Ed, having poured himself a cup of tea, took a seat before the heater. I watched him out of the corner of my eye, afraid he might turn up the gas.

"I'm all right, really. Can I go to the hospital with you today?"

"Go on with you! I should say not! I'm not even sure Ed and I'll make it today. The rain's a proper devil. Can I have a scone, love? Thanks. Ain't no one on the streets today. It's too heavy. You can see for yourself."

Nana and I turned to the window. "I feel like I'm in a fish bowl!" said my grandmother. "What about tomorrow? Think we'll still go?"

"Might not if this keeps up."

I snapped my head up. "Go? Go where?"

"Why, to your cousin Albert's. You remember."

"Is tomorrow Sunday?"

"If today is Saturday it is."

I turned to the window again. If today was Saturday then that meant I had been here a whole week already. An entire week had gone by and I hadn't been aware of it. In a way, it seemed to have passed in the blink of an eye—didn't I just arrive here last night? And yet in another, stranger way, I seemed to have been here for years . . .

"Our Ann will be coming from Amsterdam. She does want to meet Andrea."

Nana got up from the table and went to the sideboard where she picked up the little framed photograph of her other three grandchildren. There were Albert, Christine, and Ann, my cousins whom I had never met. Sitting down again, she held out the picture and pointed to each one as she spoke. "Now this was taken a couple of years ago . . . "

I let her voice fade away and the picture blurred before my eyes. I was not interested in these people. I had nothing in common with them, no bond, no desire to get to know them. It was the others, my *past* relatives, that I wanted desperately to be with.

Snatches of Nana's and Elsie's words pierced my subconscious. Something about a cottage on the Irish Sea. A tide that went miles out. Piers with restaurants and dancing. Illuminations at night.

I looked up at my nana, and then at my Aunt Elsie. How on earth was I going to be able to stand an entire day with them? How was I going to be able to leave this house and drive the fifty-odd miles to the west coast, meet strangers, talk and chat and eat with them and pretend to have a good time?

"By the way, Mum, I've brought you a few things. A nice piece of fish off the green, some potatoes for chips, and a cabbage. Couldn't find no iced buns today, sorry. Now, was there anything else?" Elsie slapped her fleshy cheek. "I almost forgot. Our Ruth called up this morning."

I swung around to face Elsie. "My mother?"

"Aye. Took me by surprise it did. Early it was, must have been about ten o'clock in Los Angeles. She says her foot is healing nicely. Wants to know how Andrea's doing and . . . "

"And?" said Nana.

"Well, she sort of wanted to know when Andrea was coming home."

"Home?" I echoed feebly.

"Oh well," said Nana briskly. "She ain't seen half the family yet has she? And you can't really say Robert's seen her yet. And now she's feeling poorly. And here's the rain keeping us from Albert's." She turned to me. "What do you think, love?"

I shook my head a little. "I can't go yet, Nana . . . "

"'Course not," she said affectionately. "How can you leave after coming eight thousand miles and only staying a week? You've got to make it a proper visit you have, see the house where you was brought after you was born and where you lived for two years, ay? And you can't rightly say you've seen your granddad, now can you? Make it a proper visit, there's a love."

The room grew suddenly hot. I felt the air close in on me, the walls loomed close as if about to topple over. Flying over the North Pole in the British Airways jumbo jet I had entertained little other thought than how soon I would be going back home. And my first day or two in this horribly cold house I had constantly thought ahead to the day when I would be getting back to L.A. But now . . . it was all different. I didn't want to leave. I *couldn't* leave.

"What did you tell my mom?"

"I said we had yet to go to our Albert's so you could see your cousins. She'd want that, you know. And I told her about Granddad's condition, how the only times he's awake he thinks you're your mum. But Sister says he'll come round soon, he often does, although it's usually late at night, and when he does you'll have a proper visit with him like. You know, Andrea, he used to love to bounce you on his knee. But you wouldn't remember that . . . "

My mind meandered off in another direction. How ironic to think of Victor's son bouncing me on his knee!

"Best be going, love," said Uncle Ed, getting to his feet and stretching. "No hospital today I'm afraid. We'll be washed out to sea in our little car. We'll be lucky if we make it home."

"Right you are. I said hello to your mum for you, Andrea, and told her what a nice time you're having here." Elsie started applying her layers of clothing. "Here, Mum, you stay by the fire. Andrea can close the front door after us, can't you?"

I accompanied my aunt and uncle to the front door where they paused before opening it. Glancing past my shoulder to be sure Nana wouldn't hear, Aunt Elsie whispered to me, "It's this house, isn't it?"

My heart gave a leap. "What?"

"It's so cold. And that little bit of a gas heater just isn't what you're used to, coming from California. You're not sleeping at nights, are you? Look how pale you've got. Listen, why don't you come and stay with us for the rest of your visit?"

I unwittingly fell back a step. "Oh no, Aunt Elsie, I couldn't leave Nana. She's all alone." The falseness of my words rang sharply in my ears. Only a few days ago I would have jumped at the offer. Central heating, colour TV, bright lights, and thick carpeting everywhere. Now, of course, I shivered with horror at the thought of leaving. Only it wasn't for Nana's sake that I wanted to stay.

"Andrea's right," murmured Uncle Ed. "Your mum's lonely now that Granddad is in hospital. Andrea's good for her right now."

"Aye, but look at Andrea. I don't think this place is good for her!"

"Thanks for the offer, but I'd rather stay."

"Very well then. But if you should change your mind, let us know. We'd love to have you. And if the rain drops off by tonight we'll stop in and take you to hospital with us. All right?"

"Yes, thanks."

As Uncle Ed yanked the door open and the gale swept into the hall, Elsie said quickly, "And we'll just have to see about going to our Albert's tomorrow. Ta ta, love."

I had to fight to close the door after them, getting wet in the process, and once it was locked I kicked the sausage into place and went back to the sitting room.

It was some time later, sitting in front of the fire and having fallen asleep under the drowsy effects of the afternoon, that I had the first erotic dream.

CHAPTER 12

*T*HE DREAM WAS, BY ITS NATURE, VERY DISTURBING. THE scenes were not fixed or orderly, they told no story, nor really made any sense other than sexual imagery. There was Victor's warmth, the tenderness of his mouth on mine, and there was the elusive smell of him, the male mystery of his body. He would come to me from out of a cloud, his arms outstretched ready to embrace; or he would beckon to me from the end of a long dark road. Sometimes we reached out, fingertips touching, or we would find ourselves lying in a field of tall grass, making love beneath a blue sky and warm sunshine. None of it made any sense; I tried in vain to ask him why this was happening, but he never spoke—there was no communication between us. Just coming together and flying apart, touching, feeling, savouring each small physical intimacy, but never reaching an understanding.

The images flashed before my eyes like scenes on a carousel, wild and unharnessed, filled with lust and sexual need. It was as though my soul were a bird trapped in a cage, fluttering, beating its wings in a frantic attempt at freedom. There was no peace in my slumber, no rest, just the rising and falling of my tethered passions, like the swelling and crashing of an outraged sea.

I awoke in a sweat. Never in all my life had I experienced such sexual desire, never known a man to have such power over me. My craving to know Victor Townsend in the flesh robbed me of sanity, of control, of *identity*. It left me, waking up in the easy chair, devoid of any other purpose than to be a slave to his power.

When I let out a moan it startled me. Quickly looking over at my grandmother to be certain she still slept, I got shakily to my feet and stumbled to the window. Outside, the rain fell even more torrentially, beating down on the earth like some demonic punishment. I rested my burning forehead against the cold pane and tried to ease the pounding of my heart.

How was it possible I should feel such things now when I had never known them before? What magic had Victor Townsend over me?

"Is he gone?" said someone behind me.

I whipped around.

Harriet was just entering the room and quietly closing the door behind her. John, who stood stiffly by the fire, said again, "Is he gone?"

"Yes, he's gone."

"You didn't tell him I was here?"

"No, John."

As Harriet crossed the room to join her brother by the fire I was startled to see how much she had changed. The flush of youth that had been her one redeeming physical trait seemed now to have been stamped out, leaving her only with the heavy features that comprised her plainness. She appeared to have been under a strain; the onus of some unseen burden had dulled and flattened her face. And yet it appeared, by her outfit, that little time had passed, for her dress was the same I had seen her in last.

John had not changed, he was the same—a vague reflection of Victor, but with brown hair and lighter eyes and features that were softer and subtler. He was, I noticed, extremely agitated. "When will Father be home?"

"Not for an hour yet."

"Good, good." He rubbed his hands together in secret thought.

"John? What's it all about? Who was that man?"

"Hm? What? Oh—" John waved his hand as if to dismiss her. "No one. Just a man."

"He's been here before. When you weren't in. Who is he? I don't like the looks of him."

"It's none of your business!" snapped the brother suddenly, causing his sister's face to widen suddenly in surprise. Immediately penitent, John forced a smile and said, "Let's just say he's a business associate."

Harriet nodded and slowly turned away from her brother. She wrung her hands as she walked around the bright green easy chair, her face puckered in worry. Not the unexplained man at the door, but something else was troubling John's sister. And from where I stood I could see how carefully she deliberated her next words.

"John. I saw Victor today."

He didn't look up. Her brother was preoccupied, staring into the fire in concentrated thought.

"I saw him on the green. He says he's terribly busy now, got a lot of patients, he said. That's why he doesn't come by. I invited him to supper. I told him Father would love to have him visit, but I don't think he'll come. John, will you ask him?"

He brought his head up. "What? What's that? Oh, Victor. I've been by his office. Not bad. Gets a lot of following from the hospital I understand, got himself in well with the surgeons there. I've asked him already, Harriet, but he don't seem anxious to visit. It's not Father, I know, 'cause they've patched that up."

"What then?"

John shrugged. "Dunno."

"John, I think Victor should come home. For good, I mean."

"Aye . . . " He turned his back on her, his face receding again into deep thought.

Harriet went on, "I don't like him having a room at the Horse's Head. He needs a proper home with proper meals. You and Jenny have lived here a year now, it's time you were moving out. If you got a house of your own then I could have the upstairs bedroom and Victor could come home where he belongs."

She paced back and forth, twisting her fingers together, her skirt making a whooshing sound as she walked past my sleeping grandmother.

"John, I want to talk to you about some—"

"I know what it is," he said irritably, swinging around with an angry expression. "You want to know where my money's gone. Well if you must know, that man who came to the door a few minutes ago was a bookmaker. My bookmaker, and he was here because I owe him a few quid. That satisfy you?"

"Oh, John . . ."

"Aye, *oh John*. I'd have done all right if I hadn't just picked a few bad geegee's. Could've bought a house last week. And don't you tell Father 'cause he'd have my hide."

"Oh John, I don't care. Stay here if you like. Stay forever. I don't care about your gambling."

"A few horses aren't gambling."

"I want to talk to you about something else. John, listen—" She rushed towards him, pressing her hand on his arm. "I need your help—"

But John shook his head. "It's that potato-eater Sean O'Hanrahan you're on about, isn't it?" he said darkly. "I don't want to hear nothing about it. Get mixed up with popery and you ask for trouble. I've told you to stay away from him, and that's final."

"But I love him!"

"You're out of your mind! The subject was closed long before now, Harriet, and I don't want to hear that name mentioned in this house again. And if I ever see you speaking to that sod again, I'll—"

"You're just as bad as Father!" she cried. "You've all gone against me! I can't talk to Victor either. He's changed, he's gone real moody and when I try to talk to him I know his mind is on something else. It's been a year, John, *a whole year* since Victor has stepped foot in this house! And you don't seem to care! And you don't care about me, either."

John only turned away from her and went back to staring into the fire.

"And you," she went on, her voice becoming that of a bewildered child. "Since you've got married you're a stranger to me. If you're not with Jenny then you're at the race track. You have no time for me any more, just as Victor doesn't, or Mother and Father. Don't you see I need your help, John?"

It was strange that the scene should fade at this point, unfinished and unconcluded, Harriet's childlike voice pleading to be heard, but I was glad it did because my legs had grown weak by the window and I had been afraid I would slump to the floor before John and Harriet were through. As it was, I barely made it to the wooden straight-backed chair at the table before I collapsed into it and cradled my head in my hands.

A few minutes later my grandmother finally stirred in her chair and opened her eyes, "Crikey," she muttered, "Drifted right off, I did. Oh but me joints do ache. It's this rain. I shall never make it up them stairs."

I slowly lifted my head to see her struggle out of her chair, leaning heavily on her cane and hobbling over to me. In the light of the room I saw again how old she was; how terribly, terribly old.

"I'm not up to cooking tonight, love, me joints hurt ever so badly. Would you mind getting yourself a bit of supper?"

"Aren't you going to eat, Nana?"

"No appetite, love. It's the rain got me down. I shall go upstairs now and read a bit of Tennyson before going to sleep. Nights like this, when the weather's so bad, I always lie abed and not stir up my arthritis. If you don't mind, love, I shall just go on up."

"Nana."

"Aye, lovey?" She kept moving towards the door, bent over her cane.

I considered what I had been about to blurt out impulsively and decided against it. Much as I would like to have sat down and told Nana everything I had seen in this house, the fear of losing it all prevented me. "Nothing, Nana. I hope you sleep well."

"I shall, lovey. Good night. There's bread and jam in the scullery. You know how to make tea. Fish tomorrow with chips and peas."

I watched her close the door behind herself and then heard her heavy steps on the stairs. When the door opened up again a second later, I thought Nana had changed her mind. But then I saw it was Jennifer coming into the room.

And when I saw who walked in behind her I nearly cried out.

"It was good of you to come, Victor," she said, crossing the room to the fire. Once again the satiny upholstery of the easy chairs reflected the fire's glow.

"I would have come long ago had it been you who asked me."

"We've all been hoping you would visit. Warrington is such a small town and yet you might as well be in another country, we see that little of you."

Victor Townsend stood with his back to the door as if afraid to come any closer. He had changed a little in the year; his hair was longer and his fine suit bespoke prosperity. But the face remained the same: impassive, unreachable with the same dark dispirited eyes.

Jenny swung around, her slender graceful body silhouetted against the flames, and folded her hands in front of her. "We've missed you."

"Have you?"

She dropped her eyes a moment, then raised them again. "Yes, I have. I had hoped for a long time you would come and visit, but you never came."

"I've been busy. It seems that the reputation of my education and training precedes me wherever I go. I don't lack for patients, and they seem willing to pay."

"You are known for your low rates, Victor, and for the fact that if a person can't afford to pay you'll treat him anyway. You're a success here in Warrington. Coming from King's College with new ideas, you've given the stodgy old doctors in this town something to think about. We're all proud of you."

"Aye, it's a good practice, mine. Adequate I should say, tending to broken bones, red throats, and vapoury ladies."

Jennifer smiled. "You make it sound so dreary."

Victor returned the smile, and it looked out of place on his face, as though he hadn't smiled in a long time. "A doctor's life is not a romantic one. Although possibly not dreary, it lacks the glamour people like to think."

"And . . . otherwise, Victor . . . are you doing well?"

He stared for a moment. "Aye, I'm doing well. And you, Jenny?"

Although I saw her stiffen, I wondered if Victor did, and yet surely he must have, for his own eyes were more rigidly fixed upon her than were mine. Her voice came out stilted. "Yes, I'm doing well."

Victor finally pushed away from the door and strode across the room. He came to a halt inches in front of Jenny, towering over her with his dark gaze. "Are you, Jenny?"

"Of course . . . "

"Come now," he said softly. "I'm his brother. I've known him all his life. John and I have no secrets. He's still gambling, isn't he?"

Jenny bowed her head, unable to reply, and studied the carpet. Placing a finger under her chin, Victor brought her head up again until their eyes met once more. "He is, isn't he?"

"Yes," she whispered.

Letting his hand drop, Victor stepped away from her and walked to the other side of the fireplace. Leaning on it with one elbow and tracing a finger over the Staffordshire dog, my great-grandfather said, "And it's got worse, hasn't it? Oh, I know. I shall spare you the embarrassment of having to tell me. Harriet's been to see me several times and has told me of it. So the men are coming to the door now, are they?"

"Can you help him, Victor?"

Once more he took a moment to study her face. Victor must have seen the same thing I saw—the large, doe-like eyes, the quivering mouth, the thinly arched eyebrows, and the overall loveliness of Jennifer. And I know how it must have touched his heart. He was still in love with her.

"Is that why you asked me here?"

"No!" She took a step forward, her face dismayed. "Oh no, Victor, you must not think that! I would never have brought up the subject of John's problem. I asked you here because I wanted to see you, and because I feared you were never coming back. It's been so long . . . " Her voice trailed off.

"It was only you who could bring me back to this house, Jenny. Harriet has tried many times. John has asked me, and even my father has broken down and asked me to come home. But it was you I was waiting to hear ask me, because you were the reason I stayed away."

The melancholy that I had seen in her photograph now swept over Jenny's face, a touching vulnerability that I felt move Victor's heart as much as it did mine. I know also that my great-grandfather was struggling with himself at this moment, fighting the impulse to take Jenny in his arms.

"I'll help John if you want me to."

"Oh, Victor . . . "

"But only because of you. John has too much pride to ask me himself, although I am not so sure I would help him if he asked. But you, Jenny, you should be in your own house now and thinking about a family. It's for your sake only that I'll help my brother."

But Jenny shook her head. "You must not do it for my sake, Victor. You must do it because you want to. Because he is your brother—"

He gave a short laugh. "Yes he is. So that makes you my sister, right? Or rather, sister-in-law, which is the same thing."

The bitter edge in his voice caused Jenny to bring a hand to her throat. Fumbling with the cameo brooch, she said, "It's not the same thing . . . "

To my surprise, Victor suddenly rushed to Jennifer and seized her by the arms, holding her tightly as if to shake her. A fury erupted on his face, a black tempest that startled both Jennifer and me and that caused us both to gasp. "Then what is it!" he said in a throaty voice that was almost a growl. "What are we if not brother and sister?"

"Victor, I—"

"Oh God!" he cried, releasing her just as suddenly as he had taken her. "What's got into me! My own brother's wife! Am I mad?"

"You can't help it," she said in a rush. Jenny's cheeks now flushed crimson and I wondered if his touch and his nearness had sent her hopes soaring for one moment. "Just as neither can I."

Although Victor glowered angrily at her, I knew that it was rage with himself that he felt and not with Jennifer. For her, this fragile woman who had filled his every waking and dreaming moment for over a year, Victor felt only a shuddering tenderness, as though he might any minute cry for want of her.

"This cannot be . . . " he whispered at last. Now Victor's face took on the look of defeat. "I have lived with this moment for a year, knowing that someday it must come, that the hour would arrive when you and I would finally confront one another. And I have often wondered in my dreams if I should be able to stand up to it and guard my dark secret. But I see that I cannot. For I am after all only a man. Twelve months have done nothing to lessen my love for you, Jennifer. A full year of working and sweating and immersing my hands in blood have done nothing to mollify the ardour I feel for you. Have I been sentenced to some ungodly punishment for a crime I don't remember committing?"

"If that is so," she murmured steadily, "then I have received the same sentence."

My great-grandfather stood so still for the next few moments that I wondered if the flow of Time had been somehow stopped. But then I saw him breathing and heard the faint tick of the Victorian clock on the mantel. And finally I heard him say in a distant voice, "I had only dreamed you loved me. I was never sure. And when I suspected it, I was afraid that it was only my wild hopes that had misread the message in your eyes. I was like a drowning man grasping for a straw. But now I see I was right after all. Then you do love me. And I wonder now if this isn't worse punishment than having you not love me at all."

"It's no punishment, Victor—"

"Oh God!" he cried. "If not punishment, then what? Just knowing that we are doomed to go through life like this, always seeing, sometimes touching, but never . . . never *loving*?"

When a tear trickled down Jenny's face, Victor stood close to her again and gently wiped it away. "I should have gone to Scotland. The night I so foolishly returned with my empty hopes for our future together and found you had married John, I should have left Warrington then and looked for far-away places to practise my medicine. But I was a fool. Just as I was a fool when, after meeting you that first night so long ago I decided I must come back and marry you, so was I a fool a year ago when I didn't leave your life altogether. For now we have this torment."

"Is it such a torment, Victor?"

"To know that I can never kiss you, to know that you must go to my brother's bed? Yes, that's torment."

"And what about the moments we do have together, like now, alone and enjoying one another. Can't a word or a smile suffice? Aren't they better than *nothing*? Think of the loneliness, Victor, if we were apart. Think of your empty years in a foreign land, and think of my lonely nights with a man I thought I had once loved but who has proved me wrong. Is it truly better for us to go separate ways, always wondering, or is it better to grasp what we can and make of it what we can?"

He spun away from her and rammed a fist into his palm. "I can't answer that! Right now I want to be with you and never leave. But when I am in my office and realize the painful truth of our situation, then I think how easy it would be to pack my bags and leave."

"Easy . . . ?"

"No, not easy! But better, by God!"

As their voices rose, the power of their emotions filled the room and surrounded me. I was drawn into their frenzy. I felt the clashing and mingling of their passions, suffering the combined anguish of both of them. It drove straight down to the core of my soul and tore me apart. I could no longer help myself. I had to succumb.

"Victor!" I screamed.

He swung around, startled.

And then they were gone.

The night became an agony. As my strength began to ebb from lack of sleep and food, I frequently drifted off into bits and pieces of slumber that left me no better rested than before. I was visited again with erotic dreams: visions of Victor, glimpses of us together, a taste of what his intimacy might be like. In my dream state his love reached out to me like tendrils of gentle mist, enveloping me, embracing me. I quivered with anticipation. But there was never any ultimate fulfilling of my desire; always it remained just at the edge of reach. My mind deceived me, toyed with me, and left me in the end utterly miserable and frustrated.

In my waking moments I marvelled at the transformation going on within me, as though a multitude of personalities were waking up. A hundred souls awoke and stirred within me, each one awakening with a different hunger, and each craving to be sated. I had never before experienced such erotic fervour, not even at the height of lovemaking, for never before had any man reached so far into my core. It was as though every single nerve in my body were charged with electricity, as though if I were to turn out the lights I would glow in the dark. There was not one part of me that wasn't alive and stimulated. And it seemed that only Victor Townsend would be able to gratify me.

At other times, when I stood by the window and felt my ardour cooled by the rain-washed glass, I reflected upon my strange dreams and wondered what they should mean. That I was in love with Victor Townsend was obvious and that I sexually desired him was also beyond doubt, but why he should be such an obsession with me, when no man in my past had ever been, was beyond understanding. The dreams seemed to be peculiarly symbolic, involving my great-grandfather as they did, and revolving mainly around sex. It was almost as if by making love with my great-grandfather I was completing the circle of life. Just as he had once given life to me, by begetting my grandfather and therefore my mother, so now was my long-dead great-grandfather receiving new life through me.

The notion was absurd and I discarded it as quickly as I did a myriad of others. I had simply fallen in love with a man who appeared to me as real as if he actually lived, and therefore my thoughts could not escape him. That he was my great-grandfather could bear no significance, for in truth I thought of him only as Victor Townsend.

But I slept again, drowsing in the chair as an unwitting victim of Morpheus, and continued to experience the disturbingly erotic dreams.

At midnight Jenny and Harriet met one another in secrecy.

Their sudden entrance awoke me, the clicking shut of the door disturbing my brittle slumber, I blinked my eyes and saw Harriet glide past me and come to a halt before the fireplace. The clock over the mantel said eleven, which I assumed to be in the evening.

Little time had passed now. Jenny looked exactly the same as she had awhile before with Victor, and Harriet was little changed from when I had seen her with John. That is, in appearance. In manner and composure Harriet had altered a great deal.

Twisting a lace handkerchief in her hands as if to tear it to shreds, Harriet pressed her fists into her stomach and she stood stiffly, jerking every now and then, and tossing her head back in a nervous affectation.

"What is it?" whispered Jenny, her face set in concern.

"Have they all gone to bed? Are you sure? Where's John?"

"He's still out. But we shall hear him come in. No one can hear us, Harriet. What is it?"

"Oh Jenny . . . " Screwing her face into a grimace, Harriet squeezed a flood of tears down on to her cheeks. "I'm so *scared*. I don't know what to do!"

"Harriet," said Jennifer in a calm, even voice. She reached out for those writhing hands and tried to hold them in her own. "Now tell me what is wrong. It can't be all that bad."

"Yes, it can. Oh Jenny . . . " she whimpered hoarsely. "Promise me you won't tell anyone. You're the only friend I have."

"Of course I won't tell anyone."

"Not even Victor. Especially not Victor."

Jenny's eyebrows rose. "Very well. I'll tell absolutely no one. Now what is it?"

Jerking her hands out of Jenny's grasp, Harriet turned away and walked a few steps. "I . . . I need to know something. I want you to tell me something."

"If I can."

Harriet worried over her next words, chewing her lower lip and attacking the handkerchief once again. She was plainly struggling with herself, trying to find the right beginning, forming words with her lips but letting no voice come out. Finally she spun around and regarded Jennifer with frightened eyes.

"Jenny," she said slowly, shakily. She dropped her eyes to the carpet, desperate to confide in her sister-in-law but bound by the rules of a puritanical age. "I need to know something and yet I have a hard time speaking about it. Please help me."

Jennifer, although the same age as Harriet, was a married woman and more mature than her friend. Seeing her sister-in-law's distress, Jennifer was easily able to adopt the role of confidante. Laying a comforting hand on Harriet's arm, she said gently, "There is nothing in all the world that you and I cannot talk about."

Harriet looked up, her cheeks flushed, her eyes bright. "It's my time . . . " she whispered. "Jenny, I've missed my time."

Jennifer stood for a moment, taking in the words and their significance, and finally breathed, "Oh, Harriet . . . "

"It's hard for me to talk about," said the distraught girl in a tight voice. "You know how it's always been. Especially with Mama. When it first happened, when I was twelve years old"—Harriet's voice dropped to a whisper—"I was frightened to death. I thought I was *dying*. I didn't know what was happening to me! And Mama was no help. All she said was that it makes me a woman and that I was to stop crying and that I was to expect it every month for the rest of my life. She never *explained* anything, Jenny. Just a few words on how often to change, the need for eau de cologne, and the strict order that we never mention it around the men. Jenny, you know all this. Mama told me I was never to complain about it, never to mention it, to just pretend it doesn't exist. But Jenny!"

Harriet's hand darted out and seized Jennifer's wrist in a desperate grip. "I was frightened when it first started. But now that it's stopped, *I'm scared to death!*"

Jennifer continued to gaze at Harriet in worried silence, her face deep in thought.

"Tell me what it means, Jenny. I think I know, but I must be sure. You can tell me."

"How long has it been, Harriet?"

"I . . . I'm not sure."

"Are you *very* late?"

"Jenny, I've missed *twice*."

"I see . . . " Jennifer maintained complete calm, her hand still resting on Harriet's arm, her face as composed as if she were discussing the supper menu. "Tell me, Harriet, have you . . . done anything that might have caused . . . this miss?"

"I think so," came the timid reply.

Jennifer closed her eyes for a moment. Oh, the delicacy of the subject!

"Jenny, I didn't know! No one ever told me!" said Harriet in a rush. Her face was startled, bewildered. With eyes perfectly round and her face now gone white, Harriet resembled a bisque doll. "Sean said it would be all right. And I didn't know, even at the time, what it was we were doing. I had always thought you could only have babies *after* you got married, not *before*. We went to the ruins of the Old Abbey. At first I was surprised. But then I liked it. And then"—she dropped her eyes and murmured shyly—"I loved it."

There was a brief flash in Jennifer's mind. A pang of envy? Fleeting, benign. Just a small stab of remorse that her own experience with John had been a disappointment. He was rough, hurried, and thoughtless of her own desires. And then the pang of guilt, recalling how she had closed her eyes to imagine Victor there in the darkness instead of her own husband. Such a small deceit, one which helped her through the infrequent attacks which were her marital duty to bear. Thinking it was Victor, wondering what it would be like with him: gentle, tender, and lingering . . .

"How long ago was this, Harriet, with Sean O'Hanrahan?"

"Well, it was . . . " The handkerchief came apart in her hands. "It was a few times. But he said it was all right. Oh Jenny! Is that what I've done?"

"It's not what you've done, it's what he's done, I'm afraid."

"No! You'll not talk of him like that. I love Sean O'Hanrahan and we're going to be married. But we shall do it secretly so Father can't stop us. Promise me, Jenny, that you won't tell Father."

"You have my word, Harriet, but you should tell Victor."

"No!"

"He's a doctor, Harriet. He can tell you what to do. Maybe you're wrong. But if you're not, then he'll tell you what to do."

"I can't tell Victor! He'd despise me for it!" Harriet broke down and started to weep.

Jennifer took the girl in her arms and held her tightly. Harriet wept until Jenny's dress was wet, then she sobbed and hiccupped until a long time had passed.

When she seemed to have control of herself again, Harriet stood back from Jenny, wiped at her eyes with the shreds of her handkerchief, and said falteringly, "Then do you think that's what I've done? That I've got a baby in me?"

"If you did something with Sean O'Hanrahan. If you're sure of what it was you did."

"It's what married people do, he said. He wanted to show me what it would be like."

Jennifer nodded gravely. Privately she mourned the passing of Harriet's sweet innocence.

"I didn't think it was possible. I really didn't. Not *before* you got married. But now it's done and I have to deal with it."

"Harriet." Jennifer held out her hands. "Please go to Victor."

"No!" Harriet fell back a step. "He would kill me!"

"Oh no—"

"Yes he would!" she screamed. "Victor would kill me! You don't know him like I do! He's just like Father!"

"Then what do you intend to do?"

"Sean and I plan to go to London and be married."

"Oh, Harriet." Tears also streamed down Jennifer's face and I sympathized with her inadequacy of words.

Harriet hesitated for just a moment longer, staring wildly at Jennifer with a look in her eyes that chilled us both, then she turned on her heel and ran out of the room.

I turned to watch her go, saw the door slam behind her, and when I turned back was surprised to see Jennifer still in the room. I would have thought the scene would have ended there, unless more was to come. So I remained in my easy chair and watched.

How extraordinary that the young woman before me should have died so many years ago! Couldn't I hear the rustle of her petticoats? Didn't I see the glitter of tear drops roll down her cheeks? Couldn't I smell the delicate fragrance of roses about her and even feel her presence in the room with me? How was it possible that she was not real?

As I stared at her and pondered these things, a strange thought quite suddenly entered my mind and jarred me. It was the fleeting memory of my last visit with Jennifer and Victor, or rather, the end of it when, so overcome with the power of their feelings, I had recklessly called out Victor's name.

And he had turned around.

My God! Had he heard me? I had forgotten that! Yes, I remembered now, I had been unable to contain myself any longer and had screamed out Victor's name. And he had spun about, startled.

Dear God, did that mean . . . ?

I kept my eyes on Jennifer now. For some reason, the time slip was lingering. She was staying longer than usual. Or possibly it was I who remained. Whatever, my glimpse into the past was lasting longer than I would expect it to, so that I began to wonder if there were a reason.

Why was I still seeing Jennifer? Was it for some purpose? She stood here alone, as real as if my grandmother stood by me, and she dried her teary eyes on a hanky produced from the sleeve of her dress. She and I were alone in this room together it might seem, and yet years apart. She was living in 1892. I was in the present.

Why, then, were we still together?

A notion occurred to me which at first I tossed aside as ridiculous. But then, after a few seconds of smelling her perfume, of hearing the movement of her skirt, of feeling her nearness, and of seeing her, I began to wonder if what I had both hoped for and dreaded all along weren't finally coming to pass: after all the *senses,* the last avenue of communication—speech—to make my involvement complete. With everything else so real, did it remain that we should now speak? And had not Victor turned around when I had called his name?

Yet she couldn't see me. She stood there, just inches in front of me drying her eyes, and was oblivious of me. I wondered, Would my speaking to her produce the magic necessary for our final confrontation?

It was worth the risk. All that could happen was she would disappear. And with Harriet gone and nothing more happening she would have disappeared anyway. So I should try it. I should open my mouth and speak to her.

Summoning up all my courage and swallowing my fears, I cleared my throat and said in a loud clear voice, "Jennifer."

CHAPTER 13

NANA MUST HAVE COME QUIETLY INTO THE ROOM, FOR it was not until she whipped the curtains apart that I awoke. "Look at that rain will you!" she said, shaking her head at the window.

I rolled my head to the side and blinked at the storm which besieged the world outside. Then I rolled back and looked up at the ceiling. My head felt as if it were made of wood.

"Slept late, you have," she said, moving about the room. "Good sign, that. It means you got your rest last night."

I tried to hide a wry smile. Nana didn't know that I had fallen asleep only at sunrise after sitting up all night.

"Tea'll be ready in a minute. Would you like some treacle on your toast this morning, love? P'rhaps it'll give you a little pick-me-up." Although Nana forced energy into her voice, I noticed how weary she sounded. "Your granddad always did like some treacle on his bread. And I shall fry you some lovely fish today with mashed peas. There's no going to Morecambe Bay, not in that wet."

I looked again at the incredible gale which whipped around the house and wondered how long we would be prisoners here. "Nana," I said, sitting up and feeling a bowling ball roll around in my skull. "Granddad had no visitors yesterday. What about today?"

"We shan't be going, that's for certain. Maybe your Uncle William will go alone. No sense in getting everyone drowned, is there? Now run up to the bathroom, there's a love."

I took the stairs two at a time, hastily washed and refreshed myself at the sink, then went into the bedroom for a change of clothes. Only fifteen minutes had passed before I was back downstairs and sitting at the table.

"You can feel the draught come right through the glass," said Nana, buttering her toast.

I watched her face in the cold morning light, saw the bluish lips, the pasty colour and puffy eyes. "You didn't sleep well, did you, Nana?"

"No, love, I didn't. Bad weather always makes me joints ache. And when they do I can't get comfortable. I shall need three hot-water bottles tonight."

"Why don't you sleep down here by the heat?"

"Get on! It's you needs the heat more than me! And I am quite used to me own bed thank you. Another cardigan and one more hot-water bottle shall do me fine."

"Your bedroom must be like a tomb, Nana."

"Elsie says this whole house is a tomb, so it don't matter where I sleep. But I like living here and won't be letting anyone take me off to one of them government flats . . . "

She chatted on. And I thought, This house is more of a tomb than you think.

No one came by to visit us, for the rain was so bad that it was impossible even to open the front door. From the bedroom window upstairs I looked down at the street and saw how dangerous it would be for a car to go even a short distance, so I knew that my relatives had suspended their visiting for the duration of the storm.

Nana and I remained by the fire, she with her knitting and I ostensibly reading a book. But my eyes only pretended to scan the pages, for my mind was racing with other ideas, none of which had to do with the present.

By midafternoon Nana's hips hurt so badly that she couldn't stand up to make the fish and chips for dinner, so instead we heated a can of soup and made do with that and some buttered bread. This was adequate for me, as I still had no appetite, but I saw how disappointed my grandmother was that she hadn't been able to fix me a treat.

Finally, after our simple meal and after an hour of silence and staring out at the formidable rain, Nana said, "I think I shall go up to bed now, Andrea. Can't sit down here much longer else I shall never get up them stairs. Bring me the bottles when the water is ready, won't you, love?"

"What will you do all afternoon, Nana?"

"I shall have on the wireless and read my Tennyson. It does relax me so. I'm sorry to have to leave you alone, love, but I'm no company now anyway. I just thank God that your granddad is warm and dry and out of draughts. And he's got good nurses looking after him. That's my solace."

For once I had to help my grandmother up the stairs, pushing her from behind as she scaled each step on hands and knees like a dog. It was a slow process, but when we reached the top I saw how impossible the task would have been for her alone. She went terribly white and had trouble breathing. "I'm eighty-three years old, love," she gasped. "I've seen better days."

She wouldn't let me help her get undressed, but insisted I return to the warm sitting room until her water had boiled. Once it had, I filled the three rubber bottles and took them back up to her room. Here, amid a clutter of Victorian memorabilia and bulky furniture, I helped make my grandmother as comfortable as I could. She propped herself in bed with several pillows, draped three sweaters around her shoulders and then a crocheted shawl, stuffed the water bottles around her legs, and then brought the portable radio near at hand on the night table. "I shall be quite comfy here, love. You go on down now."

"If you need anything, Nana, bang on the floor with your cane and I'll come up. You'll get hungry later and I'm sure you'll want me to refill those bottles."

"Aye, love. You're a blessing, you are. How I prayed God would send you to me." She readied up and embraced me with one arm. When she fell back into the pillows I saw tears well in her eyes. "Soft me!" she cried. "But you are just like your mum when she was your age. Not a bit of difference! Get on with you then, down to the warmth."

I hurried back down to the sitting room, not for the heat, since I no longer felt the cold, but in the hope that I would return to the past again soon.

My wish was answered as, opening the door, I saw the sitting room of 1892 spread out before me, glowing in the firelight, and Jennifer seated quietly in one of the easy chairs.

Very slowly and unobtrusively did I enter the room and close the door behind me. The air felt fragile, as though even my breath might shatter it, so I stepped carefully away from the door and pressed myself against the wall.

From where I stood I could see the embroidery hoop in her hands, the glint of the needle as it went in and out of the cloth, the thin streak of crimson that was the thread. Jennifer wore her hair piled on her head and held it in place with little ribbons. Her dress, a pale lavender, covered her entirely from the high-necked collar to the hem of the skirt about her feet. Stitching peacefully as she was, her face creamy pale in the glow and her small hands delicately working, Jennifer created a picture of serenity and femininity.

As I watched her I remembered my thoughts of last night and how I had wildly hoped to speak to her, and how I had even called out her name. But it had been a fanciful notion on my part, for the theory had not proved true. The minute I had uttered her name, Jennifer had disappeared.

So here she was again, sitting quietly and alone, and I sensed, even at my distance from her, that her thoughts were of Victor.

Heavy feet fell in the hallway behind me and I sucked in my breath. We were going to see him again!

The door swung open in front of me, a cold wind blew in, and then it slammed, revealing to my disappointment John Townsend. He stood still for a moment, wavering slightly, and stared at Jennifer, who had looked up from her work.

"You're soaking wet," she said, starting to rise.

"Don't bother about me," growled John, waving a hand before his eyes. I could see how bloodshot they were and could smell the liquor fumes as he spoke. "Just you worry about yourself."

"What are you talking about?"

"You!" he shouted, flinging out a hand and pointing a shaky finger. "You betrayed me, your own husband!"

"John!" Jennifer flew to her feet, letting the embroidery fall to the floor.

"You went to Victor, didn't you? You told him how badly in debt I was, that the bookies were after me, that I couldn't stop gambling."

"Oh, John . . . "

He took a step towards her and I saw the concern in Jenny's eyes turn to fright. Her hands went to her breast as he came towards her, but she stood her ground.

"It's not true, John," she said quietly. "I didn't go to Victor."

"Then how does he know so much? He even knows the amount I owe, right down to the last copper! And he offered it to me, Jenny, *he offered money to me!*"

"What's wrong with—"

"Have ya got no pride, woman?" he bellowed, coming close to her now and trembling in a rage. "Did ya have to go mincing to my brother with our private troubles? Where's yer shame, woman?"

"It was Harriet, John. She went to him, not I."

"That's a lie! Harriet wouldn't talk to Victor about tilings that weren't her concern! She's not daft ya know. It was you, Jenny, and I know it because I've seen how you two look at each other. Your eyes get like proper cow's eyes when you look at my brother and don't pretend they don't. And he ain't very good at hiding his thoughts either. He damn near salivates when he looks at you!"

"Oh my soul!" whispered Jennifer, turning around and burying her face in her hands.

"What did you have to go to him for, Jenny?"

John teetered a little on his feet; his eyes seemed not to focus on his wife. It upset me to see him so, wet from the rain and dishevelled from drinking. His greatcoat was spattered with mud and his top hat sat on the back of his head.

"Did you think I didn't know any of this, Jenny?" he said now in a softer voice, his words slurred. "Did ya think I don't know why Victor comes over every Sunday for his dinner? Crikey, woman, my brother stays away for a year, living in the same blooming town and never coming by, and then you drop him one note and he's panting on our doorstep like a dog. And he's been coming by every Sunday since. Do you think I have no eyes?"

Jenny's only response was the shaking of her small shoulders as she cried into her hands.

John reached out tentatively to her, but stopped, swaying a little, I saw in his profile the bewilderment of sudden understanding and of the frustration of knowing. He had only voiced a suspicion, but now he had his answer. And he was sorry he had.

Opening and closing his eyes a few times, as if to dispel the drunken fog, and then letting his hands drop to his sides, he murmured, "I'll not let him have you. I know you never loved me, but my brother will never—"

Jenny spun around, her face set in horror. "Oh John, that's not true! I did love you, and I do still love you! How can you stand there and accuse me of lying and deception when it isn't true? It was Harriet went to Victor about your gambling debts, John, not I. And I do still love you."

He gave some thought to her words, then said, "As much as you did when we first got married?"

She hesitated too long.

Turning on his heel, John Townsend stormed back to the door and flung it angrily open. "We shall not be taking charity from my brother!" he bellowed. "Victor has everything now, hasn't he? He's got money, he's got the reputation of a saint, and now he's got my wife. Well I tell you one thing, woman, he won't be getting far with them!"

I felt the whole room shake with the slamming of the door, and when I turned back to look at Jennifer, she was gone.

It was Nana's sitting room again. The beautiful green upholstery of the easy chairs was replaced by the Woolworth covers. The rug was threadbare again and the fire was gone. I was alone once more in the present.

These episodes were creating a strain on me, for the sudden appearance and disappearance of the Townsends was each time a shock. My nerves were beginning to tell the effect of my sojourns with the past, my hands had a tremor, I had lost my desire to eat, sleep was not to be had, and all the while my mind raced in circles.

Here was something new to puzzle and vex me. How was it that Victor Townsend had come down through the years with the stigma of evil attached to him, when from all that I saw it was John? Victor Townsend had been a good, kind, and honourable man, dedicated to alleviating suffering and devoted to loving one woman in his life. How was it then, with him being the martyr and John the drunken gambler, that the roles became reversed?

I felt the room grow hot. Despite the torrential rain outside and the biting cold that blew through the old house, I found myself despising the heat. Irritably I got up and turned off the gas heater. As I bent forward to absently scratch my shins, which were now peeling where they had been burned, I heard the distant strains of a piano drift over the air.

I straightened up abruptly.

"Für Elise" again, that haunting Beethoven melody ringing in a kind of sad melancholy, filling the room from all directions at once. The clock on the mantel had stopped. I had gone back in time again.

Slowly and cautiously I moved about the room, reaching out with invisible sensors to locate the origin of the music. As I circled the chairs and drew near to the wall which separated me from the parlour, I heard the piano grow louder. Experimentally I walked, almost tiptoed, to the door and soundlessly drew it open.

The music was coming from the parlour.

Leaving the brightness of the sitting room and merging into the darkness of the hallway, I made my way along the wall to the parlour and found the door slightly ajar. There were lights on inside.

With trepidation I pushed on the door and slid my head through, finding on the other side a room I had never seen before.

A noisy, roaring fire illuminated bright velvet chairs, papier-mâché tables, horsehair sofa, figurines, glass boxes, leafy plants in brass pots, photographs crowding the walls, and in the centre of the ceiling—to my surprise—an electric light.

I stared up at this last for a moment, with the delicate notes of "Für Elise" filling my head, and then I looked finally to my right at the small spinet against the wall.

I drew in my breath and held it.

Dressed handsomely in a maroon frock coat and black trousers with a starched white shirt and black cravat was my great-grandfather, seated at the piano and playing "Für Elise." His long wavy hair fell forward a little as he bent over the keyboard, his face masked in deep involvement.

Jennifer, seated before the fire and wearing a long satin gown, was regarding him with an expression of rapture, the sublime admiration of one whose love is as limitless as the universe which contains it.

I must have matched her look, for I, too, fell under the spell that Victor wrought, turning a mere musical instrument into a machine of enchantment. His artistry amazed me, but not as much as did the magical way in which he transformed a simple piece of music into a bewitching melody.

I remained unmoving in the doorway, torn between two minds: wanting the music to go on forever, and wishing him to stop so that he could speak to us.

When he did stop it was only to sit for some time and stare at the keyboard, as though requiring an interval to draw himself back to the present. Victor had set his soul free with the notes of "Für Elise" and now he had to draw it back in again and be its master once more. Jennifer also sat suspended, reliving the song in her mind, holding herself still and not wanting the moment to end. I felt her adoration fill the room.

"Can you play it again?" she asked after a length.

Victor swung around on the piano seat and placed his hands on his knees. "I haven't much time. The others will be home soon."

"They should love to hear you play."

He shook his head. "They must never find us alone like this, Jenny, or else they will believe what they fear in their hearts and read into our actions something that has not taken place." His face darkened. "Or never will."

"Please come and sit by me."

Victor filled the small room with his stature, striding to the chair next to Jennifer and sitting down, stretching his legs before him. He crossed one foot over the other, his boots shining in the firelight, and said, "My brother has accused us of indiscretions. How ironical, when not even a handshake has passed between us."

"Don't be bitter, Victor."

"Why not? To come here every Sunday and sit in the same room with you and pretend that I am not thinking what I am thinking? You seem content, Jenny, to rest satisfied with what we have together. But you see, I am not. How cruel fate can be." He let out a short, dry laugh. "And what practical jokes are played on us! If only I had told you long ago that I was going to return to Warrington, then you would not have gone ahead and married John and right now you would be the wife of the most prominent physician in Warrington! But instead you are married to a man who spends his days at the race track and his evenings at the pub."

"Please, Victor," she said softly.

"I think John should face up to his vices and try to straighten himself out. He's running from his creditors now, and it's only a matter of time before they catch up with him. He borrowed money yesterday to repay Cyril Passwater today because of money he borrowed last week to pay off Alfred Grey. How long can he keep that up? He won't take my money, and God knows I've enough, but instead he keeps up this dangerous game of robbing Peter to pay Paul. John should stand up like a man, face his creditors, and work out some sort of arrangement with them. And at the same time put an end to this gambling business."

"It's easy for you to say, Victor, but John doesn't see it that way. Each day he thinks he'll have the one win that will pay off everyone and give us the house we need."

"And each day he falls deeper into debt. Jennifer, you don't dig one hole to fill another! If it were up to me—"

"It isn't up to you. John's his own man and although he may not have much else, he does have his pride. Victor, you mustn't interfere."

"If he weren't married to you I wouldn't give a hang. But he is and he's making your life wretched for it! It's only for your sake, Jenny, that I want John to clean up this business."

"Then for my sake as well leave him alone. John must find his own way."

"He needs a shock, needs to be forced to show his hand—"

"Victor . . . "

He regarded Jennifer, the furrow between his brows deep and angry. Victor's cynicism was difficult to curb; his frustrations too frequently mastered his tongue. It was not only the problem of his brother and the woman he loved, it was his own life as well that drove Victor Townsend to trenchancy.

"Promise me," said Jenny quietly, "that you won't interfere with John."

He scowled into the fire. "If it is your wish, then I promise."

As I watched his face I had some idea of the thoughts that went on behind it, for I received brief glimpses into his mind. I saw the results of Victor's medical genius, the reputation he had earned in the year and a half since returning from London, the improvements he had brought about at Warrington Hospital, the lives he had saved, the pain he had relieved, and how he had been rewarded. At this moment Victor Townsend was the personal doctor of the Bishop of Warrington, and also attended upon the family of the Lord Mayor. His youth, his innovations, and his success had led Victor to certain public accolades that had then earned for him the high esteem of influential figures.

Yet it was not what he wanted.

There remained in my great-grandfather still the desire to explore the world of test tubes and microscopes and discover through science the road to greater medical advances. I saw in his mind the frustration of being unable to help the victims of tumours of the brain or of failings of the heart. Victor Townsend, though a practitioner of great acumen, was helpless in the face of countless incurable diseases that continued to decimate the innocent population of the world. Here was where he was needed, here in the blind spots of medical care. Victor Townsend wanted to be one of the men who lit lamps in the dark corners of medicine.

"What are you thinking about?" whispered Jenny.

"A man named Edward Jenner. Do you know who he was?" Now Victor turned to her, the darkness gone from his face and replaced by an urgency. "Edward Jenner was a man who one day wondered why milkmaids never got smallpox. He also noticed that milkmaids almost always came down with the cowpox at one time or another. Now, Edward Jenner wondered if there was a connection between the two; what if it was possible to inoculate a person with the lesser disease and thus save them from the killing one? Everyone laughed at him, Jenny, but Edward Jenner's smallpox vaccine has made us all able to live free of fear of that dreaded disease that once took whole cities at a go. But what about the others? What about pneumonia, cholera, typhus, polio?"

He leaned forward and seized her hands. "What am I doing here? Prescribing syrups for coughs and tranquillizers for hysterical women. Even in surgery I have no satisfaction, for I am limited by my own knowledge. So much remains yet to be found! Do you see what I am saying?"

"Yes," she said in a small voice. "You should have gone on to Scotland."

He dropped her hands and flew to his feet. "That is not what I am saying. The laboratory that awaited me in Edinburgh can just as easily be constructed in Warrington."

"Then what are you saying?"

"That I am a man running about in circles. I have allowed my bitterness and my frustration to immobilize me. Why should I struggle and fight when the one true thing I want in all the world will be forever denied to me?"

Jenny also came to her feet and she placed a light hand on his arm. "Am I to be the cause of your downfall as well?"

My great-grandfather looked as if he had been physically struck. Shock and horror crossed his face. Overcome by the significance of her words, he relinquished himself to an insane impulse and drew Jenny hurriedly into his arms.

She did not protest. Dropping her head against his chest and closing her eyes to savour the moment, my great-grandmother fought the tears of her own twisted unhappiness.

"What have I been saying?" he murmured into her hair. "How can I have been so selfish as to wound you with such ravings? There is nothing more important to me than your happiness, Jenny, oh Jenny . . . " Victor drew her harder to him, as if to drive out the anguish. "How can I have been so thoughtless to say such things when I know that your own life must be as miserable as mine! And you suffer so silently while I indulge in self-pity! Truly, truly I don't deserve you . . . "

They clung to one another for a long moment, cutting a tragic silhouette against the firelight, until, with great reluctance, Jenny drew back a little and looked up at him.

"To feel your touch," she whispered. "To feel your arms about me like this is . . . is . . ."

Victor bent his head as if to kiss her, but stopped.

"You must go now, my love," she said. "They will be home soon. These things are forbidden to us, Victor, for no matter what he is, John is still my husband and I must remain true to him. It is not for us to know one another's kiss. And if we allow this one thing, then where will it lead us? What will we allow next time, and the time after that until there is no time left?"

Jennifer pulled completely away from his embrace and faced him gravely. "We must not be alone again, Victor, for I shall not be able to control myself. And then we can add guilt to the rest of our misfortune."

My great-grandfather stood like a graveside mourner, his arms hanging at his sides, his face a mask of insensitivity. Jennifer continued to stare up at him, her small frame trembling, her eyes filling with tears, and they remained thus as they faded from my view.

I stood for some moments with my back to the open door before I realized that the parlour of long ago had disappeared and that I was once again in the dark mustiness of Nana's storeroom. There were the sheets draped over the furniture, the rolled-up rug, the dust-covered desk, the dingy walls. It had taken me only a few seconds to make the journey back from 1892 and yet I felt as drained and fatigued as if I had walked all the way.

Closing the parlour door, I stumbled into the hallway, seeking its coolness and appreciating now its encompassing darkness, like a shroud that comforts, and continued to hear in my ears the echo of their last words together.

How lucky Jennifer had been to have been loved by a man like that! It was something I had never known. Or . . . had I? Was this what Doug had tried to offer me, and what I had been foolish enough to shun?

A sharp thumping overhead brought me out of my thoughts. Remembering Nana and that her signal to me was to be her cane, I quickly went upstairs. Turning on the overhead light, I went to her bedroom door, quietly opened it, and stuck my head in.

Nana was fast asleep in the pillows.

Another thump brought me to draw my head out of her room and close the door. Of course! The sound was not of the present but of the past. And it was coming from the front bedroom.

The door already stood wide open, revealing the Victorian interior. Once again, everything was new and bright, the walls decorated, the rug and drapes no longer faded but their original colour, and a fire in the fireplace. I also noted with interest that the gas lamps had been replaced by electric ones, as with the one in the parlour, so I assumed that the modern age had made one small conquest over the indomitable Mr. Townsend.

I stepped all the way in and looked around. By the fire was a red-velvet wing chair, white doilies draped over its arms, and in it sat Jennifer, her small feet on a little red-velvet footstool, staring ahead.

Watching her for the moment, wondering if I should try again to speak to her (how inconceivable it was that I should be able to see, hear, smell, and almost feel these people without being able to communicate with them!), I soon felt a cold draught at my back and saw through the corner of my eye someone enter the room.

It was Harriet. She said, "Jenny."

Stirring out of her daydream, Jennifer turned a little in the chair and then smiled. "Hello, Harriet. Please come in."

But the girl hesitated beside me. Her hair, I noticed, seemed haphazardly stuffed under her feathered bonnet and the cloak which hung over her shoulders and hid her dress seemed to have been thrown carelessly there. I also noticed that Harriet's face was a peculiar grey and that her lips were completely white. "Jenny," she said again.

Now also seeing the same signs of distraction about her sister-in-law, Jennifer rose to her feet and took a few steps forward. "What is it, Harriet?"

"I . . . " She stepped forward, faltered, and then swayed a little, as if she were going to faint.

"Harriet!" Jenny rushed forward, put an arm about her shoulders, and led the distraught girl to the wing chair. Harriet was like a rag doll in Jenny's hands, flopping down into the chair, allowing the cloak and bonnet to be pulled from her. There was a curious detachment in her eyes, a dazed look that was of someone who had suffered a great shock. She appeared so much younger than Jennifer now, sagged in the chair as she was, her homely face a queer white, her eyes glazed over. Harriet moved her lips but no words came out.

Taking the other chair in the room and drawing it up before Harriet so that their knees touched, Jennifer took the girl's hands and rubbed them between her own. "You've got cold. Look how white you are! Where have you been in this weather, Harriet?"

Bringing herself around, Harriet said in a muted voice, "Where is everyone, Jenny? Where are Mother and Father?"

"Father's still at the mill. Mother has gone to visit poor Mrs. Pemberton, who is bedridden. And John, well, I don't know where John is just now. What's the matter?"

Harriet turned that peculiar gaze to the fire and stared blankly at the flames. Her lips, which were grey, moved again without saying anything.

Jenny narrowed her eyes in concern. As I watched, the whole room took on an oblique aspect, almost a dreamlike atmosphere that was created in part by the silence and the soft shadows but mostly by the strange manner of Harriet.

"I went to him . . . " she whispered at last.

"What did you do, Harriet?"

"I went to him. Just like you said I should."

Harriet brought her head around and, shaking it, seemed to focus her eyes on Jennifer. Then she said in a slightly huskier voice, "I went to Sean and told him about my trouble."

"What did he say?"

Harriet's voice was as expressionless as her face. "He said it was my fault and that he had nothing to do with it and that he is going away."

"Going . . . " Jennifer fell back in her chair. "Sean O'Hanrahan is going away? Where to?"

"I don't know. Even while I was with him he was packing his trunk. He said something about going back to Belfast."

"But . . . but you *did* tell him about—"

"About the baby? Oh yes. And proper mad he was, too. As if I had sat down and done it all by myself. I reminded him of how he had spoken of weddings and such when we were at Old Abbey, how he had said he wanted to marry me as soon as possible. But that was then, Jenny, and I guess there's no reason for him to want to marry me any more."

"Oh Harriet . . . " Jennifer worked her hands over Harriet's, trying to massage some life back into the girl. Not even the flicker of the yellow and orange flames in the fireplace could paint the imitation of life on Harriet's face. She was deathly white.

"Harriet . . . " murmured Jenny again, her heart going out to the victimized girl. Although her own age, nearly twenty, Harriet was very childlike. But the education she was receiving about life and reality was beginning to show on her face.

"And then I went to him," she whispered again, her eyes once more staring into the fire.

"Back to Sean?"

"I went to *him,* just like you said I should. I had nowhere else to turn. I couldn't tell Father, for he would punish me ever so awfully. You don't know what he did to me when he found out Sean and I were writing letters. But this time he wouldn't just lock me in the wardrobe. He'd do something much worse."

"The wardrobe—"

"He used to do that to me, you know," she continued in a distant, detached voice. "To punish me he used to lock me in the wardrobe and it got so bad that I would behave not out of respect or of a sense of right and wrong but because I was afraid of going back in there, I couldn't stand it, Jenny, if he did that to me. I used to squat inside that dark wardrobe, with not the slightest bit of light coming through the cracks, and hear him turn the lock, and then wait and wait for the time he would open it up and let me out. I used to be afraid he would forget me and I would die in there. I would scream at first, and then I would just whimper and beg and scratch at the door. I had the feeling I was being buried alive. But he always did come back for me. There was once . . . when I howled so bad that he came and got me, clouted me insensible, and then threw me back in for the whole night. I thought I was going to go insane that time. But I didn't. He'd do that to me now, Jenny, and worse. Father's very proper and very strict. If he knew about this, he'd say I did it to shame him. You know that, Jenny, you know what he's like. You've seen how frightened Mother is of him, and how John obeys his every word. John never wanted to stay in Warrington and be a clerk. But he had to because Father said he had to, Victor was the only one who stood up to him . . . "

When Harriet seemed to have forgotten what she had started to say, Jennifer urged gently, "So who did you go to, love?"

"My brother. I thought he might be able to help me. And I guess . . . I guess . . . he did . . . "

As though unaware of what she was doing, Harriet absently held out her right arm, rolled up the sleeve, and presented her white forearm to Jennifer. In the hollow of the elbow joint was a red blotch, and leading from it were purple stripes.

"Harriet, what is this?"

"It's from a needle. What do you call it . . . a hypodermic needle."

"How did you get it?" Jenny bent close to examine the small wound. "It looks infected."

"It is. But it'll go away, he said."

"Harriet, I don't understand. What happened? Who did this?"

She had to take hold of the girl by the shoulders and give her a little shake. Harriet turned her face around again but the blankness of the gaze remained.

"I'm homely, aren't I?" she said in a small voice. "I'm too plain for gentlemen to look at. I shall never be married. Not now. I loved Sean O'Hanrahan. He was all I wanted. But now I shall be a spinster until I die."

"Harriet, tell me about the needle."

She drew in a long breath, but it rattled and her skin grew even paler. Jennifer thought briefly that Harriet looked like someone who had just touched death. "It was to put me to sleep, he said. He wanted to put me to sleep. But it didn't work somehow . . . maybe I was too frightened. Maybe he didn't give me enough. He made me lie down on the table. I tried to get up but there were straps. I told him I wanted to go to sleep. I begged him. I pleaded with him. But he was angry. That must be why he did it. He said I had disgraced the family."

"Harriet, what are you—"

"He had an instrument. I saw it flash in the lamplight. He held it in his hand and told me to lie still. My own brother . . . "

"Oh God . . . " moaned Jennifer. "Oh dear sweet God . . . "

"He said it was the only way. He said he was saving me from future suffering. He said I wouldn't feel anything—oh, Jenny!" Harriet suddenly slumped forward and buried her face in her hands. The crying sounded like that of a kitten; she trembled in a pathetic way and tried to talk through her fingers. "But I was awake the whole time. I felt the whole thing. The pain, oh, Jenny, the pain was incredible! You have no idea! It was like torture, feeling that instrument, so sharp and so crude, scraping the life out of me. Jenny, it was only when I could no longer stand the pain that I finally mercifully passed out."

"Harriet, Harriet," murmured Jennifer, falling forward and burying her face in Harriet's hair. "Oh my poor sweet love. Harriet, Harriet."

They cried for some time this way, Jennifer cradling Harriet in a protective embrace, trying with her voice to drive out the anguish, trying to soothe and mollify. But finally Harriet lifted her head and gazed at her sister-in-law with the bewildered, innocent eyes of an injured animal. "What shall I do now?" she whispered.

But Jenny was at a loss for words. Her shock was too great.

Removing herself from the embrace, Harriet struggled to her feet and out of the chair. She stood uncertainly before the fire, her body quivering. The pallor of her face startled me and when I saw her try to take a few steps, I started forward to catch her fall. But Jennifer was up and holding on to her, steering her to the bed.

"I just want to die," said Harriet. "My own brother. How could he have done that to me? Oh dear God, let me die . . . "

When they took a few unsuccessful steps towards the bed, Harriet paused and looked down at the floor. With shaking hands she slowly lifted the hem of her long skirt. And there on the carpet spreading quickly in its warmth and freshness, was a pool of blood.

CHAPTER 14

HERE WAS TO BE NO REPRIEVE FOR ME THIS NIGHT, FOR although I was nearly prostrate with exhaustion as I fumbled my way down the hall towards the stairs, I was soon to be drawn back to witness yet another event of the past.

The horrible crime that had been committed upon Harriet had shocked me with equal force as it had shocked Jenny. Although everything pointed to Victor, I could not believe him capable of such an atrocity. And yet, even John I could not suspect it of. He might have been wayward and weak, but he wasn't evil.

As before, I was granted no time to puzzle this out or to recover from the blow, for just as I reached the head of the stairs I heard again the sounds of commotion coming from the front bedroom.

Events were happening rapidly now.

I returned to the doorway, leaned on the jamb, and watched John pace the floor before the fire with Jenny again seated in the wing chair. Her dress was different so I knew it to be a different day.

"Must it be so?" she said in an agonized voice. Her eyes followed her husband as he stalked back and forth like an animal in a zoo. The Townsend fury was etched on his face, darkening his eyes and tightening his chin. At this moment, John looked more like Victor than he ever had before.

"I have no choice," he mumbled. "I have no choice."

"Couldn't you face them? Couldn't something be worked out? Must you run off like this?"

He whipped about. "And what would you have me do? Run crying to the sods and expect a little tea and sympathy from them? Jenny, they're a rotten bloodthirsty lot! They don't care a hang for my personal life. All they want is their money."

"Then let Victor—"

"No!" he boomed with such ferocity that it startled both of us. "I shall not accept charity from my brother. And I especially want nothing to do with him now."

"John, surely you don't believe—"

"Leave that blackguard out of this. After what he did to Harriet I want nothing to do with him! As for me, I'm going to run because that's the only way I can keep my hide."

"Then I shall come with you."

"No you won't, my love," he said in a gentler voice. "You must stay here and wait for me. I will be gone in a few days, but I can't say where. Nor can I tell you when I'll return. I have to hide for a little while and let the heat blow over and find a way to get a few pounds together. In the meantime, you'll wait for me, won't you, Jenny love?"

She stared up at him helplessly.

Suddenly John was on his knees before her and grasping her hands. "I love you, Jenny, even though you don't love me. No, don't say anything, let me go on. I've thought about it a bit now, and I've seen what my neglect of you has caused. And of my own sister as well. If she'd have come to me instead of going to Victor . . . " John shook his head. "Don't want to think of that now. It's over and done with. But us, Jenny, we still have a chance. I'm planning a little trip, and I don't know how long I'll be gone. But you'll see, when I come back I shall set things right between us. Be a different man, I will, and I'll pay off those sharks and leave the horses alone forever. You'll see, Jenny love."

"John," she murmured sadly. "I wish you didn't have to go."

"But I have to and that's the end of it. But I'll be safe because no one knows I'm leaving. It will be a nice quiet slip-away. Now remember, Jenny, it's a secret. They're not to find out, 'cause if they do then I shall be in danger for me life. You do understand, don't you? Right now I'm one step ahead of them. But if those sods were to learn that I was planning to run . . . I hate to think of it. Between me and you then?"

Her shoulders slumped forward. Jennifer seemed to collapse inward. "Yes, John. I shall tell no one."

When my head finally cleared I was back downstairs and sitting by the window looking out. The barest trace of a morning showed through the rainstorm, and even of that my eyes perceived little. It was the sound of the rain pelting on the window that brought me out of my reverie, and I was not surprised to find that I must have been sitting like this for some time. Vaguely, in the murky pool of my memory, I recalled finding my way downstairs and staggering wearily into this straight-backed chair.

I looked around. The room held no warmth, no comfort for me now. It was cold and grey, like the watery world outside, and I felt a oneness with it. There was no light in my soul, just dead coals. The night had been too much to bear. It was not merely that I was a witness to all that I saw and heard, but rather that I was in some way forced to *feel* it all as well. Whatever emotions my dead relatives could conjure, I seemed to become infected with them. Helpless victim that I was, I was being inflamed by passions that no longer existed except within these bizarre slips in Time. Why was it, I wondered, that while I could shield myself from the forces of living people, the dead ones seemed to find a way in? How much more was I expected to suffer before I would be set free? If ever I should be set free.

And then again, did I want to?

Wearily I pushed myself to my feet and dragged myself over to the gas heater. Nana would be up soon and she would be exclaiming again about the faulty pipelines or some such. To save myself from having to hear once again about the mucky products British manufacturing was producing these days, I lit the heater, set it at its lowest possible setting, and wandered away.

Eventually I felt the sofa give way beneath my weight and I let my head fall back.

Did I really want ever to leave this house and go back to my previous existence? I wondered bleakly. How could I turn my back on the sweet devotion of Jennifer or the excitement of Victor's nearness? Even John's frenzy and Harriet's anguish had made me come alive and had made me feel, for the while, that I was finally a complete person. Was this their magic, their ability to bring me to life, to wake up to feelings that I had never before experienced?

I was now thriving on the brief episodes in the past as a drug addict lives only for his fixes. While I lived in the moment of my ancestors, despite what torment the instant might hold for me, I was truly alive. Whereas the periods in between, left to myself and without their spark, were interminable limbos.

The hours dragged by this morning. I looked at the clock frequently, each time wondering how five minutes could seem like an hour.

Nana did not come down.

When, by eight o'clock, my grandmother still did not appear, nor did she make any sound overhead, I decided to go upstairs and see if she was all right.

I moved sluggishly. I saw the hairs on my arms rise and noticed that my fingernails had turned blue. It must be like a deep freeze in this house, and yet I did not feel it.

At the top of the stairs I paused and listened. No sound came from her bedroom.

Now I became alarmed. Startled back to life and remembering for the minute who I was and where, I also recalled that the day before Nana had not looked at all well.

I knocked on her door. No reply.

"Nana? Hello, Nana?"

No response.

I slowly pushed open the door and peered in. The room was in total darkness. I stood still for a second, listened, and still heard nothing. With mounting concern I hurried across the room, banged against some furniture, and finally was able to pull the curtains aside.

The bed was empty.

"Yes, love?"

I fell back against the dresser. "Nana!"

"I was in the bathroom, love, didn't you hear me?"

Her sudden appearance had made my heart jump. Now it thumped irregularly against my rib cage. "No. I didn't hear you. I also didn't hear you get out of bed."

"Yes, I went very quietly. I thought you might still be asleep and I didn't want to wake you. How do you feel this morning? I see you're up and dressed already."

"Yes . . . " I stammered. "I . . . I feel okay. Gosh, you startled me."

"Your nerves are proper edgy, love, I don't like that. Let's go down and have some nice hot tea, shall we?"

Back downstairs and sitting once again by the window, with my face fixed towards the billowing storm, I realized the sharp truth of my grandmother's words. My nerves *were* edgy. They were more than that. They were taut, ready to snap.

And what else could I expect? No sleep. Too little to eat. Spending the night first with my loving Victor, desiring him and knowing I could never be fulfilled by him, and next with Harriet and the memory of her grisly ordeal, and lastly with John preparing to run from his adversaries. In one night I had lived a lifetime.

"I don't know what's wrong with you. Got me worried, it has. Look at that rain, however shall I get a doctor here?"

"I don't need a doctor, Nana. Just some . . . tea will do. Thanks." I forced the sweet brew down my throat and tried not to gag. The toast, however, was beyond my acting ability.

"Is it your bowels again?"

"No!" God, I should *never* be able to get that horrible white stuff down my throat. "My . . . bowels are fine, Nana. It's just . . . it's just . . . "

"I think I shall fix you some cherry cordial and wrap you up good and proper before the fire. You need heating up. You're freezing to death! Look at you!"

She leaned over and touched a hand to my arm. She shrieked. "God help me if you don't feel like a proper corpse!"

I looked down at my arms.

"It's a wonder you haven't come down with pneumonia by now! How can you stand the cold? It said on the wireless that the temperature's dropping. It must be thirty degrees in here! And here's me with four cardigans on over me jumper and still shivering! And you there half-naked. I don't know how you can stand it!"

It's this house, I thought wildly. It's trying slowly to kill me . . .

We sat before the fire and, although it made me suffer to sit so hot and wrapped up, I managed to keep still for Nana's sake. Although my shins now itched terribly, what with the burn peeling off, and although I felt as if my body were on fire, I maintained my silence for Nana's peace of mind.

She tried to ply me with any manner of oral balms, but nothing would go down. Not the cordial, nor hot milk, nor tea, nor the unlabelled chalky white stuff. With any of them, as soon as the odour hit my nose, I had to turn away and gag.

In the end, Nana merely shook her head and took up her knitting.

We sat thus for most of the day.

In the early evening, Nana had been sufficiently warmed to be able to move her joints around the kitchen and cook us up a small supper. How I managed to get it all down was a feat that astounded even me. Yet I chewed and swallowed mechanically, tasting nothing, and was able at the end of it, to keep it all contained within my stomach.

Following this, more food than I had eaten in many hours, I began to feel drowsy. Despite the jumpiness of my nerves and the carnival of thoughts in my head, I finally succumbed to the effects of the heat, the blankets, and the heavy food.

When I awoke, the first thing I did was look up at the clock. It said nine. Then I turned to Nana. She was dozing peacefully in her chair. With the storm raging beyond the window and with only one lamp burning in the corner there was a sort of diffuse halo-light in the room. And it centred on John, who stood by the fire.

We were alone for the moment, John Townsend and I, and the thought went through my head, What an unfair trick of Nature to have made him so little like Victor.

Vaguely the family traits were there. The large nose, the square jaw, the furrow between the brows. John Townsend was a handsome man in his own right, but he lacked the mystery and intensity that so endeared me to his brother. Possibly he was aware of this, John, a weaker and more superficial man, possibly aware of how drastically he fell short when measured against his brother.

John stood nervously by the fire, ramming a fist into his palm each time he looked at the clock. There was an urgency about the way he stood, an agitation in his eyes.

Presently Jenny slipped into the room, closing the door surreptitiously, and I saw that she carried a valise.

Taking this from her, John said, "Thank you, love. Anyone hear you?"

"They're all asleep. Father and Mother retired an hour ago, and Harriet's asleep in our bed. I shall take her place on the day bed in the parlour."

"Jenny . . . "

"I've put my garnet earrings in there as well," she went on stiffly. "They originally cost five pound so you could fetch perhaps a guinea or two for them. You'll need it."

"Jennifer." He reached for her, his hands clumsy and uncertain. "Truly it pains me to go off like this so sudden like. I'd hoped for a few days grace and a better leave-taking. But that sod brother of mine has called the wolves on me, so if I want to escape with my hide I shall have to leave tonight."

Jenny's face was impassive as he kissed her cheek.

"I shall miss you, Jenny, more than I can say, I'll be thinking of your lobster mousse. No one I know can whip it smooth as you do and still have all the flavour in it."

She regarded him stonily.

"No tears for me then?"

"I shall wait for you, John."

"Of course you will. No fear you'll go running off to that swine brother of mine. Now he's disgraced the family name, I suppose you see him for what he is."

While Jenny held herself erect and regarded her husband with a starched expression, I felt the cold winds in her heart blow through mine as well. They swept over me as had Harriet's pitiable thoughts, in bits and pieces, telling me of the pain and shock of Victor's ruinous fall. The name Megan O'Hanrahan now blew through our mind, bitter and acrid. It was she who had leaked out the rumour of Harriet's abortion and of the brother who had committed it. I saw in Jenny's mind the memory of her entreaties to him to repudiate the claim, and the memory of his silence. One by one his patients had fallen away, his titles robbed from him, his honour stripped away. Not once had Victor opened his mouth in his own defence as the story of the abortion had run through Warrington like a killing plague. In short time there had been nothing left of Victor Townsend.

In Jenny's mind there also flitted the vision of Mrs. Townsend retiring to her bed in shame and humiliation, afraid to walk the streets. And there was proud Mr. Townsend, holding his head high every morning as he made for the mill, coming home each night crushed and defeated.

He had heard the words whispered behind his back, indiscreetly loud enough for him to hear. There he goes. His daughter's a common slut (with an Irishman, too!). His eldest son is an abortionist. His youngest is a drunk and a gambler.

"You don't believe me, do you?"

"No, I don't."

"Well, it's true. Victor went straight to the bookies and told them I was planning to leave town. So they came after me they did, threatening and demanding all their money. So I had to fob them off with a lie about giving them it all tomorrow. Aye, it was Victor all right, getting back at me for his own fall from grace. Couldn't stand to see me escaping. And it had to be him, you see, 'cause no one else knew. You and him was all I told, and I don't think my own wife would set the dogs on me, would you?"

Jenny did not reply. Another voice was echoing in her ears now. It was Victor's. The two of them were in the parlour, he had just finished playing the piano and he was saying, "He needs a shock, needs to be forced to show his hand."

And then her own voice saying, "Promise me that you won't interfere with John."

And Victor saying, "If it is your wish, then I promise."

Now John was smiling with the confidence of one who knows he's going to win a card game. "Your words say one thing but your eyes say another. I can see it in your face, Jenny, that you've lost your love for Victor."

But what he saw, it was clear to me, was the repugnance she felt for this family and this town for what they had done to Victor. They had all been quick to condemn him before they had even heard his defence. If you want to blame someone for this whole nightmare, her eyes said, blame Harriet for getting into trouble in the first place, and then for telling the whole thing to Megan O'Hanrahan.

All that John Townsend read on his wife's face was bitter disillusionment. "You'd better go, John."

"Aye, love, I'm going. But I want you to know something. I'll be back. Quicker than Bob's yer uncle, and I shall have sovereigns in my pocket, just you see."

When he spoke I detected a trace of excitement in his voice and saw a light behind his eyes. John Townsend was finally escaping. It might be at the risk of his own neck and he might be running in disgrace, but he was finally doing what he had always envied Victor for doing: breaking away from this house.

"Then we shall be well off and have our own house. And I shall have a maid for you and even a telephone. What do you think of that, Jenny love, a telephone?"

"It's late, John."

Saying no more, he picked up the valise, kissed her roughly, and then hurried from the room. She stood immobile before me as we heard him close the door behind himself, and then the front door after that. When she was certain he was gone, when the house was totally silent except for the ticking of the clock, Jennifer finally released a sob and crumpled to the floor. As her hand hit my foot she disappeared.

Nana, having roused herself some time around nine-thirty, gathered herself together and muddled upstairs. She muttered something to me on her way out about fixing myself a late snack since we hadn't had any supper, then she filled the water bottles from the hot tap in the bathroom and crawled into the cosy comfort of her bed.

Down in the sitting room I heard the bedsprings speak. Then there was the whisper of a wind, as if the whole house sighed, and I settled down for my next encounter.

It came only a few minutes later.

Having had little time to ponder the wretched condition the family had been reduced to those many years ago, I heard someone moving about in the parlour.

I went slowly, uncertainly. A few days before, I had witnessed only happy scenes, normal family settings in which the Townsends had been like any other household. But then the episodes had taken a turn. They were becoming increasingly frightening. There was a touch of the macabre to them now, hinting of criminal deeds and of family shame and ruination. What would I witness this time? How far was this family prepared to go in its self-destruction?

It was Harriet, sprawled on the horsehair sofa and sobbing into her arms. I stood dispassionately in the doorway feeling some measure of pity for the child who had blundered so witlessly into the adult world. I wondered what day it was now, or what year. How much time had passed since the abortion; what had happened in the meantime? Where was Victor? What had become of him after his disgrace? And had Sean O'Hanrahan disappeared? Had John come back already, his pocket full of sovereigns? Or had something new taken place, now to be revealed to me?

"Oh God, oh God, oh God," muttered Harriet over and over again. "It's my fault. I told him, I told him, I told him. I should have kept silent. I didn't have to tell him."

Harriet was talking to herself in the way that anyone who is self-chastising will do. With no one to give ear to her self-rebukes she must in the end turn to herself.

The fire was low in the fireplace, almost out, and the room had a gloomy aspect. Harriet lay as if she had flung herself there in a fit of despair. "He's angry with me now for telling. That's why he did it. I can't blame him. I can blame only my own stupid self. Oh Harriet, you idiot."

The rest was incoherent. She wept into her arms and prattled on and on, every now and then throwing out a clearly audible invective. "If only I had remained silent he wouldn't have done this! Now I am ruined forever!"

Could she still be talking about Sean? Or did she mean Victor?

When Harriet finally sat up and wiped her eyes, I fell back, stunned.

All her hair had been cut off.

Rising from the couch and going to the gilt mirror over the fireplace, she stood with a boiled face and scrutinized herself with disgust. "You can't blame him for doing it," she muttered to the deplorable reflection. "He's angry. And it's the only way he knows to get back at you. You should have just killed yourself at the very beginning and then everyone would be happy now. He wouldn't have his reputation ruined, Mother wouldn't be confined to bed, and John wouldn't have run off. Now look at me. Who can blame him?"

There was less bitterness in her voice than a pathetic kind of plea, like a torture victim begging to be let go.

Yet what startled me most was her appearance. While Harriet had been a plain girl, the one saving characteristic about her had been her lovely hair, full and thick and wavy and of a rich chestnut colour. And she had always worn it as if she had taken great care and pains with it. Now it was gone. Instead, her skull was fitted with a sparse little cap of uneven tufts, at some points showing her bare scalp. It was almost comical, she looked like a tonsured monk, and her face was so swollen, her eyes rimmed with red, and with the ridiculous fringe of hair to add to the distortion, that Harriet remotely resembled an organ grinder's monkey.

I immediately regretted these comparisons, for I saw how tormented she was. Someone, wielding dull scissors and a great deal of brute strength, had obviously got her head under his arm and had whacked off all her lovely curls.

My heart went out to her. And I also wondered who had committed such a horrible deed, and why.

"I deserved it," she whimpered before the mirror, examining closely the comical tufts and bald spots. "I had it coming to me for what I did to him. He had the right. Oh God . . . *he had the right.*"

Unable to bear the sight of herself any longer, Harriet flung herself away from the mirror and back on to the sofa where she wept anew.

Standing in the doorway and watching her as I was, compassion filled me for this unfortunate girl, a child I had once observed as innocent and sensitive and full of idealistic notions. It was a pity she had been initiated into reality in such a brutal way; Harriet had suffered her share of cruel torments.

A thought occurred to me. It was an insane impulse. Recalling that just a short while before, when Jenny had crumpled to the floor, that I had felt her hand hit my foot, I suddenly heard myself saying to the girl on the couch, "Harriet, what happened?"

And she snapped her head up, staring at me.

CHAPTER 15

*S*o . . . IT WAS HAPPENING AT LAST. THE THING I HAD BOTH dreaded and hoped for had now come to pass; I was going to communicate with the past.

Was this then the ultimate reason for my being a part of it all? It seemed to come to me all at once, like dark clouds suddenly parting to reveal the sun. *Was this my purpose then?*

When I had spoken those words, Harriet had stopped crying and had looked up. Her face had held that startled expression of someone caught doing a private thing. Yet she had not seemed actually to see me. Her eyes had narrowed in my direction, as if trying to focus on something, and then her face had relaxed. What had I been to her at that moment? An optical illusion created by a play of light; a shadow on the opposite wall? What had Harriet seen when she had lifted her head and squinted at me?

It couldn't have been much for, after tilting her head to one side in a quizzical manner, she had put her face back into her arms and had continued crying. Yet the fact remained that *she had heard me.*

I had spoken her name and Harriet had heard me. And then she had seen something . . . *something* in the open doorway.

This meant only one thing to me. That the Time window was somehow widening, that the last of the senses—that of *touching*—was finally coming about.

Wandering back into the sitting room, I went over and over the last week and a half here in Nana's house. I recalled my first visions, Victor at the window, "Für Elise" behind the bagpipes. And it all fit a pattern. First sound. Then sight. Then smell. Then vague sensations such as cold or the nearness of one of them as he or she brushed past. And finally, tonight, Jennifer's hand hitting my foot.

We were starting to touch.

And with touching would come communication. Hadn't Victor once turned around when I had called out his name? And now Harriet. Harriet interrupted with her crying by the sound of her name and squinting at (what?) something in the doorway.

So it was finally happening. There remained no doubt with me now that I should soon be able to speak with them, or make myself seen and felt. This was what it had all led to, the final moment when I should actually become a part of *them*.

But why? For what reason? Was I ultimately to play an active part in the drama of the past? Was I intended somehow to step in and intervene?

That had to be it—I could think of no other explanation. For some reason I had been chosen to play a part in the Townsend drama.

Drilling my mind with questions that could not possibly find answers within myself, I stormed about the sitting room as if I were in a rage. And in a way I was, frustrated with my lack of comprehension, angry that I could not see clearly what all this was leading to.

I went into the scullery, found Nana's bottle of cherry cordial, and poured myself a large glass. It was a mild liqueur, not adequate for the relief I would have preferred, but it was something. And it was as I was closing the scullery door and pushing the sausage into place that a thought struck me with such force that I staggered and fell back against the table.

And what hit me was this: If I had just now been able to bridge the gap with Harriet, however feebly, and if I were so certain that this gap would narrow in time, then did this not also mean that I should soon somehow, in some way, also be able to communicate with Victor Townsend?

The significance of this drove me to the sofa, where I fell down hard and nearly spilled the cherry cordial.

Soon to show myself to Victor! Soon to talk to him! Inconceivable!

And yet . . . if I were so willing to accept the idea with Harriet and Jennifer, why was it so unreasonable that it should happen with him?

Because it mustn't, said my frightened mind. *I must not let him see me.*

This new notion upset me more than anything else that had happened so far. I had felt Jenny's hand touch my foot. I had interrupted Harriet's crying with my voice. What would the next step be? Would I find myself materializing in their midst, speaking to Victor, feeling him touch me . . . ?

"It's been two months," said a voice nearby.

I snapped my head up. Jenny and Harriet were seated in the easy chairs before the fire.

"We should have had a letter or something by now," said Harriet. "John's been gone exactly two months."

I was alarmed by the change in Jennifer. The loveliness and freshness were gone, replaced by a patina of melancholy that had painted shadows under her eyes and deep lines on either side of her mouth. By the stoop of her shoulders and the careless way her hair was dressed Jennifer appeared years older. And yet she was not. We had moved along only two months in time.

Harriet, embroidering the edge of a handkerchief, sat with her hair bound in a kind of lacy house cap, completely concealing her head and the haphazard growth of her tufts and fringes. Both girls appeared sullen and glum.

Jennifer, with no work in her lap and her long slender hands dangling uselessly over the arms of the chair, said, "Perhaps he isn't where he can dispatch a letter. Or possibly he has gone far away and the letters he has sent have been lost."

"There is still the telegraph."

"I don't know, Harriet, where John is. Perhaps he is on his way back and wishes to surprise us."

Harriet shook her head. "I just don't know how Victor could have done that. To his own brother."

"None of us in this family is entirely without a blemish, Harriet."

Sitting as close to them as I was, almost a member of their company, I tried to open my mind to their thoughts, tried to unearth the unspoken information there. But all I received was one simple message from Jennifer: I haven't seen Victor in nearly three months.

It caused me to shiver. This accounted for her appearance and the listless way she stared into the fire. The room was so still and quiet that the faint little sound of the needle puncturing the linen could be heard as Harriet concentrated on her handiwork.

I wished there was some way I could have spoken to Jennifer just then, to Jennifer alone and without Harriet to overhear. For I wanted to tell her that Victor was going to come back, that their time together was not yet up, that they both had an unavoidable appointment with Destiny.

Nana's words of several days before now rang dimly in my ears, sounding like a worn phonograph record: "Victor came home drunk one night and *forced* her."

Yes, I thought sadly, your time with Victor is not yet over.

"I think Victor has been bitter ever since he gave up that Edinburgh appointment," Harriet went on. "He was different when he came home, wasn't he? And he's been different ever since. That was two years ago, but I remember that night as if it were just last week. How shocked he was to hear of your marriage to John. And the way he stormed out, taking lodgings at the Horse's Head and all. I never did understand why he gave in to Father and came back. The appointment in Scotland was all settled. And then all of a sudden, here he was."

"People do change their minds."

"Aye, they do. And maybe John has, too. What if he doesn't come home then? What will you do?"

Jennifer shrugged. It didn't matter. Without Victor around nothing mattered.

The scathing tone of Harriet's voice disturbed me. In the three months since she had lost the baby, Harriet seemed to have grown bitter and hard.

The unspoken condemnation of Victor led me to wonder if he had not had something to do with the cutting of her hair. What had I heard her say to herself just a short while ago in the parlour? "He's getting back at you for telling. His reputation is ruined. It's the only way he knows to get back at you."

I shook this off. Condemn him though the others might, I could not bring myself to believe Victor the evil and brutal man his descendants made of him. How Nana had vilified him, blaming Victor alone for the tragedy of this family. He was as much the victim as were the others, and certainly not the one responsible.

My head began to throb. Rubbing my eyes with my fists, I tried to fight off the feeling that there might be some truth to what everyone said. Especially his contemporaries. While Nana might be dealing with handed-down gossip, I was listening to the words of those who had been closest to him. What had really happened in these last three months?

When I brought my hands away I saw that Jenny and Harriet had left me. I was alone again in the dismal sitting room, my head aching terribly and my entire body crying out for sleep.

I gazed forlornly at the rain-spattered window. How much longer was I going to be a prisoner of this house and its past?

At first I thought the thumping was inside my head, but as I opened my eyes and saw the watery morning pour in through the windows, I recognized the sound of Nana's cane striking the floor overhead.

Struggling to my feet and trying to shake myself out of a fog, I managed to look at the clock and see that it was nearly eight. While it would seem I had slept most of the night, I certainly did not feel as though I had.

My body silently screamed and rebelled against this rough treatment, making the climb up the steep stairs harder than usual. How on earth did Nana manage it? And when I went into her room to find her sitting up among her pillows, it was she, not I, who exclaimed, "By God, you look awful!"

"How do you feel this morning, Nana?"

"The arthritis has got me, love. This rain can't last forever. The wireless said it should end tonight. Then we shall have some sun. Elsie or William should be coming round after that, we need some food in the house. And your granddad's not had a visitor in a few days. Mustn't worry him."

"Can't you get out of bed, Nana?"

"Andrea, what's the matter with your eyes?"

"I don't know. Why?"

"Go and look at yourself."

I crossed over to her dressing table and took a good look at myself in the mirror. Puffy and red and looking as if I had walked into swinging doors, my eyes were startling evidence of the strain this house was putting upon me.

"And I've never seen a body so white! You look drained. Absolutely drained. It's like someone's sucked all the blood out of you. How do you feel?"

"All right, I guess. Just tired."

"You shall want to be getting home soon then. Once this weather lets up you should be getting over to Cook's and reserving your passage back."

I forced a smile. "You sound like you want to get rid of me."

"Never! But I am worried about you, love." Now my grandmother's face took on such a serious aspect that I had to turn away. Deep inside myself I felt the change taking place. I knew there was something wrong with me, yet I was too afraid to admit it. If I could just ignore it, glide over it, pretend it isn't there . . . But Nana's heavy concern made me uncomfortably aware of the fact that something was definitely, terribly wrong . . .

"I'll make you some tea, Nana. And some toast?"

"If you can manage. I didn't have you here to be a maid, you know. Who'd have thought a rain like this would have come along, ay? Take your time, lovey, and let me know if there's a break in the weather. You know that as soon as there is we shall be seeing Elsie or William."

I felt her eyes sharply on me as I crossed the room and went out to the hall. Once there, away from her penetrating gaze, I leaned against the wall and took some deep breaths. I felt on the verge of collapse.

It was no trouble making tea and toast, as long as I kept my mouth open and didn't allow the smell up my nose. Because when that happened I would gag and have to leave the kitchen. But I quickly mastered my revulsion for the food and was able to set a decent tray for my grandmother. She looked it over with delight and asked, "Where's yours?"

"Downstairs, Nana. If you don't mind, I'll eat alone."

"Of course. Get on down to the heat. And be sure you turn it up. Oh I do wish you would wear one of my cardigans."

"I'm okay in the sitting room."

"And you've gone thin, too. What will your mum say when she sees you? She'll wonder what we've done to you here! Why, you've gone like a skeleton!"

I nodded and thought, Yesterday you likened me to a corpse. Maybe that's what I'm becoming. Slowly dead.

Back down in the sitting room, I slumped into an easy chair and felt all the life go out of me. All I could do was wait for the next episode to happen, for my next precious moments with the past. Unhappy as they were, tragic as they were, I longed to be back with them. They were my reality.

But why were they robbing me of sleep and food? Was that necessary? How long could I keep this up before I did in fact collapse? When Elsie showed up tonight or tomorrow, she would be sure to be alarmed (*I* had been after seeing myself in the mirror) and would try to cart me off to her house.

Would I be allowed to go? Or were they keeping me here, slowly killing me, so that I could join them . . . become one of them?

In the afternoon I was in the past again.

I had fallen asleep, although it was not the slumber of peace and rest but of disturbing, grinding dreams and of a deathly chill that sank through my skin and filled my bones with ice. I had shivered and tossed and turned all through my afternoon sleep so that when I awoke, to find Jenny sitting before the fire by herself, I was more tired than I had been before.

She was writing a letter this time. I found that if I moved to the edge of the couch, sitting as far forward as I could with my elbows on my knees, I could read what she wrote.

July 1894
Dearest Victor,

I write this letter in the hope that it will be forwarded by some kind person who knows your whereabouts and that it will reach you before long. I have written three letters to you now with no response. Perhaps you are not receiving them; perhaps you choose not to reply. In any case I shall endeavour to maintain my hope that you are alive and well and able to respond.

It has been four months since last I saw you. Well I recall that day. How Air Johnson publicly condemned you from his pulpit, and how you sat so straight and proud in the church, your face not betraying the hurt. And when later that afternoon I went to plead with you to speak up in your own defence, you said not a word to me but began packing your bags. I shall never understand why you silently let this town crucify you, and yet there were those who stood by you. It was not for me to judge, Victor, whether or not you committed the Deed, or if you did, your motives behind it. All I know is that the day you left Warrington something inside me died.

I want you to come back, Victor. Or send for me from wherever you are. You must be made to understand that there are those who love you yet and cannot bear your absence.

John has also not returned, nor has he written, and it is my fear he shall never do so. Wherever your brother is, perhaps he is happier. Yet I wonder if you are.

Jennifer stopped writing suddenly, her pen poised above the paper, and with one swift, angry motion seized the page, crumpled it in her hand, and flung it into the fire. Then she brought her hands up to her face and started to cry.

I was now on the very edge of the couch, barely staying on it, and was so close to Jennifer that I could smell her rose perfume. Watching her weep quietly, her thin shoulders trembling, my heart went again out to her. I had the knowledge that would give her consolation, for I knew Victor would return. And yet how could I convey it to her?

So I tried again.

With a swallow for courage and a deep breath to brace myself, I said in a normal voice, "Jennifer."

She snapped her head up. This time she did not resume her crying as Harriet had done but instead narrowed her eyes at me as if trying to focus on me.

"Jenny," I murmured, not moving. My heart was flailing against my chest. This was it, *this was the moment I would break through.* "Jenny, don't cry. He'll be back. Victor will come back."

She sucked in her breath. "Who . . . who are you?"

I thought I might faint from the strain. "A friend."

"You look familiar . . . "

"He's coming back, Jenny . . . But as I spoke to her, Jennifer faded before my eyes.

I slid off the couch and on to the floor in a heap, not quite fainting but not quite retaining consciousness. The room swam about me, the floor heaved up and the ceiling swung down. I felt the walls draw in close and then fly far apart. My fingers dug into the thin rug, trying to keep me from falling into space, for I felt the floor drop away and the odd sensation of floating came over me.

When I regained my balance again and the room was still, I found an acrid taste in my mouth and knew that my stomach had tried to vomit, but its emptiness had proved unproductive. With a groan I lifted myself off the floor and marvelled at how weak I had grown. The effort to bring myself to my feet took all powers of concentration and strength so that, coming to a stand, I was not strong enough to stay upright and so slumped again on to the couch.

I had broken out in a fine sweat all over my body. The T-shirt clung to me. My damp hair was plastered to the back of my neck. And I felt sick all over.

For one fleeting moment I had crossed the bridge of Time.

Jennifer had seen me, had spoken to me. I must have, for one brief instant, been clear and sharp to her, for she seemed to think she knew me. Was it my Townsend likeness? Or was it something else?

The enormity of what had happened began to sink in. *I had crossed the bridge of Time.* For one blink of an eye I had been back in the world of 1894.

I knew now beyond a doubt that my next encounter would be longer, more intense. I would speak with them, touch them, and . . . what else? And with whom? Victor?

Perhaps if I had been in a stronger state of body my mind would have had the sense to be frightened. But as it was, weakened to the point of exhaustion and helplessness, my beleaguered mind could only go around and around on the phenomenon I now faced. For there was no doubt in my mind by now that there was a purpose in my going back in time.

There was a reason for my being sent to the past.

But what was that reason?

I lay back breathing shallowly and letting the mild warmth of the room dry my skin and clothes. And as I lay sprawled, too limp even to wipe off my forehead, I saw the dim beginnings of an idea start to form in my mind.

It had something to do with changing things.

Already I had gone back for one instant and had interrupted the normal passage of events in 1894. I had interrupted Jenny and I had told her Victor was going to return.

What would I do next time? What would I say to the next dead Townsend I would meet?

Of course. That was it. That was my purpose. And my choice—if choice I had.

I could go back and change history.

Already I had taken one small step towards that end. I had stopped Jennifer from crying and had told her that she would see Victor again. If I had not, then she would have gone on crying and would have been utterly miserable until the time he did indeed return. But now, I felt certain, she was sitting in the sitting room, at this same moment, back in 1894 on a July evening, wondering about the strange prophetic words she had heard from the mouth of a ghost.

And she must be harbouring some small spark of hope that, had I not intervened, she would never have known.

What next then? When I encountered the next Townsend, what would I do or say to him or her?

Here was something that perplexed me. While it seemed I had no choice about going back in time, indeed I had no choice about even leaving the house, it still remained to me whether or not to communicate with them. I had not been forced to utter those words to Jenny. I had spoken them of my own free will. Therefore, it appeared that the choice of whether or not to intervene still remained to me.

But what was the purpose then? Why had I been chosen to go back and then given the choice of stepping in or remaining out of the sphere of their drama? Why should I intervene, why should it even occur to me to do so?

Unless, of course, it could serve some good purpose.

Suddenly I saw the answer.

Bringing my head up and squinting at the window in the opposite wall, I saw the rain continue to fall in torrents outside, and I thought, It is within my power to change the ultimate fate of this family.

It now seemed so simple really, not a problem at all. Suddenly, with the realization of that idea, the mystery was dispelled. I knew why I had come to the house on George Street. I knew why I had been chosen and what I was intended to do.

"While he was alive, Victor Townsend made this house a living hell for everyone in it."

Those had been my grandmother's words to me on my second morning in this house. She had mentioned "unspeakable acts," something about Victor being a demon, that he had had dealings with the Devil.

Of course, it was all clear to me now.

Victor Townsend, somehow unfairly maligned by his brother and the whole of Warrington, had disappeared with his anger and bitterness and frustration. After having given up the Scottish appointment and having lost Jennifer, the ignominy of what he had done to Harriet and then to his own brother must have driven Victor to extremes.

Sitting on the sofa now and gazing blankly at the rain-spattered window, I imagined him coming home a totally different man. I saw him returning with a vendetta in his heart so black with the lust for revenge that I saw him a cruel, violent man, turning against those who had vilified him and repaying them for the suffering they had inflicted.

Was that it then? Had Victor, coming home after months of being alone and allowing his vengeance gradually to poison his mind, returned bent on destroying those he had once loved?

My God, was there truth after all to Nana's words?

The hours passed sluggishly and yet I remained on the sofa in the same position, flagged by my own physical weakness but now also oppressed by my twisted thinking.

In the time that had passed, spent only in the same thoughts over and over again, I had come to the realization that it was within my power to save, if not Harriet, then possibly Jennifer from the retribution of the demented Victor Townsend. If indeed he was to return as I imagined, then was there some way I could step in and protect Jennifer from the fate she was destined to suffer?

Was it possible to go back and change history?

And if I did, what then would become of me? Jennifer was my great-grandmother. She had been raped by Victor and then had given birth to my grandfather. But what would happen if I were somehow able to step in and prevent the attack? It would mean that my grandfather would never be born.

And, following that line of thinking to its ultimate consequences, would that not also mean that I, too, would cease to exist?

It must be, then, that the choice I had to make was one of self-sacrifice. I had to decide which I would do: stand by and watch Victor return to work his vindictiveness on his family, or step in and prevent it.

And if I prevented that final calamity, then I would be committing suicide.

The riddle, like a maze that has no outlet, drove me deeper and deeper into myself. I walked previously unexplored regions within my soul, saw aspects of myself that I had never known to exist. I felt myself tilt out of my body and fly up to the ceiling where, hovering up in the corner, I could look down and watch myself writhe on the couch. I shrank down and became the size of an atom, or I flared out and sailed to the distant pillars of the Universe.

And I also wondered, Could I be wrong about Victor?

If I am wrong, then what if I commit a staggering error by preventing the coming together of Jennifer and Victor, two very dear and beautiful people, and blunderingly bring about my own extinction? My grandfather, my mother, Aunt Elsie, Uncle William, my three cousins, my brother, myself . . . all gone in an instant. I had but to step in and stop Victor's ultimate crime.

But can you change history? Was I only deluding myself? Were these the maniacal ravings of someone who hasn't slept or eaten in a few days and who is at the point of nervous and physical collapse? How could I be sure?

How could I be sure?

The thumping overhead awoke me to find myself sprawled out on the floor in the middle of the sitting room. It took me some time to orient myself, and when full consciousness returned to me and I heard the thumping on the next floor up, I wondered if it was Nana in need of me or some visitor from the past. I was able to struggle to my feet and stumble to the door.

The hallway was dark. The stairwell ascended into a blackness that seemed deeper and more formidable than ever before. The silence was palpable; it clung to my skin and worked its way down my throat. As I mounted each step I had to fight for breath, for my body rebelled against the power that impelled it. And with each step I thought, If I am right and Victor comes back a tormented man bent on revenge, shall I be able to stand by and watch his tortures upon those I've come to love or will I have the courage to step in and avert the tragedy and also erase my own existence?

At the top of the stairs I leaned heavily against the wall, gasping for air. It seemed thin and icy up here, as if I had climbed to the polar regions, and as I stood gathering more strength, I thought further, And if I can intervene, how will it be done? For now I have seen that I have attained solid form with these people and can speak to them. In the next visit I will seem even more real to them. So how will I prevent the crazed actions of Victor? Will the mere sight of me, suddenly appearing, send him off? Will I be able to stop him long enough for Jenny to get away? How will I do it?

I turned and gaped down the dark hall. The thumping was coming, of course, from the front bedroom. My grandmother's room was still and quiet.

Before I started forward on that inevitable path, I thought, And what if I am wrong? What if Victor merely comes home sad and defeated and searching for love? And what if I step in and prevent a harmless, loving event from taking place? What if I make the wrong decision?

A thousand questions and no answers, I had only to walk down the hall, step into the bedroom, and let fate work its hand.

CHAPTER 16

*A*GAIN, THERE WAS THAT EERIE, HALO-LIGHT FILLING THE room, coming from an unseen source and in its appearance chilly, giving off no warmth.

As I stepped across the threshold I felt a presence at my side. It was Jennifer. She had stepped through the door with me, although she seemed unaware of me. Her eyes were fixed on the clothes wardrobe, and she hesitated, just as I did, for a moment.

The scene was hauntingly familiar. I had been here before. The same aura hung in the room, that of lurking horrors and hellish imaginings. Perhaps it was only a fancy, but this time the shadows seemed to hang at odd angles, making the room appear distorted, at a tilt. I had the vague impression of entering a fun house; there was a cold draught where I—we—stood, coming from all sides, chilling not my flesh but the marrow of my bones. The play of light robbed the room of all colour, filling it with contrasts in black, white, and grey. It was queer, twisted, dreamlike . . .

Jennifer and I walked forward. Her face was strangely set, looking first this way and then that, and returning her stare to the wardrobe. She seemed to have come in here looking for something, although I sensed that she knew, that she feared, it was in the wardrobe.

We were both drawn to it, keeping our eyes on its polished surface, on its swirling grain, on the shiny brass locks. While Jenny may have glanced about the room, I did not, for I was terrified of what I might see in the shadows. A horror gripped me that so filled me with dread that I wanted to cry out. Yet my feet continued to move forward, keeping apace with Jennifer.

Presently we stood before the wardrobe. We stood and gazed at it, feeling the little hairs on our necks prickle up. We both had a sense of wanting to turn and run from this place, yet we could not, for we had to know what was in the wardrobe.

I saw our hands reach out. Jenny's, long and pale, touched the little brass knob. My own hand merely remained outstretched in an imitation of her action. We continued to hesitate, feeling the eeriness of the room, shuddering with the terror that crawled along our skin.

Jennifer grasped the brass knob and started to turn it.

I thought I would faint.

On the floor, by our feet, were drops of blood leading up to the wardrobe, and there on the bottom, staining the wood, was a fresh ooze that came from within.

Stiff with fright and unable to stop herself, Jennifer slowly drew the wardrobe door open.

We both screamed. We screamed together, almost in harmony, our hands flying to our faces, muffling the sound as soon as it came out. I knew that Jenny's heart pounded in unison with mine, that she felt a faintness wash over her, that she saw the room tilt.

But then it passed and we collected ourselves, stunned by what we saw, but allowing some ancestral instinct to take over and command our bodies.

We were staring down at Harriet.

Crumpled in the corner of the wardrobe like a discarded doll, she gazed up at us with unseeing eyes and an expression on her face that was a mixture of shame, surprise, and acceptance. Her poor head of hair, matted in parts where the blood had dried black, stuck out in different lengths, framing her homely face in grim parody of a clown.

I felt myself kneel, just as Jenny did, and although we leaned close, we could not bring ourselves to touch. We already knew that Harriet was dead.

Jenny and I stared at her, too bewildered to move, feeling our minds go mercifully blank in a kind of mindless shock.

There was a knife in the centre of Harriet's breast, a large bread-chopping knife that had done unnecessary damage to her flesh and rib cage. The blood no longer gushed, but we could see where it had, and it was congealing in pools around her hands and feet and in her lap.

Tucked into her left hand, sticking out halfway and with the name "Jenny" written on it, was an envelope.

We waited an interminable time, gazing at the mutilated body of poor Harriet, glancing dispassionately over the many wounds inflicted all over her body, thinking how a meat grinder could have done no worse. It appeared that Harriet had lived some time before she had finally, mercifully died.

At last, feeling our senses return, Jennifer reached out to Harriet's hand. Not gingerly, but sadly, lovingly. She took hold of the envelope and yanked it free. Then, with a feeling of resignation, she stuffed the letter into her pocket and rose to her feet.

I also rose, but when Jenny turned and left, I continued to stand and stare down into the wardrobe until it was empty and all I was looking at in the end were some balls of fluff and the cuffs of my blue jeans.

When I awoke sometime later, with no idea of the time, I found myself lying on the bed. I was fully clothed and on top of the covers and could not remember how I had got there. After a moment of remembering who I was and where, I managed to push myself up on my elbows and look around the room.

It was again 1894.

There was the clothes wardrobe, looking like new and standing wide open with a few of Jenny's gowns hanging inside. There was a fire in the fireplace and the electric lights glowed unevenly. And there was Jennifer, sitting quietly and alone in the wing chair.

Am I stuck here? I wondered in alarm. Did the Time portal close behind me when I crossed over? Will I never go back to my own time?

I continued to lie on my back, propped up on my elbows and watching Jennifer. The strains of her morbid discovery were starkly evident on her face. Thin and pale, with shadows beneath her eyes, Jenny looked like a woman who had given up. I saw how she stared into the dying fire, how little life shone in her eyes. She had surrendered, retreated.

I did not hear the footsteps on the stairs until Jenny, hearing them, sat up and turned abruptly to the door.

When I turned, hearing the steps now in the hallway and drawing closer to the bedroom, I gaped at the doorway until I thought my eyes would pop out of their sockets.

And after a long moment, there in the doorway appeared Victor Townsend.

Jenny and I both gasped. But while she flew to her feet I did not move. I could only remain as I was and marvel at the change in the man. It was the same as when I had seen him after returning from London: strangely austere, his face a mask of dark secrets, his eyes heavy with disillusionment. He stood motionless in the doorway, making no sound, no emotion written on his face, and regarded Jennifer across the room with an air of sorrow and resignation.

I looked over at her. She stood as if she were seeing a ghost. Her hands hung at her sides, her face was frozen in shock, her mouth partly open.

The moment that passed between them was infinite, and yet it was filled with so much. In one look, everything was conveyed.

Finally, Victor said, "I knocked at the front door and when no one answered I let myself in. I had seen from the street the light in this window, so I knew someone was home. Jennifer . . . "

She could not speak. Her body inclined itself a little towards him, her hands coming up to her waist and clasping there, but still she could not speak. It was as if she were gazing upon someone who had returned from the dead.

"I received your letters . . . " he said in a manner which suggested he was searching for the right thing to say. "But I couldn't answer them. Jennifer . . . I have missed the funeral, haven't I?"

"Yes . . . " she breathed. Her eyes continued to behold him with shock and disbelief.

"About John . . . " Victor seemed uncertain of his words. "Have you heard . . . "

Mechanically she shook her head.

"They found him, Jenny," said Victor in a flat, detached voice. "In the Mersey. The bookies caught up with him. I'm sorry."

Her face remained expressionless. "It had to happen," she whispered. "I guess I've always expected it . . . "

"Jenny . . . " he began falteringly. "I have come to say goodbye."

Jennifer's body began to tremble; she was slowly regaining her senses. "Goodbye?" Her voice was like a soft breeze.

"My God, Jenny, how this pains me. You don't look well. You're too thin! Leave this house, Jenny, get away from this family before you perish!"

"Why have you come to say goodbye?"

"I stayed away from you, Jennifer, to protect you from my own black name. You've been so innocent in all of this. And look what it's done to you. I had hoped you would forget me in time, think of me as dead."

"Oh no, Victor . . . " Now she took a step towards him.

"And it must be so again. I came when I heard about Harriet. I wanted to go to the funeral. But I came late. Where is the family, Jenny?"

She licked her lips, trying to remember. "They've gone to Wales. The shock was too much for your mother. She collapsed, Victor. She can't walk. And your father blames himself for Harriet . . . Well, they had to get away for a while, you see . . . "

"And you didn't go with them?"

"I . . . couldn't. I've been—"

"Waiting for John to return."

"No, Victor. I've been waiting for you to return." Her voice drew strength now, as reality sank in. "I had lost hope for John, and wherever he is now, I hope he has found peace. But you, Victor, I have lived with the hope that you would return. How could I go off to Wales when you might come back? As indeed you did . . . "

They fell silent once more, staring at one another, filling their eyes and their senses with one another. And as they did so, I felt myself slowly rise from the bed. I swung my legs over the edge away from Victor and cautiously drew myself to my feet. Without thinking, I went to stand beside Jennifer.

Now we both stood and watched across the room the man we loved.

"Why have you come to say goodbye?" whispered Jenny.

"I will go away now for good. I can no longer call England my home. I am a disgraced man, I have no right to live among decent human beings. Perhaps France—"

"Stay, Victor." Not passionately, not pleadingly. Simply: "Stay." And I saw how it moved him. Visibly unnerved, my great-grandfather swayed uncertainly in the doorway.

"I had not come home for you and me to be alone together. I intended to visit my mother and try to grant some small comfort to her." Now that she has lost two of her children, he thought grimly. "I had hoped only to see you in their presence. But not . . . not like this."

"And why not like this?"

"Because I can bring you only unhappiness."

"As you have done to everyone else?" Across the room I saw him nod. "Then . . . " I felt Jenny reach into the pocket of her dress and pull out an envelope.

Taking my eyes off Victor for one minute, I saw that it was the letter she had taken off poor Harriet's battered body. And now I also saw, with a pang of grief, that it was the same pathetically sweet stationery Harriet had used to write her secret letters to Sean O'Hanrahan.

"Read this," she said, holding it out to him. Victor eyed the envelope.

"What is it?"

"Please read it."

After a moment of consideration, he approached us slowly, standing as far from us as he could and reaching out for the letter. As he pulled the page out of the envelope and unfolded it before his eyes, I saw the delicate handwriting of Harriet before my own eyes. I read the letter with him.

Dearest Jennifer,

I know that as you read this, my one true friend, you are in a distressed way and that I have caused you a most grievous harm. And yet it had to be done this way. I must tell you why. I have known for some time that I must make my end this way, in the manner that you found me, for I have always believed this is how Father would want it.

My time is short, I will not prolong your misery. When my father refused me the right to marry Sean, calling him a papist and other wretched names, I disobeyed him and went with Sean to Old Abbey. You know about this. And when I was in a family way, even then I held the hope that my sweet Sean would still marry me. But I learned otherwise. I was disgraced. But more than that, I had been rejected.

I suppose that is when, dearest Jenny, I became a person other than myself. It was as though another woman had entered my body and manipulated me. I say this not to exonerate myself of the deeds I committed, but to give you some small explanation of why I did it.

Victor performed no abortion upon me. That was by my own hand. I was seeking to hurt him. I had hoped to hurt all of you, thinking that this would lessen my own pain. And then I sought to ruin John and so went to the bookies and told them of his plan to leave Warrington. I will not say now, my loving friend, that I did not derive some sinister pleasure out of the misery I wrought, for in my demented mind this is what I truly thought: that I was equally able to inflict misery upon others as it had been done to me.

When, however, I had a lucid moment and I saw what I had truly done to Victor, the one person I have always loved and worshipped above all else, it struck me a blow. For I had not intended to *ruin* him, merely to cast a shadow upon him in your eyes. Yes, Jennifer, I had wanted to make you unhappy, too. For your beauty and grace and for all the things I could never have, Victor among them. For being my brother, he was more beyond my reach than any other man.

And when I saw how I had driven him away, and then John, and how I had sent Mother to her bed as an invalid, I could take it no more. In my vindictive moments I was relishing the destruction I had wrought. But in my sane moments, I was beset with remorse. And when Father cut off all my hair as punishment for what I had done with Sean, I knew then that there was no other way out than to rid you all of the instrument that had caused so much grief.

Forgive me, dearest Jennifer, for I did truly look upon you with affection and it was only some darker aspect of myself that was jealous of your beauty and of Victor's love for you. Forgive me that I have caused you to find me in this manner. It could not be clean. Father would have wanted it this way.

God forgive me. Harriet.

"You knew all of this, didn't you?" said Jennifer, now standing very close to me. Victor continued to stare down at the letter long after he had read it. A barely perceptible nod of his head answered her question.

"Then why didn't you speak up? You were so terribly wronged, Victor."

To this he did not reply. Instead he raised his face to me and when I saw the depths of sadness in his eyes, the loss of spirit and the gentle grief, I wanted to cry.

Finally, reading the letter once more, he held it out to me. When Jennifer's hand stretched out to receive it, my own arm also rose. And when Victor placed the letter in my hand, I was not surprised.

"No one else has read this," I heard Jennifer say very close to my ear. Although I had not moved, we seemed to be almost touching. "I found it on Harriet's body when I discovered her in the wardrobe. I have kept it all this time, in the hope of showing it to you one day. There was no doubt that Harriet's death was a suicide, because of the manner of the wounds and . . . that she had not been placed in the wardrobe but had put herself there. That's . . . what the police said . . . and Dr. Pendergast confirmed it. But no one knows of this letter or what it says."

"Burn it," he said flatly.

"Why? It releases you, Victor," said Jennifer. And I added, "It clears your name. You can come back to Warrington a free man, I will not burn it, Victor."

His eyes probed mine with an intensity that needed no words. When he held his hand out to me, I wordlessly surrendered the letter to him and was not surprised when he crumpled it up and tossed it into the fire. I watched it catch flame and burn.

"Yes I knew all these things, yet it would do no good to protest my own innocence when it would mean the condemnation of my sister. She came to my office on that day and told me about her condition. I suggested she see the term through and give life to the child. I had thought perhaps you and John would take it and give it a name. But later I found the instrument missing and I somehow knew . . . "

"You have burned your only chance for redemption."

Victor shook his head. "What good would it serve now to show the world what my sister had become? What good can come of having my father read those last words, telling him that he was responsible for her death? I can bear what has been done to me. I can go to a foreign country and start anew. In time it will all be forgotten. Future Townsends will know nothing of what went on in this house, the taint that is in their line."

A voice, sounding strangely like my own and yet mingled with Jenny's, asked, "And will you come back to England again?"

"I don't think so. My life here has ended. All that I sought to accomplish has been dashed. It would be useless to try again. But in France or Germany . . . "

His voice faded away. I saw in his eyes the conflict there, the bitterness and the sadness. It made me reach my hand out to him.

And when he lifted his own hand and our fingers touched, it seemed so natural.

Jennifer was no longer with us. I stood alone before the fireplace, the hem of my long skirt brushing my ankles. I felt the heat of the flames against my bare neck, for my hair was now swept off my back and on top of my head.

Across the years, across the miles and through the mysteries of time and space, our fingers touched.

"No one else has read the letter, Victor dearest"—how good his name felt upon my tongue!—"no one knows but you and I. It has been a torment without you these past months. I went to your office and then to the Horse's Head, but no one could tell me where you had gone. I have lain awake at nights, thinking you dead, thinking you alone in some miserable slum, finding solace in gin or other deplorable conditions. But now . . . to see you standing before me. It's like a dream . . . "

"Jenny," he murmured, his fingers curling about my hand.

Yes, I'm Jenny, I thought. *I am Jennifer.* And I have loved you for so long, desired you and wanted you, that I thought I should die of it.

"I had thought for a while I was going out of my mind with worry. It has all happened so fast. The sleepless nights. And I have been unable to eat."

"You're too thin, Jenny. And pale."

"I've had the strangest imaginings! I've thought this house haunted, Victor. I've seen a young woman . . . "

"Poor Jennifer," he intoned, stepping close to me now, drawing both my hands into a tight grip. His voice, deep and thrilling, said, "I should leave now, Jennifer."

And I heard my voice—our voice—say to him, "Stay, please . . . "

And if I am trapped in this time frame with the door to the future closed forever behind me, would it be so bad?

"I shall spend my eternity with you, Victor . . . " I whispered.

When his arms encircled me and I felt his body against mine I thought I should cry out. The electricity that shot through my body made me at first stiffen and then slump against him, moulding myself to him as though this was where I belonged.

And it was where I belonged. It was here, with my mouth pressed against Victor's, feeling the breath squeezed out of me, feeling my legs go weak and the need to cling to him, that I knew this was where I had always belonged. I had come so far . . . so far . . .

The years of abstinence, of holding ourselves back, crumbled beneath his most violent kiss, as he devoured me and held me so tightly that it seemed he would merge us into one being. I did not need to be guided towards the bed, knowing that was where we must relinquish ourselves to the power of our sexual need.

I have never before experienced such passion within myself nor ecstasy with a man. One part of my brain, Jennifer, could only marvel at the excitement and gentleness of Victor compared with John, while the other half, myself, saw the empty years of my past and the endless string of bed partners who, all put together, could not measure up to this one man.

These were my erotic dreams fulfilled. I had known all along it would be like this with Victor Townsend, that our final coming together would be the end of my searching and give meaning at last to my dormant soul.

I was struck with the truism that this was the first time I had given myself to a man I truly loved.

And later, after our sojourn into Paradise and the uniting of our souls for all time, I knew also the purpose of my being here. It was all so clear now.

It was all intended for this one moment.

The episode of the past days, the witnessing of moments in the past, the wondering, the puzzling, had all been only to prepare me for this one moment. So that I may understand.

So that I may understand.

I had been wrong. My theories of a short while ago had been very far off the mark. I had not been brought here and forced into the past to prevent some imaginery tragedy. I had been chosen not to prevent this event, but *to be a part of it*. And the reason was clear to me now.

Lying in Victor's embrace, his warm breath on my neck, his face set in the first repose it had known, I knew that there lay another man, on the other side of town in a hospital terminal ward, who needed to be told.

What followed our lovemaking is very unclear to me. When it seemed that we had spent all night in each other's arms, my great-grandfather and myself, I awoke at one point to find that it was only midnight. And I recall somehow making my way down the stairs and back into the sitting room, walking in something of a trance, with no feelings within me except the lingering euphoria of Victor's love. Gone was the turmoil I had known all these days in Nana's house, and gone were all the questions and riddles that had plagued my mind. Instead I had the sensation of sweet resignation, of *acceptance,* and of knowing that I had spent one night with the only man who would ever have any true meaning for me.

I believe that I then went to the couch and lay down, for it seems that I slept after that, deeply and soundly, like someone whose mind is free from worry and whose body has scaled great summits. And it was during this slumber that I had my last, remarkable dream.

In it, Victor came to me, standing over me as I lay there, not in the solid and real sense he had been to me earlier, up there in the bedroom, but more as the spectral form he should have been. A ghost. And he stood smiling down at me, although a little curiously. And I felt myself gazing up at him with no sense of fear, no sense of wonder, merely the deep-seated warmth of knowing that I had been privileged to know this man.

And in the dream the hazy form of Victor said to me, "Who are you?"

And I replied, "Your great-granddaughter."

This seemed to surprise him. "How is that so?"

And I replied, "How is it that you are talking to me now? Am I dreaming?"

But all he said was, "How is it you are my great-granddaughter when I never married and never had children?"

I giggled a little at this, thinking, How absurd.

"Your one night with Jennifer," I heard my voice say to him from a great distance, "produced a son. She named him Robert. And when he became a man he had a daughter, my mother. That's how it is you are my great-grandfather."

His face cleared a little. And as he stared down at me, I thought his eyes seemed to have a light behind them, as though hope had crept into them and lifted the veil of cynicism and disappointment. As Victor Townsend looked down at me I thought his face grew calmer, became untroubled and younger-looking, appearing now as he had before the London hospitals had aged him before his tune. "I had a son . . . " he murmured.

"What happened to you?" I heard myself ask.

"I went to France after that night. I promised Jennifer I would come back for her. I went to France to find a home and a medical practice and then I would be worthy of making Jennifer my wife."

"Did you?"

"I died a year later on a ship while crossing the Channel. She never knew I was on my way back, for I had not written ahead, intending to surprise her. She must have gone through life thinking I had abandoned her."

"She died shortly after, Victor. It must have been grief that did it."

"And I never knew she had a child."

"Your child," I said.

"So why are you here? Why are *we* here? I have been brought out of a grey . . . dreary place . . . "

"I don't know. I guess to make everything right again."

"What was his name?"

"Robert."

"Robert . . . " he repeated.

"But he's dying now."

"We all die," said Victor.

"Tell me something. Tell me about Time. How did it happen? Are you still alive somewhere . . . "

But my great-grandfather was not listening. He turned his head and glanced over his shoulder. And I saw sunlight wash his face and a smile so bright that it made my heart move in my chest. "She's here . . . " he murmured.

"I guess we're all here."

But he heard me no more. Victor Townsend turned away from me once and for all and walked off into the mist which surrounded the couch.

And the last word I heard him utter was "Jennifer . . . "

CHAPTER 17

*W*HEN I CAME TO AND OPENED MY EYES, I SAW A SITTING room that I had never seen before. And I wondered in my muddled state, Where am I now? But, rolling my head to one side and seeing the sunlight pour through the window, I knew.

"The rain's stopped," called my grandmother from the kitchen.

I sat up. The smell of frying bacon and toast met my nose. And I was instantly hungry.

"What day is it, Nana?" I called out.

"What day is it? Why, it's Wednesday, love."

Wednesday! I had been in this house twelve days. "Gosh, I'm hungry," I said, springing to my feet. I felt wonderful! My body was relaxed and refreshed. And there was something else, too . . .

Nana poked her old grey head through the doorway. "Ah, you're looking better, lovey. Storm's over. Can go to the hospital today. And after that it's Cook's for you with your plane ticket."

"Sorry, Nana," I said, quickly gathering up my blankets and pillow and extra clothes strewn about. "You can't get rid of me that fast.Go to Cook's yourself, if you want, but I have some people to visit yet."

She said something more, but I didn't hear. I bounded up the stairs and headed for the bathroom.

She didn't have a shower, but the bathtub sufficed. Filling it with hot water and scrubbing myself all over, and then sticking my head under the force of the taps, I washed away all the debris of the past eighty years.

I felt I had been born again.

Dressing in the biting air of the bedroom and rubbing my arms against the cold, which I now sharply felt, I took a moment to pause before the clothes wardrobe. I looked down at the dusty floor of it and at the dismal darkness, and I recalled what Jennifer and I had found there. Then, brushing out the wetness of my hair, I looked over at the bed and smiled.

We ate a hearty breakfast of bacon and eggs and toast, and I ate enough for three people.

"Well, you've got your appetite back I see! You're eating like a horse!"

"I feel great, Nana!"

"And your colour's back, too. Well, I'm glad to see you've finally got one of me cardigans on."

"Had to. It's cold in here." I grinned at her and gulped down my tea.

Beyond the window was the most perfect day I had ever seen, with a blinding blue sky and tufts of white clouds and singing birds and grass so green that you could smell it without going outside. It made my heart rise to the rafters. I wanted to cry out with joy.

We had all been born again.

"It was the flu you had," said Nana. "And it's gone. See? No need of doctors. Not when the body knows how to take care of itself."

"Oh yes, Nana." I smiled to myself, thinking of Dr. Victor Townsend and his remarkable cure. "And I see your arthritis is gone, too."

"Not gone, lovey, just asleep till the next storm."

We laughed a little and got back on to our old footing again. We listened to the radio and agreed with each other that British economy was plummeting fast. When Aunt Elsie and Uncle William showed up at the door shortly past noon, I bounded over to let them in and greeted them with hugs.

They were Victor's grandchildren. And look at Uncle William, wasn't there a resemblance?

We bundled up and struck out into the biting cold day. Sunny and bright, it was still winter in Warrington and it felt good to shiver.

Granddad was just as we had left him several days before: lying flat on his back and staring blankly at the ceiling. Aunt Elsie went through the ritual of opening biscuits and bottles of juice for him, chatting all the while about the horrible storm that had kept us away and about the new baby that had been born to the Duchess of Kent, while I remained in my seat staring down at him.

Here was Victor's son. Here was the result of that night in the front bedroom, a night that had not only given him life but myself as well. For I knew that as long as I lived, I should always look back and know that, despite whatever I might encounter in years to come, I had known what it was like to be truly loved by one man.

We sat for an hour at my granddad's bedside, myself not speaking, Aunt Elsie and Uncle William talking in their usual manner, pretending that he could hear. And I noticed that the offensive odours were gone, that the sourness that had initially repulsed me about this old man had disappeared.

And as I looked down at him I thought, I'm glad it's over. There was a time when I had wanted it to go on forever, when I had feared losing Victor and having to face the present once more. But all that has changed now. For I am a child of the present, not of the past, and Victor belongs where he was born—in the past. We can never meet again.

But I am glad, for I would not trade that one experience for anything in the world. I do not mourn its passing, I rejoice in it. For now I can go on in life a more complete person at last.

There remained only one act left to me.

When Aunt Elsie announced that it was time to go and started packing up her things, I said, "Wait a minute, Aunt Elsie. I want to tell Granddad something."

She gave me a surprised look.

"Can I tell him in private? Please? I'll be leaving soon and I don't think

I'll be back to England for a long time . . . well, you know, so I just want to have a little chat with him before I go."

She looked at Uncle William. "You mean you want us to leave?"

"If you wouldn't mind."

"But I don't think he can hear you—" She cut herself off and shook her head. "Of course you can talk to him, lovey, he'd enjoy it, William and I'll be at the car. Take all the time you want."

"Thanks, Aunt Elsie." I watched them fold up their wooden chairs and push their way through the swinging doors. Waiting until I saw them emerge from the hospital and walk across the parking lot towards the Renault, I then fell on my knees at my grandfather's bedside and murmured to him, "Granddad? Can you hear me? It's Andrea."

His eyes remained fixed on the ceiling, blank and lifeless.

"Granddad," I said again, soft, compelling. "It's me, Andrea, your granddaughter. Can you hear me? I think you can. But I think you're trapped. You're trapped in a body that can't move, but you can hear me. Is that right?"

I watched him again, that placid face, the shallow breathing. There was no sign that he heard me.

So I went on, "I've got to tell you something, Granddad, before I go back to America. It's about your father, Victor. I want you to listen to what I have to say."

I don't know how long I knelt at that musty bedside, whispering into the ear of a comatose man, but I went slowly, carefully, and told him everything that had happened to me in his house on George Street. I left nothing out—from the very first night when I heard "Für Elise" right down to my last night's dream in the sitting room, and my final words with Victor. I told him about every episode, skipped no details, took my time and made sure that he would understand. And I ended by saying, "So you see, Granddad, your mother didn't despise you. She loved you. She loved you very much. In fact, you were the only joy in her life. And she didn't die because of the memory of your conception, as you had been told, she died of a broken heart; she thought Victor had forgotten her. And when you always thought that she must have hated you, Granddad, that she hated even to look at you because you reminded her of a horrible moment in her life, it was just the other way around. You reminded her of the one moment of happiness in her whole life. Granddad, you were the child of a union of love—a love child."

I hung at the bedside, not knowing that I had talked to him for fifteen minutes or that a change had come over him. All I saw before me was the face of a tormented little boy living with his invalid grandmother, Mrs. Townsend, who had, because of her twisted mind, pounded into his head horror stories about his father that gave him nightmares at night.

So I leaned close and whispered one last thing. I told him that his mother and father were united again in that other realm which we don't understand, but which Granddad would soon be entering, and I told him that they would be there, waiting for him.

Finally I raised myself up and sat back on my heels, wondering if I had got through to him. His face remained fixed, his eyes glassy and staring. But then I saw his thin lips working over toothless gums and it seemed he might be trying to say something.

I leaned forward and said, "What is it, Granddad?"

His lips were trying to form a word, clumsily and with effort. And as he struggled, a tear fell from his eye and rolled down on to the pillow.

Then the most peculiar light came into his eyes as they looked at a point somewhere between the bed and the ceiling, staring searchingly as if they saw something, and more tears fell.

His chin trembled, but the word would not come out.

"What is it, Granddad, tell me."

He tried to raise his head, his eyes fixed now on some object hovering above the bed, and when at last some freak imitation of a smile curved his lips and he said in a normal voice, "Dad," I knew what it was my grandfather saw.

He died at that moment. And he died with that smile on his face.

I never told my relatives about what had happened in the house on George Street. It was not for them to know. And yet, ironically, it was the very thing which drew me close to them, realizing as I did after my grandfather's death that my aunt and uncle and cousins were just as much a part of Victor Townsend as my mother and I were.

I found a new capacity within me to love these people, whom I had at first regarded as strangers with funny speech and alien ways, just as I found whole new aspects to my soul that had never been there before.

The next Sunday we went to Morecambe Bay and I met my cousins, and I can't remember when I have had a nicer time. It thrilled me to meet these people who were part of Victor's legacy, and I found myself quickly endeared to them for the fact that we shared something stronger than mere chance friendship.

On the day that I left my grandmother's house, she said to me, "You mustn't be sad for my sake, lovey, now that your granddad's dead. We had sixty-two lovely years together, him and me, and I wouldn't trade them for anything in the world. No woman could have asked for a better man. And let me tell you something. Growing old isn't hard, not when you've got faith in God and an afterlife. You see, love, I believe that my eighty-three years on this earth have only been a kind of beginning to what really lies ahead. And while a modern young thing like you might think this the belief of a foolish old woman, I quite expect to see your granddad after I die. And that's a fact. We shall be together again, because nothing so simple as death can keep us apart. Not after all this time. We'll keep on going, your granddad and I, and I shall go to my final rest with no fear."

She gave me a gift as I was about to leave, and it was the leather-bound copy of the book *She* that I had looked at weeks before. And holding it in my hand I recalled the dismal philosophy I had pondered upon reading one particular passage—that the only future which awaits us is decay and dust. Only now I had a different thought on the matter, so that reading the words "Mortality is weak and oppressed in the company of the dust which awaits upon its end" I thought, How foolish we mortals can be! Because I knew at that moment that Victor and Jennifer still lived on somewhere and that my grandmother would indeed be united with my grandfather after a time, and that we all would, in the end, rendezvous with our own special eternity.

As for me, I knew where my own destiny lay. Just as I had been allowed to go back and change the past, so was I also being given the opportunity to change my future. I didn't want to throw away the chance to have what Jenny and Victor had wanted but could never have. The chance was being offered me; I wanted to seize it before it was too late. I could only hope that Doug would still be there when I returned, for I had so much to say to him. For one thing, I had learned to utter the words "I love you."

As for explanations, I have none. *How* it all happened is a matter of speculation. And *why* it happened . . . well, that too can be debated, although I am certain that it was preordained long ago. Granddad was dying, he had to know the truth. And Victor was existing in some "grey, dreary place" not knowing what had happened after his death. And Jenny, too, had died not knowing the truth. So I had been the catalyst. I like to think I helped set things right.

I had gone to the house on George Street as a person without much of a past and with no future to look forward to. But now I came away with the treasures of a past that was rich beyond imagining, and a sure feeling for the brightness and the hope that the future would hold.

At the kerb, before I climbed into Uncle Edouard's Renault, I stopped to glance back at the house. My eyes travelled up to the front bedroom where, in the window, hung the familiar white lace curtains.

They seemed to flutter farewell.

FROM

THE DIVINING

A NOVEL BY BARBARA WOOD

NOW AVAILABLE

1

SHE CAME SEEKING ANSWERS.

Nineteen-year-old Ulrika had awoken that morning with the feeling that something was wrong. The feeling had grown while she had bathed and dressed, and her slaves had bound up her hair and tied sandals to her feet, and brought her a breakfast of wheat porridge and goat's milk. When the inexplicable uneasiness did not go away, she decided to visit the Street of Fortune-Tellers, where seers and mystics, astrologers and soothsayers promised solutions to life's mysteries.

Now, as she was carried through the noisy streets of Rome in a curtained chair, she wondered what had caused her uneasiness. Yesterday, everything had been fine. She had visited friends, browsed in bookshops, spent time at her loom—the typical day of a young woman of her class and breeding. But then she had had a strange dream . . .

Just past the midnight hour, Ulrika had dreamed that she gotten out of bed, crossed to her window, climbed out, and landed barefoot in snow. In the dream, tall pines grew all around her, instead of the fruit trees behind her villa, a forest instead of an orchard, and clouds whispered across the face of a winter moon. She saw tracks—big paw prints in the snow, leading into the woods. Ulrika followed them, feeling moonlight brush her bare shoulders. She came upon a large, shaggy wolf with golden eyes. She sat down in the snow and he came to lie beside her, putting his head in her lap. The night was pure, as pure as the wolf's eyes gazing up at her, and she could feel the steady beat of his mighty heart beneath his ribs. The golden eyes blinked and seemed to say: Here is trust, here is love, here is home.

Ulrika had awoken disoriented. And then she had wondered: Why did I dream of a wolf? Wulf was my father's name. He died long ago in faraway Persia.

Is the dream a sign? But a sign of what?

Her slaves brought the chair to a halt, and Ulrika stepped down, a tall girl wearing a long gown of pale pink silk, with a matching stole that draped over her head and shoulders in proper maidenly modesty, hiding tawny hair and a graceful neck. She carried herself with a poise and confidence that concealed a growing anxiety.

The Street of Fortune-Tellers was a narrow alley obscured by the shadow of crowded tenement buildings. The tents and stalls of the psychics, augers, seers, and soothsayers looked promising, painted in bright colors, festooned with glittering objects, each one brighter than the next. Business was booming for purveyors of good-luck charms, magic relics, and amulets.

As Ulrika entered the lane, desperate to know the meaning of the wolf dream, hawkers called to her from tents and booths, claiming to be "genuine Chaldeans," to have direct channels to the future, to possess the Third Eye. She went first to the bird-reader, who kept crates of pigeons whose entrails he read for a few pennies. His hands caked with blood, he assured Ulrika that she would find a husband before the year was out. She went next to the stall of the smoke-reader, who declared that the incense predicted five healthy children for Ulrika.

She continued on until, three quarters along the crowded lane, she came upon a person of humble appearance, sitting only on a frayed mat, with no shade or booth or tent. The seer sat cross-legged in a long white robe that had known better days, long bony hands resting on bony knees. The head was bowed, showing a crown of hair that was blacker than jet, parted in the middle and streaming over the shoulders and back. Ulrika did not know why she would choose so impoverished a soothsayer—perhaps on some level she felt this one might be more interested in truth than in money—but she came to a halt before the curious person, and waited.

After a moment, the fortune-teller lifted her head, and Ulrika was startled by the unusual aspect of the face, which was long and narrow, all bone and yellow skin, framed by the streaming black hair. Mournful black eyes beneath highly arched brows looked up at Ulrika. The woman almost did not look human, and she was ageless. Was she twenty or eighty? A brown and black spotted cat lay curled asleep next to the fortune-teller. Ulrika recognized the breed as an Egyptian Mau, said to be the most ancient of cat breeds, possibly even the progenitor from which all cats had sprung.

Ulrika brought her attention back to the fortune-teller's swimming black eyes filled with sadness and wisdom.

"You have a question," the fortune-teller said in perfect Latin, eyes peering steadily from deep sockets.

The sounds of the alley faded. Ulrika was captured by the black Egyptian eyes, while the brown cat snoozed obliviously.

"You want to ask me about a wolf," the Egyptian said in a voice that sounded older than the Nile.

"It was in a dream, Wise One. Was it a sign?"

"A sign of what? Tell me your question."

"I do not know where I belong, Wise One. My mother is Roman, my father German. I was born in Persia and have spent most of my life roaming with my mother, for she followed a quest. Everywhere we went, I felt like an outsider. I am worried, Wise One, that if I do not know where I belong, I will never know who I am. Was the wolf dream a sign that I belong in the Rhineland with my father's people? Is it time for me to leave Rome?"

"There are signs all about you, daughter. The gods guide us everywhere, every moment."

"You speak in riddles, Wise One. Can you at least tell me my future?"

"There will be a man," the fortune-teller said, "who will offer you a key. Take it."

"A key? To what?"

"You will know when the time comes . . ."

CPSIA information can be obtained
at www.ICGtesting.com
Printed in the USA
JSHW021650220523
42075JS00002B/371